The Lost Art
of Letter Writing

MENNA VAN PRAAG

Allison & Busby Limited
12 Fitzroy Mews
London W1T 6DW
allisonandbusby.com

First published in Great Britain by Allison & Busby in 2017.

Copyright © 2017 by MENNA VAN PRAAG

A CIP catalogue record for this book is available from
the British Library.

First Edition

ISBN 978-0-7490-2100-9

Typeset in 10.5/15.5 pt Adobe Garamond Pro by
Allison & Busby Ltd.

The paper used for this Allison & Busby publication
has been produced from trees that have been legally sourced
from well-managed and credibly certified forests.

Printed and bound by
CPI Group (UK) Ltd, Croydon, CR0 4YY

For Ash,
With love for giving me goosebumps with her talk of stationery shops
and with thanks for all those beautiful letters

&

For Clara,
With thanks for being the namesake
and with love for always knowing when I need cake

Chapter One

The shop is tucked down a little side street, missed by most people, except those few seeking it out or accidentally stumbling upon it on their way to somewhere else entirely. The shop has a little green door, requiring customers to stoop upon entering, and tiny windows so cluttered that it's impossible to peer through and see what's going on inside. Which is exactly how Clara wants it to be. She doesn't desire great wealth or prestige; she doesn't dream of attracting crowds of students and tourists passing through Cambridge, as other shop owners do. No, Clara wants those who have wandered away from the crowds, those who are feeling distracted and disconnected, those with bruised hearts, those who don't know how to undo the past and soothe their pain, those who doubt it's even possible.

Until, that is, they wander along the tiny street and come upon the tiny shop. In one of its tiny windows is tucked a tiny note, written in tiny, but elegant, handwriting, inviting them to venture inside and:

Learn the lost art of letter writing . . .

Most can't remember when they last sat down to press the nib of a pen to paper, when they last inscribed an envelope, found a stamp and dropped a letter into a postbox, imagining the person who'd open it, grateful for the gift of thought and time sent from afar. And yet, even if they've never written so much as a postcard before, still they'll step inside – seized by a sudden, silent urge they can't understand – and gasp.

The walls of the little shop are lined with letters, hundreds and hundreds of letters, in every colour of ink and paper and every style of handwriting. Dark oak cabinets contain writing papers in a thousand different designs: papers lined with silver leaf, embedded with roses and violets, papers studded with glittering foil stars, or painted with watercolour sunflowers – each unique and furnished with matching envelopes. Shelves sit above the cabinets, weighed down with a rainbow of notebooks: bound in leather, swathed in silk, embroidered on linen or cotton, some made of paper stitched with flower petals but none the same as any other.

Only one corner of the little stationery shop is clear of any papers, pens or other writing paraphernalia. In this corner stands a delicate ornate Victorian writing desk made of mahogany and inlaid with mother-of-pearl, containing a dozen drawers – one of them curiously locked and impossible to open – and accompanied by a chair cushioned with dark-green velvet.

It is here that Clara's particular magic takes place.

Upon the lettered walls hang half a dozen glass cabinets lined in crimson velvet, each just large enough to contain a single pen. Clara has held each of these pens, except one. Her grandfather made them all, buying them back at great expense years after he'd sold them. One was used by John Lennon to compose *Imagine*, another by Daphne du Maurier to write *Rebecca*, another by Quentin Blake to illustrate *Matilda* . . .

The only pen Clara hasn't touched is the one her grandfather made especially for her. The nib is gold, the inlay platinum, the barrel plated in silver, the cap topped with a small, single pink diamond. It was a gift on her thirteenth birthday and, with it, Clara's grandfather attached a promise that one day – when she was ready – she'd use it to write her own great novel. He'd seen it in her spirit, he whispered, the day she was born he had seen that literature was her destiny.

So far, however, Clara has never been able to write anything longer than a letter. She's planned plenty of books and begun (with the assistance of lesser pens) a great many of them. She's written millions of words, constructed thousands of sentences, even completed a paragraph or two, but hasn't yet managed to finish a first chapter. Every day Clara tries in vain to realise her grandfather's prophecy but lately, twenty years after he gave her the pen, she's starting to wonder if he didn't make a mistake.

Clara is sitting behind the counter (carved by the same carpenter who created the writing desk, in dark mahogany and mother-of-pearl and topped with an antique black-and-gold cash register) when her next lost soul walks into the shop. For a moment the woman seems confused, as if she's trying to remember why she's standing in the doorway of a stationery shop at all. Then she glances up and catches Clara's eye.

'Welcome to *Letters*,' Clara says with a smile, grateful for the excuse to put down her unresponsive pen. She stands, walks around the counter, and stops at the cabinet on the other side of the room. Then she turns back to the woman. Clara waits for a moment, then speaks into the silence.

'So,' she says gently, 'to whom are you writing?'

'I'm sorry?' The woman seems confused again.

'Well,' Clara says, 'you've come here to write a letter . . .'

The woman frowns. 'I have?'

Clara smiles again. 'Just give me a moment.'

She glances at the cabinet again, her eyes slowly scanning each unlabelled drawer in turn. Then she stops, bends and opens a drawer close to the floor. Clara picks carefully through the papers, until she selects one and holds it out towards her new customer on her open palm.

'If I gave you this paper, to write something you needed to say to someone you haven't yet said it to,' Clara says, 'then who might that someone be?'

The woman reaches out to take the paper, holding it as if it were made of gold, which, indeed, it is: a sheet of cream linen flecked with tiny slices of gold leaf.

'My sister,' she says, so softly that Clara almost can't hear. 'I'd write a letter to my sister.'

Clara's smile deepens. 'Perfect.' Crossing the room, she ducks behind the counter again, pulling open unseen drawers and closing them again. 'I'll find you the perfect pen, so you can sit down and write.'

'Oh, no.' The young woman shakes her head. 'I can't.'

Clara looks up, her fingers curled around a long, thin, silver pen. 'Why ever not?'

The woman stares at her feet. Her voice, when at last she speaks, is as soft as falling leaves. 'Because she's . . . dead.'

Clara nods, as if she'd expected exactly that answer which, indeed, she had.

'I'm sorry to hear it,' she says. 'But I wouldn't let a little thing like death stop you. And don't worry, I have a special postbox for letters like that.'

'You do?'

'Oh, yes,' Clara says. 'Of all the letters written in this shop, perhaps half of them are written to people who won't ever read them. At least, not in a way that we might understand.'

'Really?'

'Take this,' Clara holds out the silver pen. 'You don't need to know what to write. The desk will help you with that. Almost as soon as you sit the words will start to come, I promise.'

Tears fill the woman's eyes. She steps forward and takes the pen, tentatively, between her thumb and forefinger. 'Thank you.' She presses the paper to her chest. 'I want—I never had the chance to say . . .'

Clara nods, taking a step back to allow the woman to walk to the writing desk. She has read hundreds, possibly thousands, of letters to ghosts in the last decade of owning the stationery shop. Each letter has touched her heart, and each writer has captured her curiosity. And yet, there is something about this woman that particularly intrigues Clara. She wants to sit and drink cups of tea and listen to her life and learn why her pretty blue eyes seem so very sad. But, of course, she can't.

'Sit,' she says instead, as the woman hovers by the desk. 'Take as long as you want. No one will come into the shop until you are done.'

The woman does so then, placing her paper carefully on the square of green felt, smoothing it over with her palm. 'Thank you,' she whispers, just loud enough to be heard, then curls her body over the desk, takes a deep breath and presses her nose to the paper.

Clara watches as the woman slips slowly into the past, her

breath and memories mingling in concentrated puffs. Later, her breath comes in silent sobs as she wipes tears from her cheeks before they fall onto the paper, while still clutching the immobile pen tight in her fist. Clara watches the woman's shoulders shake. Then a stillness comes over her and she begins again to write. Clara watches the pen race across the page, inky black letters sliding out at such speed that every word surely obscures the next. The air crackles with the burst of energy just released, the nibs of all the other pens twitch excitedly, impatient for their turn. A thousand papers rustle in a hundred drawers and Clara watches, a smile on her lips and a wish in her heart that one day she will be possessed to write like that; only a book instead of a letter. Unfortunately, and frustratingly, the magic of the writing desk doesn't seem to lend itself to anything other than letters.

When the speeding pen is finally still again and the air is silent, Clara pulls her gaze away and pretends to be studying the empty page of the notebook on her lap. She's staring at it when the woman is standing in front of the counter, wiping her blue eyes.

'I didn't . . . I don't,' she mumbles. She takes a deep breath. 'I don't know what to do with . . .' She folds the letter twice in half. 'Will you read it, if I give it to you?'

'Only if you want me to,' Clara says.

'Oh,' the woman says. 'But why would I . . . ?'

'Some people feel that letters aren't really letters until they've been read,' Clara explains. 'Even if it's by someone who isn't the intended recipient.'

The woman considers this. 'Yes, I suppose . . . Well, I'd like to leave it with you. But I'd rather you didn't read it, if that's all right.'

'Of course.' Clara nods, hoping the disappointment doesn't show on her face. 'Then I'll find you an envelope.'

She walks across the carpeted floor to the cabinet of closed drawers, bending down and opening the same one where she'd found the linen paper flecked with gold leaf. When she stands, Clara offers her customer the matching envelope.

'Thank you.' The woman slides her letter inside then licks and seals her secret.

'Would you like to post it?' Clara asks.

'Where?'

Clara points to the small, flat face of a dark-red postbox embedded into the wall behind the counter. 'Just there.'

A slight smile dimples the woman's cheeks. She walks to the box and drops her envelope inside – kissing it quickly before letting it go. She turns back to Clara. 'I can't . . . I . . . Thank you . . . But, how much do I . . . ?'

'That depends,' Clara says. 'Would you like the pen, or only the letter?'

The woman glances down at the pen in her hand, as if she'd forgotten it was there. She looks at the small leather bag hanging at her side.

'I—just the letter, please.'

'Okay. Then that's four pounds and fifty-five pence, please.'

The woman opens her bag, pulls out her purse and thrusts a ten-pound note into Clara's hand, along with the pen.

'I'd give you more, if I could, but' – she grasps Clara's hands tightly – 'thank you, thank you, thank you so much.'

Then she lets go and, without looking Clara in the eye, turns and hurries out. As the green door falls closed behind the unknown customer, Clara walks back to the counter and rings the money into the till, feeling a slight tug of sorrow knowing that she'll never see this particular woman again. Clara feels this way each time a customer leaves, wishing the connection could last just a little longer but, of course, it can't.

With a soft sigh, Clara slides the silver pen back into its drawer.

Clara wrote her first letter when she was four years old. It contained three sentences and was addressed to her cat. Now she writes nearly every day, letters long and short, addressed to people she doesn't know and will never meet.

Although Clara only lives a few minutes' walk from her shop, she never goes straight home after closing time. Instead, whatever the weather, no matter how wet or cold, she takes long detours through town, sometimes (on long summer nights) venturing along winding country roads and across fields into the surrounding villages. While she walks, Clara glances into the windows of the houses she passes, looking for the recipient of her next letter. Then she'll stop and take a closer look. One day she'll see an exhausted mother rocking a crying child, another she sees an old man gazing sadly at the wall, or a bachelor eating a TV dinner for one. Some days Clara sees no one, but it doesn't matter because there is always the next day and the day after that.

Clara knows when she sees someone she can write to, someone who will open her letter – her anonymous, unasked-for letter – and, instead of tossing it straight in the wastepaper basket, will sit down and spread the paper open on their lap, gazing in wonderment at the words – words that are, somehow, exactly what they need to hear in that moment, words that will heal, motivate, inspire or console, words that have clearly been chosen by someone who can see straight into the darkest nooks and crannies of their souls.

They will sit a while longer then, pressing the paper beneath their fingertips, letting the words soak off the page and into their hands, until a tiny spark of hope ignites in their chest and they stand, filled with renewed determination and a sense of self-belief and faith they haven't known since childhood. They'll put the letter away in a safe and secret place, returning to it again and again over the coming days, weeks, months and years – whenever they need to remember, to reignite that spark of hope they felt upon first reading it, until they've imbued it so many times that the words have knitted together into the cells of their blood and the marrow of their bones.

When Clara sees such a person she feels it in the tips of her fingers – a tingling sensation akin to a slight electric shock – then she notes down their address in her notebook and continues walking.

Sometimes the letter takes a week to write, sometimes only an hour and Clara has a ritual accompanying the start of each one. First of all, she sits at the counter, remembering the person she saw, the look on their face, the layout of their living room, the wallpaper on their walls . . . Then she slides off her chair and hurries across the dark wooden floorboards to the cabinets containing the writing papers. Usually, Clara instinctively knows the drawer she needs, immediately plucking out the perfect piece of paper, though sometimes she has to search a little longer before finding the right one. Choosing the envelope follows and, finally, the pen. Although she has thousands of papers to choose from, and hundreds of pens, it never takes Clara more than a few minutes to make her selection. Which is a shame really, since she enjoys the moment of anticipation so much.

Once she has her instruments, Clara sits at the little writing desk and, much like her customers, waits for inspiration to strike. Sometimes this takes only moments, sometimes a little longer, though, no matter how long it takes, Clara doesn't find the waiting a frustrating experience but a meditative one. She enjoys the silence, the tentative sense of connection with a complete stranger, the expectation of hope and healing to come.

And when, at last, she starts to write, Clara doesn't select the words herself, doesn't carefully craft sentences of specially tailored wisdom and inspiration for the intended recipient, since she has no idea what she ought to say and what they need to hear. Instead she allows the magic of the desk to take over. So the pen skims across the paper, leaving a loping trail of purple ink in its wake, and Clara just holds on. She's hardly aware of what she writes and never reads the letters back when they are finished. She simply sits at the desk until the pen stops and she knows she's done.

Chapter Two

His letter arrives on a Tuesday morning. Edward sees it as he bumps down the stairs in his tatty tartan slippers, the ones Tilly bought him three Christmases ago and he's worn every day since. He walks past the mail on the mat and heads towards the kitchen. As he steps onto the cold stone floor, he pulls his dressing gown cord tighter round his waist. The gown is still too big (he lost a lot of weight three years ago) and too feminine (paisley silk in shades of purple) in his humble opinion, but Greer made it for him the summer she died so he'll wear it until it falls off, which won't be long now. Tilly has sewn so many patches on the threadbare gown that it's virtually become a quilt, but Edward ignores his daughter every time she begs him to throw it out. He also ignores the two flannel dressing gowns sitting in the bottom drawer of his wardrobe – still in their plastic wrap – birthday gifts from Tilly, gentle attempts to help her father heal and move on.

Edward flips on the coffee machine. The hum follows him across the kitchen as he drops four slices of pre-cut bread into the oversize toaster, then loads up his arms with milk, margarine, orange juice and jam. A twinge of guilt hits Edward's stomach as he unloads his flimsy breakfast goods onto the table. He should be making scrambled eggs and baked beans to accompany the toast, perhaps with slices of bacon, or porridge with fresh fruit and nuts – something substantial and nutritious for a growing girl. Edward can't remember the last time he ate a piece of fruit, though he knows he must have done since his favourite sister's frequent visits are always accompanied by healthful snacks.

The toast pops up and Edward spreads jam (strawberry without seeds is all Tilly will accept) on two slices of toast and pours a glass of orange juice, warming the glass in his hands before setting it on the table, to soften the chill of the juice.

'Till! Breakfast!' Edward aims his voice at the ceiling – also the floor of the bathroom, where his daughter now spends most of her time. Isn't thirteen too young to be caring about make-up, dresses and boys? He can't remember either of his sisters caring about such things so young, one of them still doesn't and probably never will. Sadly, Tilly seems all too acutely aware of such things. Last night, to Edward's absolute horror, his daughter refused rice pudding after dinner on the grounds that she was 'watching her weight'. As these three words hit the table and rolled towards him, like bowling balls careening towards his chest, Edward was at a total loss for what to say. Unfortunately, Tilly had taken the silence as validation of her need to diet.

'See,' she'd declared, pushing her chair away from the table, scraping its wooden feet on the stone floor. 'I knew you thought I was fat!'

'I . . . I . . . What?' Edward had fumbled about in the fog, trying to grasp hold of something that made sense. 'Of course I don't think you're fat,' he'd said at last. But it'd been too late, his

18

daughter had already slammed the kitchen door shut behind her.

In light of this rather horrifying turn of events, Edward has been feeling the loss of his wife in a different way. For the first few years, he simply felt as if a large slice had been taken out of his heart, along with the breath from his lungs, leaving something fundamental missing, a gaping hole from which to view what remained of his life. But for the past few months, as Tilly has somehow mutated from a sweet, shy little girl into a mercurial, bolshie teenager, Edward has longed for Greer even more as a mother than just a wife. He wants her to hold his hand during these strange, unbalancing experiences, wants her to explain what's going on, to come and take charge, before it all gets any more out of control.

Generally, before Tilly turned strange, Edward thought he was doing okay. Not wonderfully or brilliantly, but okay. He'd learnt how to live, how to function from day to day, without his wife. He'd learnt, until recently anyway, how to single-parent his child. He'd learnt how to skirt around the edges of his loss so that, while he still saw the gaping hole, he no longer fell into it.

'Till! You'll be late!' Edward tips his head back towards the ceiling, noticing, for the first time, a large crack in the plaster snaking across the surface. It's not the first crack he's discovered, the house (a beautiful three-storey Victorian terrace with bay windows and red-brick walls, found after they left their home on Hope Street) is riddled with them – along with patches of mould, creaking floorboards, flickering lights and jammed doors. Last Christmas, when she was still a sweet little girl, Tilly suggested these physical quirks were in fact the ghosts of her mother and stepmother trying to send messages from beyond. Edward can't remember what words of parental wisdom he'd responded with, though he knows he didn't admit he'd had the thought more than once himself and only wished it were true. Now he stares at the crack and sighs, having neither the energy nor inclination to deal with any of it right now, or indeed in the future.

A hairdryer blasts on above his head.

'Tilly!'

Taking a bite of toast, then pulling his dressing gown cord tighter, Edward heaves himself out of the kitchen and into the hallway. He rests his foot on the first step of the stairs and leans against the bannister.

'We'll get stuck in traffic if we don't leave in ten minutes,' he shouts. 'So get your skinny self down here, now!'

Above him, the hairdryer flicks off and the house is suddenly silent. A moment later, Tilly pokes her pretty face out onto the landing.

'Hold your horses, I'll be down in a sec. And I am not skinny. I wish!' She rolls her eyes, before disappearing again.

But Edward can tell, by the flicker of a smile on the edge of her lips, that – for once – he's said the right thing. He takes his foot off the stairs and turns to head back to the kitchen, when he notices the mail again, the little pile of letters lying on the mat. Just underneath the telephone bill at the top, Edward sees an envelope – the paper embedded with flower petals – addressed to 'The Homeowner' in purple ink. He stoops to pick it up, leaving the other letters untouched, and sits on the first step of the stairs, his silk dressing gown slipping open and exposing his legs to the chill of the unheated hallway. Not that he notices.

Gently, Edward pulls a single sheet out of the envelope and rubs the edge between his fingers. Dozens of flower petals he can't identify are scattered through the paper – red, mauve, pink, yellow – and suddenly he remembers. Greer's wedding dress looked just the same. She'd sewn it from a fabric that had also been embedded with petals: roses, violets, peonies, primroses . . . She'd pointed out each one to him with her slender, clever fingers while he had watched her mouth move around the words, still in awe that his soon-to-be wife could create such incredibly beautiful things.

Edward skims the letter, searching for the subject, glancing down to see the signature – slightly startled to see that there is none – then stops and reads it properly once, and then again.

Tilly is kicking the step above him before Edward realises she's standing there. He shifts sideways so she can pass by. Tilly hops down the stairs then pauses at the bottom to look up at him.

'Are you okay, Dad?'

Edward nods.

'You look a bit weird.'

Edward manages an almost-nonchalant smile. 'I'm fine.'

'Okay,' Tilly says with a shrug. 'If you say so.' Then she bounces off towards the kitchen, leaving her father gazing at the paper of pretty flowers and startling words he still holds in his hands.

There is one person Clara writes to regularly: her mother. These are not anonymous, unasked-for letters but accounted-for, anticipated letters.

'I don't know why you don't just call to arrange things, like everyone else,' is Sophia's most common complaint.

'Because letters are more personal, more thoughtful than phone calls,' Clara protests. 'Calling is . . . perfunctory; I like to write.'

'*Your* calls are, and that's whenever I can actually get you on the phone,' her mother says, 'but I like to chat. You can discuss things properly that way, share ideas, talk . . .'

'Well, we can do that now, can't we? Now that we're actually together.'

'I suppose.' Sophia adjusts her teaspoon so it sits just at the edge of her saucer. 'But I like to be spontaneous. I don't see why we always have to make appointments.'

Clara looks into her own cup, as if searching for the right response in the murky depths of her milky tea. Instead, she says nothing. Sophia reaches for another scone and soaks it in butter, then adds a dollop of clotted cream.

'But you do make the best scones I've ever had,' she says. 'And I've had plenty.' She glances down at the folds of her stomach, under the shelf of her breasts.

'Thanks,' Clara says, deciding to accept this unexpected compliment graciously.

'It's a shame we didn't inherit your granddad's genes,' Sophia continues. 'That man could, and often did, eat entire afternoon teas without putting on a single ounce. Mum was like me, though, more's the pity.' She casts an eye over her daughter. 'You didn't stand much of a chance, what with me and your father, did you? It's a shame, but still . . .' She shrugs, adding a little more cream before taking another bite of the scone.

Clara studiously ignores both her own stomach and the remark, and takes another sip of tea. She'd been about to have a second scone herself, but won't now.

'Your grandma was a fabulous cook, though, I'll give her that. She published a cookbook once. Did I ever tell you that? Dad was proud as punch. Or is that pleased as . . . ? At any rate, he was thrilled.' Sophia beams as she munches. 'He used to sell signed copies in the shop. He made her one of his special pens, so she could sign them all in style. I think he bought half the

22

publisher's stock, gave them as gifts to everyone we knew.'

Clara stares at her mother. 'You've never told me that before.'

'Didn't I? Oh, I thought—'

'What's it called?'

Sophia holds her scone in mid-air. 'You know, I don't remember. Isn't that funny? I must have read the recipes hundreds of times, 'til I had them memorised, but I can't recall the title.'

'But you must have a copy,' Clara says. 'I can't believe I've never seen it.'

'Actually, I don't. I had my own, signed, of course. But it got so stained over the years – I suppose at some point, I must have thrown it out.'

'You threw away Grandma's book?'

'I'm sorry, sweetie.' Sophia shrugs. 'You know I'm not very attached to things. Your father taught me that.'

Clara winces but says nothing.

'And,' her mother continues breezily, 'once I had all my favourite recipes memorised, I didn't really need the book any more now, did I?'

It's not about needing, Clara wants to say, *it's about treasuring*. But she knows there's no point. Her mother is so unlike her in this respect (and most others) that they simply aren't able to understand each other. Sophia's house is all cream and chrome, plain carpets, unadorned walls, sleek modern appliances, without a sign of past or personality, and everything looking – at least on Clara's rare visits – as if airbrushed for an imminent magazine photo shoot. By contrast, Clara's house (inherited from her grandfather) is a homage to chaos, clutter, colour and old-fashioned living. No two rooms are alike, though they share common themes – vintage clocks, weathered Persian rugs, velvet cushions, potted purple orchids, stacks of books,

23

framed letters written by famous people – and all are unified by the fact that everything appears to be dated c.1900 and it seems that nothing once arrived in the house had ever left again.

Clara tries to keep cordial relations with her mother, which means keeping visits fairly frequent (or Sophia starts texting pointed remarks about feeling abandoned and unloved) but as short as politely possible. It bothers Clara sometimes, if she ponders on it for too long, that she isn't close with either of her parents and that she doesn't have any siblings. But then she thinks of her grandparents and decides that the two things – one unfortunate, the other not – balance each other out fairly enough.

'I'll bet there's at least a few hundred copies in this house, if only you could find them in the mess,' Sophia says, finishing off her scone in another bite.

Clara shakes her head, not rising to the bait. 'If there was a single copy I'd have found it. I know every book in the house. It's not here.'

Her mother pauses, teacup at her lips, to consider. 'Have you looked in the attic?'

Clara frowns. 'What attic?'

Sophia raises an eyebrow and doesn't attempt to hide her smile. 'I thought you knew everything about this place.'

'I've only lived here ten years, you grew up here,' Clara says, trying not to snap.

Sophia slips off the breakfast stool she was perched on, her feet encased in expensive dark-brown suede boots, alighting with a determined thud on the wooden floor. Another way in which Clara differs from her mother is in appearance, not in size, perhaps, but in presentation. Sophia is always impeccably put together in muted monochrome silk, satin, cotton and cashmere –

so her clothes blend with her kitchen – while Clara favours cheap, cheerful prints in bright colours, so she stands out like a sore thumb in her mother's sterile surroundings but blends seamlessly with her own oriental rugs.

'Follow me,' Sophia says as she disappears out of the kitchen.

Clara hurries after her. After the second flight of stairs, Sophia stops halfway along the landing. She points up at the ceiling.

'It's here.'

Clara looks up at a beautiful oriental rug attached to the ceiling, mirroring the one on the floor beneath it. 'Where?'

'Underneath that rather hideous rug, I presume.'

Clara flinches.

Sophia stands on tiptoe, takes hold of the closest corner of the rug and gives it a sharp tug.

'It's nailed in place,' Clara says, 'we need a ladder.'

Ignoring her, Sophia gives another tug and one end of the rug rips off the ceiling. She sidesteps the cloud of dust that showers down upon them.

'Pass me that garish umbrella,' Sophia says, waving her hand in the direction of a polka-dot umbrella leaning against the wall. 'Goodness knows what it's doing all the way up here, but for once your clutter is useful.'

Clara hands her mother the umbrella. Sophia turns it upside down, using the curved wooden handle to unhook the brass ring fixed onto a large square of wood in the ceiling. It springs open and, after another tug, a wooden ladder uncurls to the landing floor. Clara peers up into the dark hole above her head. 'I can't believe I never knew about the attic.'

Sophia mounts the stairs. 'Well, don't stand gaping like a goldfish, come on.'

The words land like pebbles on Clara's upturned head. She shakes off her confusion and follows her mother up the steps. When Clara emerges into the attic – to see her mother already rooting through a pile of cardboard boxes in the corner – she lets out a little gasp. The attic is large and, like every other room in the house, full to the brim with everything one could possibly imagine, and a few things one couldn't: books, boxes, furniture, leather suitcases, racks of clothes, cracked teapots and piles of papers . . . Everywhere she looks Clara sees something new.

'What is all this?' she asks, under her breath.

'It's probably all rubbish,' Sophia says, without glancing up. 'But we might find the odd gem worth selling – I doubt it, but you never know.'

'Maybe we shouldn't be looking at it,' Clara ventures. 'Perhaps it's private, perhaps that's why they didn't tell me.'

'Oh, don't be so silly.' Sophia abandons the cardboard boxes and casts her eye about for something more promising. 'Anyway, they're dead now, so the issue of privacy is moot.'

Clara raises an eyebrow. 'Do you feel that way about your own death?'

'Don't be so morbid, Clara,' her mother says, fingering the edge of a bright-yellow satin swing dress. 'Oh, I do wish my mother had had better taste. I wouldn't have minded a few vintage gowns to go dancing.'

Clara regards her mother. 'I didn't know you danced.'

Sophia smiles. 'What you don't know about me, dear, is a lot.'

Clara is about to reply to this remark when her curiosity is snagged by a box a few feet away. The box is set apart from the general cornucopia of bric-a-brac and appears to have somehow escaped the thick sprinkling of dust coating everything else. The

26

box is twelve inches tall and deep, made of shining mahogany, intricately carved in a pattern Clara recognises but can't quite place. And then she realises. The box must have been made by the same carpenter who created the writing desk. Her mother's chatter drops to a background hum as Clara steps towards the box, carefully picking her way over the piles scattered across her path.

Clara sits, squeezing herself between a rack of dresses and a low wall of cardboard boxes, and passes her palm gently over the top of the box, tracing her forefinger along the swirls and swells in the wood. She finds the catch and very carefully, very slowly, opens the lid. Then she's staring down at a package wrapped in brown paper and tied with string. And, on top, sits a note, yellowed, worn and barely readable:

For Clara,
If you haven't found your first story yet,
I have one here for you.
I hope, too, that it might make up for all the family you have lost.

Chapter Three

After dropping Tilly at school, Edward returns immediately to the letter. He'd left it propped up on the kitchen counter by the kettle but has been thinking of nothing else since – as if he'd left pieces of his skin behind on the pages and needed to return to reattach them to himself. When he's at last sitting with the letter in his hands again, Edward feels a deep sense of relief he can't explain.

For months after Greer died, he'd felt that sense of loss all the time: every second of every minute of every day. He'd be walking along the hallway and stop and turn around, trying to recall what he'd forgotten. Then he'd remember: his wife. The idea that she'd gone in any sort of absolute and permanent way wasn't something he could make sense of – neither his mind nor his body could comprehend it – he felt instead that she'd wandered off somewhere and neglected to tell him where she'd gone while, at the same time, taking a part of him with her. Eventually, Edward had managed to overcome this extremely disturbing phenomenon by shutting down every feeling part of himself, so there was nothing to miss any more, whether he'd ever had it or not.

Now he slowly unfolds the letter, half expecting the words to have evaporated in his absence. It's not addressed to him by name, simply beginning with a sentence at the top of the page, but there's absolutely no doubt in his mind that it's intended for him.

Monday 1st May '17

I know that you have given up hope of ever feeling happy again. I know you're just shuffling through your days now, trying not to make any major mistakes, waiting until it's all over, until everything is at an end. And, should you want to pass the rest of your life like this, you won't be judged for it. And yet, there is a tiny part of you that still flickers brighter than the rest, a dim spark of hope that lingers on. I know you feel it flare up sometimes: when you step into an unexpected patch of sunlight, when your daughter laughs, when you chance upon a deer who's wandered into your garden and, instead of skittering away, he stops and looks you right in the eye.

I know you've suffered great tragedy twice in your lifetime, twice more than any man should have to suffer and I know that, even then, you still experience little moments of glory and wonder – hidden bubbles that burst up unexpectedly amid the madness and misery. I know, too, that occasionally – usually at twilight, when the veil between the magic and the mundane is nearly lifted – you see that a choice is open to you, and that the life you choose is up to you.

Edward folds the letter on his lap twice in half, smoothing the edges across his knees. He knows he'll open it up many times again, that he will reread and reread, but for now he needs a little silence.

He needs to make sense of this mystery, to figure out who sent him the letter and why. It must be someone he knows, since the writer clearly understands him so well, better in fact than he understands himself. Which is rather strange and, in fact, slightly scary. Has someone been watching him, following him, spying on him? But even then, how could they see so deep into his heart? Perhaps it's from his sister, Alba. Yet it doesn't read as if it's written by a sister, being both too impersonal and yet too intimate all at once.

Edward takes a deep breath. He already feels different, despite himself. In the past three hours, since he first read the letter, his cells have started to shift about, his blood has begun pumping a little faster, his bones are realigning, minute cracks are creeping across the ice encasing his numb heart.

Edward puts his hand to his chest, feeling an ache in his muscles and bones, as he sometimes does when he stands after kneeling on the floor for too long. He wonders, for a moment, whether he might be about to have a heart attack. So he sits, waiting for the pain to pass, glancing about the kitchen, wondering what his wife would have thought of the state of this house. He asks this of himself often, though he knows the answer: she would have hated it. She would have thought it boring and bland, the opposite of the magnificent multicoloured costumes she created which, Edward reminds himself, was exactly the point. A few months after she'd died he'd suddenly decided that he had to find a new place to live, a place that didn't remind him of her every single second of every single hour of every single day. It was a decision he's regretted in a million moments since.

Edward stares at the oven. And then, for some reason, after studying a rogue spot of strawberry jam on the marble worktop, Edward glances up at the ceiling, at the thick black crack snaking across the plaster. He feels a sharp tug in his chest and presses his hand closer to his heart. And then, for the first time in a very long time – almost three years, in fact – Edward feels the urge to *do* something, something useful, something ordinary and insignificant.

Edward stands. He will mend the crack in the ceiling.

Clara sits with a box of papers in her lap. Her mother chatters away in the background, something about swing dancing and high heels, while Clara presses her fingers to the first page, the heat of her skin making marks on the black leather. She's torn between a desperate desire to read and devour every word and a longing to save the pages forever untouched, so keeping a little piece of her grandfather always alive and unwrapped.

Clara has never been a particularly curious person. She's never kept awake at night wondering what's happened to all those people who receive her letters. She doesn't want to ask her customers what they write in their own letters. She's never tempted to open the ones she's promised not to read. Once, when Clara was thirteen, she had a deep crush on a boy and, while they sat in his bedroom listening to records, he left to go to the bathroom. She shifted to lean against the wall and felt something hard under the duvet. It was his diary. She hadn't read it. Perhaps, Clara sometimes thinks, this lack of curiosity accounts for her lack of success as a writer of fiction. And yet, she knows now that, no matter how much she longs to hold on, no matter how greatly she wants this moment to last for ever, she will, of course, read this diary.

Every inch of the first page is enveloped with her grandfather's handwriting, a small, slanting script in twilight-blue ink from the nib of his favourite pen. She can imagine him, hunched over the writing desk in the shop, scribbling away. He only ever wrote with one pen, the very first he ever made, when he was an apprentice in Amsterdam, before his family came to England. And he'd never allowed her to write with it, no matter how much she'd begged.

'A perfect pen falls in love with a single hand,' he had said. 'Its love is lifelong and loyal. In the hand of another it will dry up, it will scratch out words and turn everything into an illegible mess. It isn't fair to put it through that pain. So you may hold my pen, my sweet, but I'm afraid I can never allow you to write with it.'

A sigh of sorrow rises in Clara's chest but she swallows it down, knowing it'd arouse comment from her mother. Her grandfather's twilight words blur. Clara blinks and brushes her fingers over her eyes. Then she takes a deep breath and begins to read:

My dearest Clara,
You've found this because you're looking for a story and, I'm guessing, because you're lonely and longing for a connection – with yourself and with others. Well, I can offer you both. Enclosed in this box are letters. They belong to our family; they tell of a great love story. I won't say anything more than that, since I'd like you to discover the rest without my help.

I believe, if you should want to find out more, that the adventure will do you great good. It will ignite desire in you, it will set you on a path to grand adventures – out in the world and inside your own heart – that will ultimately bring you great joy. Of course, if you already have this in your life now, then you may not want to venture down the rabbit hole to which these letters will lead you. But, I have a feeling that, when you find this note, you'll still be hiding away in your little shop of letters, writing to those who call upon you, offering your magic

to transform their lives yet neglecting your own. Of course, if
I am wrong, you can ignore your silly, fussing grandfather. If
I am right, however, then please read these letters. And please
follow where they will lead . . .

With all love,
Granddad xox

'Dad! What on earth are you doing?'

Edward looks down from where he's standing on the tabletop. He brushes plaster out of his eyes, then wipes long dusty white streaks across his jeans.

'I'm mending the crack in the ceiling,' he says.

Tilly raises an eyebrow. 'It looks like you're making a massive hole in the ceiling.'

'Don't worry,' Edward says. 'It's all part of the process.'

The arch of Tilly's eyebrow rises higher. 'Ok-ay.' Dropping her school bag on the floor (then shifting it a safer distance from underneath the large hole) Tilly walks over to the cupboards and starts searching for biscuits.

'Pass me that hammer,' Edward says, 'and stop doubting your father's skills. I am an architect, you know.'

Tilly sticks her head out of the cupboards and picks up the hammer with her free hand, the other clutching a packet of dry digestives. 'Dad, you haven't done that for years.'

Edward takes the hammer and taps at the jagged edge of the hole. A little shower of white powder dusts his hair. 'I know. But, I'm thinking maybe it's time for me to start working again.'

Tilly, with half a biscuit sticking out of her mouth, looks up. 'But you sold the firm.'

Edward shrugs. 'That doesn't mean I can't get a job working for someone else's firm, or doing freelance jobs,' he says, still gazing up into the hole. 'Anyway, it's just a thought I had today. I haven't made any plans, I was just thinking.'

'That's great, Dad,' Tilly says, swallowing the biscuit, then nibbling at another. 'You should get a job. It'll do you good to do less thinking and more actual living.'

Edward pulls his attention away from the hole to regard his daughter. How can you be so wise, he wants to ask, did you grow up while I wasn't looking? But the realisation of just how much he's been neglecting Tilly since his wife died brings tears to his eyes and he has to say something else instead.

'I'm glad to see you're eating today. Does this mean you've come to your senses and no longer think you're fat?'

'You're so lame, Dad.' Tilly rolls her eyes. 'These biscuits only have twenty-eight calories each. I can have three.' And, with that, she leaves the kitchen.

Edward gazes after her as she skips purposefully along the corridor, and suddenly thanks every lucky star he never thought he had – quite the opposite, in fact, if there are such things as unlucky stars – that his darling daughter seems so relatively unscathed by everything. If only he was so robust himself.

As Edward's gaze returns to the hopelessly gaping hole above his head, another thought comes to him: after fixing the mess he's made of his ceiling, he will have to, somehow, track down whomever sent him the letter.

Chapter Four

Ava's days are shaped by *The Times* cryptic crossword. She begins it in the morning, unfolding the paper as she sits with her cup of milky Earl Grey and marmalade scraped thinly over slightly burnt toast. While drinking the tea and nibbling the toast, Ava scans the little black-and-white squares, digesting each of the clues. By the time her cup and plate are empty, she's usually filled out three or four answers. And the rest of the unanswered questions have soaked into her mind and memory, allowing her to revisit them throughout the day.

Words float up at unexpected moments. Ava will be washing dishes when she hears: *Bemuse – 7 Down: Play goddess to stupefy (6)*. She'll be checking in library books when: *Bittern – 14 Across: Bird pecked bird (7)* pops up. She'll be running for the bus when she'll realise: *Rayon – 10 Down: Light shed on synthetic material (5)*. And each time Ava will smile, a secret little smile, then make a mental note of what to fill in later . . . In truth, though Ava tells herself she's driven by the desire to finish the crossword as fast as possible – the competition with oneself being the point – actually an ideal day is when the final answer arrives at bedtime. This way she can spend most of her moments concealed in the comfortable confines of her own mind, almost able to pretend the rest of the world doesn't exist at all.

Ava's other hobby is gardening. She enjoys being with her plants whatever the weather. She loves springtime, of course, witnessing the resurrection of so many of her beautiful flowers, coaxing them on with soft words, gently touching the light-green leaves of new shoots as they push their way through the wet, dark earth and into the cool sunlight. But she loves the winter as well. On even the coldest mornings Ava wraps herself in thick wool, slips her socked feet into sheepskin boots, curls her fingers around a large mug of coffee and ventures out onto crisp, crunchy grass. She'll take a few crossword clues – tucked safely and snugly into the corners of her mind – out into the frosty air and mull them over as she slowly circles the frozen lawn. Ava doesn't touch the solid earth during the coldest months but she brings the warmth of her body into the garden and stays with her plants for as long as she can. She strokes a bare finger along the stripped branches of the bushes and trees, reminding their hibernating leaves of the warmth of life to which they will one day return.

But, of all the seasons and all the months, May is Ava's favourite. When a symphony of bluebells explodes across her flower beds, she can't stop smiling. Sometimes she'll stare at them for hours. She'll be preparing dinner, or doing the washing-up and just look out of the window. Then, finally, she'll tear her gaze away, catch sight of the clock and realise an hour has disappeared. And, during the months when her garden is plump with colour, the combination of the beauty and silence is so soothing that Ava often forgets to think about her crossword puzzles at all.

Today, as she steps outside in stockinged feet, Ava senses a shift in the air. She sniffs her cup of lukewarm peppermint tea, shivering slightly in the cool morning breeze as she glances around her garden. She should probably slip on a pair of shoes – the soles of her stockings will soon be damp from the dewy grass – but something stops her and Ava walks onto the soft wet lawn. Instead of circling the garden she stands in the middle, shuts her eyes and wonders what feels different. It takes a while before she can pinpoint it. It feels as if something is about to *happen*.

And then, in the next moment, it does. A sound, like Ava has never heard before in her life, soars through the air – a flood of notes from a violin. It pierces Ava's heart, stopping her breath in her throat. Then the sound dies and the air is still again. But, after a few minutes the music begins again and, as it plays, something inside Ava stirs, as if her heart is a hibernating bear slumbering all her life and only just now waking up.

Finn O'Connor was three years old when he heard his first concerto. It was Vivaldi's *Four Seasons* and Finn was absolutely transfixed. He was a boy who loved to run and jump. He'd never been able to sit still for more than a second – his mother having to employ great skills of persuasion whenever she sat him down for a meal – but as he'd watched the musicians and their instruments he hadn't shifted from his chair for a moment. Through every bar of spring, summer and autumn Finn stayed glued, still as a statue, while the notes of a dozen instruments soared above, around and vibrated within him. But when winter arrived and the violin solo came to a crescendo, Finn was literally capsized by the music. He fell off his chair.

Six days later, finally exhausted by his unrelenting begging, Finn's mother spent the family's weekly shopping budget on a second-hand violin. Then after he lived, breathed and slept with it for another two weeks, she took two extra cleaning shifts at the school to pay for lessons. He hadn't been able to read by sight or play pieces perfectly without practising, but what he lacked in innate talent Finn made up for in tenacity. His enthusiasm only increased as he grew. He practised all day, each day, every moment he could. He woke early and stayed up late. He pelted into the living room after school, snatching up his violin, his most precious, prized possession and holding it against his heart. He stood with it, whispering his secrets into the wood before cocking his ear to the bridge to better hear the soft replies.

'Finn, please. Not at the dinner table,' his mother would protest, half-heartedly. 'Can't you let go of that instrument just long enough to eat?'

Finn's answer to this plea was always the same. He'd cast a reproachful glance out from under furrowed brows and tighten the fingers of his left hand around the scroll of his violin.

'You're spilling your peas,' his mother would object.

In response, Finn would press his lips to the table and inhale the offending peas, to which his mother would sigh and mumble something unintelligible. Then she'd start muttering about their father.

'It's all my fault . . . I'm not enough . . . If only your father hadn't left, you wouldn't be so . . .' And tears would fill her eyes and Finn would pretend not to see them.

'Don't be stupid, Mum,' Byrne – Finn's older brother – would snap then. 'Dad left cos he's a bastard philanderer. And Finn would still be a weirdo, even if that man, or any man, was here. I'd just consider yourself lucky you've got one normal son.'

At eleven years old, Byrne didn't have any slightly strange

40

obsessions. He didn't even have any passions – excepting video games and spaghetti. He viewed the world through the jaded eyes of someone who knew what he liked and what he didn't – most things in life falling into the latter category. So when Finn serenaded him at bedtime with Beethoven's Fifth Symphony, Byrne slammed the door and stuffed his head under his pillow. And when Finn trundled along the pavement to school, humming the violin solo from *Aida*, Byrne told him to 'shut the hell up'.

But, despite all her concerns and half-hearted protests, for the most part Mary O'Connor took great delight in her younger son and his music. She asked him to play when she did the dishes every night and while she was making breakfast every morning. At other times, when she was scrubbing someone else's linoleum floors, for example, she found herself humming along as if Finn were standing beside her, bow in hand. His music seeped into her dreams so she woke smiling, even though her bed was bare and bereft of the man she wished was still sleeping beside her.

It was only when Mary most longed for that man and turned to her youngest son instead, that she hated the violin. When she read to Finn at night and felt the sudden urge to cuddle him close and squeeze him tight, she glared at the instrument wedged between them, momentarily wishing it would spontaneously combust. Of course, she never said anything against it. Indeed, Mary was eternally grateful that Finn had something he loved so dearly he might not miss an absent father quite so much.

Finn was twelve when a tragedy occurred. As he ran across the road on his way home from school, clutching the violin under his arm, he stumbled and dropped the case. A car blasted its horn and Finn sprang away. He survived. The violin didn't.

'I'll buy you another one,' his mother promised. 'As soon as I can find another job. It won't be long, don't worry. I've got another interview next week.'

She'd been let go from the cleaning job at the school after the council had made budget cuts. Sadly, for both Finn and Mary, it took her an entire year to find a new job. During this time, while he couldn't play, Finn took to scratching at scabs on his skin until they bled, over and over again, until they scarred. He sucked his thumb so fiercely it got blisters and twisted his hair so hard it shed in clumps. When, at last, his mother was gainfully employed and quickly saved to buy him another violin, Finn clutched it to his chest so tightly he could barely breathe and wept with relief.

Finn plays every morning at daybreak. Sometimes he serenades the birds singing outside his bedroom window, other times he accompanies them and, occasionally, he lets them take the lead. It's his meditation, his inner settling before being thrown into the fray of the day. Finn doesn't do well with people. He's okay with kids, which is why he teaches music four days a week at the secondary school across town. He relies on the stable income, as well as enjoying the biweekly injection of unadulterated enthusiasm the kids give him.

Today, Finn steps over piles of cardboard boxes to reach his open window. It's all new to him: the house, the window and the little garden beneath. He'd moved in the day before but it already felt like home. Really, all Finn needed was his violin to feel at home. He could have been pitched up in a tent in a field or in a sleeping bag under a bridge and, as long as he had the sweetest part of him, he'd be all right.

Cool spring air blows through Finn's fingers as he plays, warming up with Vivaldi's *Four Seasons* – autumn and winter – as he always does, before mixing in a little Mozart and Beethoven, then letting himself go into a free style of his own making. As he plays Finn glances out of the window onto his garden below. It's a bit of a mess – the previous tenant clearly hadn't cared much for gardening – but the garden next door to his is absolutely glorious. He keeps playing as he lets his eyes flit from one flower to the next until, finally, they alight on a woman standing at the edge of the lawn, holding a cup of tea, staring up at him. She's beautiful, with long black hair and big dark eyes. Instinctively, Finn darts away from the open window, clutching his violin tight to his chest, as if the woman had been intending on snatching it from him. He waits in the shadows behind his curtains for a while, before finally peeking out of the window again.

This time he sees something else entirely. The woman with the long black hair has gone but, as Finn glances around, he sees another woman standing at the bottom of his other neighbour's garden. This woman has red hair that curls and spirals in the wind, freckles scattered across her bare skin – of which there is quite a lot – and an air of serenity he's rarely seen in another person. Indeed, Finn is so mesmerised by this woman, so enchanted, that it takes him a while to realise that she isn't actually standing on the lawn but hovering a few inches above it.

Chapter Five

Of course, Clara, even with her languid lack of curiosity, reads the letters. Or, at least, she tries to read the letters. Unfortunately, she isn't able, since they're all written in a language she doesn't understand. It doesn't help too that the handwriting is virtually illegible but, even once she's deciphered each letter of the first paragraph on the first page, she's still made no progress at all.

Since Clara is a committed Luddite when it comes to technology, refusing to own a computer, or dabble with the attendant evils of emails and the like, whenever she has to use the Internet she visits the library and makes sure to check out a few books at the same time. It's a sort of equivalent, she considers, to cutting down a tree and planting another in its place – if only everyone would balance their embracing of modern technology with an equal expenditure on and employment of real books, pens and paper. The world would be a better place.

Today, instead of tackling the computer herself, Clara asks the librarian for assistance. He informs her that the letter is written in Dutch. Meaning, Clara reasons, that they came from her grandfather's family, of whom she knows little to nothing about. Only that most of her family had fled from Amsterdam just before the outbreak of WWII and most members of their Jewish family who'd stayed behind had perished.

Since discovering that the letters are in Dutch, Clara keeps them by her bedside – so they are the last thing she sees as she switches off the light and the first thing she sees when the sun through her curtains wakes her. Somehow, even the feeling of keeping the letters close, though Clara can't make any sense of them, gives her comfort. She's always missed the fact of having very little family – once her grandparents died, her mother was all she had left. Clara has no father to speak of and no siblings, so the notion of a few extra family members is an appealing one.

Clara knows it'd be fairly easy to find someone to translate the letters in Cambridge – it's a city of students, after all, some of whom no doubt read multiple languages – but she's holding back. Perhaps because she's a little nervous about embarking on this adventure and also because she wants to hold on to the mystery – full of potential and possibility – for a while longer. The mystery gives her imagination free rein so Clara can bask in images of reunions and love and joys to come. And she's not yet willing to let go of these delights, however unreal, for the probable disappointing bump of reality.

On the rare occasions she's not thinking of the letters, Clara finds her mind drifting to the man whose name she doesn't know. When she'd seen him in his living room, sitting on the sofa with his daughter – at least, Clara presumed it was his daughter – reading a book, she'd been so touched it'd almost brought her to tears. Clara can't rightly say why; she had no urge yet to have children and hadn't found the man himself especially alluring, so hadn't been moved by maternal or romantic feeling. And yet, for some reason, the image of them returns to her.

Clara doesn't usually think of the people to whom she sends letters. After the letter is written and posted, she closes that mental file and moves on to the next one. Very occasionally, years later, Clara might find herself writing to the same person a second time – most people usually experience several ups and downs in their lives, after all – but she'd rarely thought of them in the intervening years. With this one, though, it's different.

Clara wonders if it might be because her own father left around the same time, when she was about the same age as the young girl. And, even though this other father seemed so sad, he also seemed solid. He wouldn't desert his only daughter, he would stick with her through thick and thin. He'd make her hot chocolate late at night, he'd run to her bedroom when she had nightmares, he'd make her favourite breakfast of French toast on a Sunday morning. Of this Clara was absolutely certain. She couldn't say how she knew, but she knew. Clara's own father had left when she was twelve. He'd been leaving in increments for years before that, so Clara wasn't actually very surprised to find him gone one morning. Her mother, on the other hand, had been rather more surprised and thus had remained considerably more bitter. But Clara hadn't felt the presence of her father for a long, long time – as if he was slowly fading away like a ghost – and so, she always imagined that, one day, he'd simply evaporated into thin air. Her mother, if she knew any different, never divulged the particulars and Clara, knowing it would get her nowhere, had never asked.

Of course, Clara has thought of her father often over the years, wondering where he might be and what he might be doing. But since he's never tried to contact her, never written with his whereabouts, she confines her wonderings to the realms of unreality. And since

47

it's less painful to think about a virtual stranger, Clara thinks on this other father instead. Sometimes she'll be sitting behind the counter, waiting on her next customer, doodling on paper with one of the special pens, and find that she's quite accidentally begun writing him another letter. She'll look down and see the words:

How are you? How's your daughter? What are your names? (Why does that matter?) I hope you're both well . . .

And then she'll snap out of her reverie and pull herself back to attention.

Once Edward has mended the crack in the kitchen ceiling (a task that took him a good few days longer than he'd anticipated, after he initially made it a good deal worse before at last making it better again) he moves on to other long-neglected DIY projects. Now that he has surveyed the house with a critical eye, he can't believe that he's let it get into such a state of disrepair. Every room is in serious need of a good lick of paint, gutters are cracked and overflowing with leaves, the garden is overrun with weeds and Edward can't even bear to acknowledge, let alone begin to confront, the obscene levels of dirt and dust on every single surface in every single room.

As he tours the place, taking inventory, it increasingly strikes Edward that the state of his house reflects the state of his life: neglected, broken and shabby. Which is embarrassing and, considering that he's raising his daughter here, more than a little shameful. So Edward makes a list and sets to work. He starts at the bottom and takes each project room by room. Five days after he starts, Edward reaches the bathroom.

The bathroom, he's sorry to see, is probably in the worst state of all the other rooms in the house. Eleven items, on his list of forty-eight, relate to the bathroom. The first that must be dealt with are the tiles. It's the biggest job and should be done as soon as possible in order to allow enough time for the grouting to dry before Tilly takes one of her infinite showers the next morning. The amount of time teenage girls spend in the bathroom seems, to Edward, to bear an inverse ratio to the amount of time they actually need. Still, what does he know? So, with a shrug, Edward sets himself to work. And, as the hours pass in clouds of dust and humming and sweat, he finds that he's smiling while he sings and, for the first time in a very long time, all of a sudden he belts out a note:

'Waterlooooo . . .'

'Hey, Ed.'

Edward instantly stops. This behaviour would definitely fall under the category of 'embarrassing things that fathers aren't allowed to do'. He glances up guiltily from grouting the bathroom tiles. But, as he does so, he realises that Tilly only ever calls him 'Dad'. Still confused, it takes Edward a moment to realise who he's seeing, sitting on the loo seat with her legs crossed. For there, even more beautiful, but significantly more transparent than Edward remembered, is Greer Ashby, his dead wife.

Edward has no idea how long it takes him to speak, anywhere between an hour and a day, or just a full fifteen minutes. All he knows is that the pathways between his brain and his mouth seem to seize up for rather a long time. He's always been a very practical, pragmatic man – not entirely an atheist, perhaps, but certainly leaning heavily in that direction – and has never been inclined to flights of fancy, certainly not in the direction of his dead wife.

Although, that's not entirely true, as he now recalls. In the weeks and months after her death he'd kneel on the bathroom floor – on the floor of every room in the house in fact – and beg a God he didn't quite believe in to send her back. Every night he'd sob into the darkness, pleading for Greer's spirit to return to him.

'It's you,' he says.

She smiles. 'It is.'

Edward continues to stare at her, confused. 'But, but . . .' Edward stares at her, open-mouthed, since, even when he'd asked her the question, he still assumed that she was an apparition, a figment of something, an ethereal gift from a finally benevolent universe, but not one that could actually speak. And she sounds exactly as she did and looks so similar too, with the exception of the extra dose of beauty and transparency.

'But what?'

'But, why are you here?' he asks, still not entirely convinced that she actually is.

Greer gives a little shrug. 'I'm not entirely sure.'

'B-b-but . . .' Edward stutters, trying to gather his colliding thoughts and still not quite certain he isn't hallucinating. 'If you're here – then why . . . why did you wait so long?'

Greer is silent.

'Why did you come back now?' he asks. 'When, when . . .'

'When you don't need me any more?' Greer finishes.

'No,' he says, a little too quickly. 'That's not what I mean . . .' He pauses for several moments. 'Well, okay, yes,' he admits. 'I just, I literally just started putting my life back together. I just began learning how to live without you and now, and now . . .'

His wife watches him, waiting.

'Why? Why couldn't you come back when, when' – his eyes

swell with tears as he remembers – 'when I couldn't bear to be alive without you?'

'Oh, Ed.' Greer doesn't move, though she seems to shift forward in her seat, as if wanting to go to him but being unable. 'I'm so, so . . .'

'I hate that you're being so Zen about all this, like it's the easiest thing in the world, while I'm falling apart on the bathroom floor.' Edward finds a small smile. 'And I've done more than my fair share of that in the past few years, don't you think?'

Greer nods. 'I know, sweetheart. And, if I could have made it any easier for you, I would have. In a second, in a heartbeat.'

'So, why didn't you?'

'I don't know,' his wife admits. 'But, if I had, would it really have made it easier for you to let me go?'

Edward snorts, then shrugs. He's a little surprised at his own reaction, even as he's having it. He'd always imagined that, if he ever saw his wife again, he'd either weep uncontrollably or be overwhelmed with joy. As it is Edward feels so strangely conflicted that he isn't exactly sure what he's feeling at all.

Greer continues to look at him from her position on the loo seat.

'No,' Edward admits after a while. 'No, I suppose not. Though that doesn't make it any more forgivable.' He knows, even as he says it, that, of course, it does.

'I think, perhaps, I had to wait for you to heal,' Greer says softly. 'I think I had to wait for you to be okay before I came back.'

She says this to comfort him but, in truth, she really has no idea at all.

Chapter Six

Finn is late for work. He's cycling madly across town, hoping to hell he doesn't get hit by a car or, worse still, a bus, and knowing that – no matter how fast he goes – his legs aren't able to get him to the school on time. He's late because he always stays too late in the morning, playing. Although, he's not simply playing, he's also watching the woman (actually, the wom*e*n) who come outside every morning to stand in their gardens and listen.

Having another point of attention while he plays is entirely new for Finn. He's always been completely and utterly focused before, to the point that major natural disasters could have befallen his surroundings and he'd never have noticed. He's always put himself so completely into his playing, feeling the birth of every note quiver through his fingers and every echo hum long and deep in his chest. It's the very reason Finn loves to play – loves it more than any other experience he's ever had, even sex, though that's admittedly been a limited foray so far – because when he plays he forgets himself so entirely. It's almost, though Finn isn't a religious person, a spiritual experience – in that he feels his body disappear and his spirit rise up to merge with and melt into wherever it has come from, the energy that had created everything in the first place. Playing music, for Finn, is so much bliss, joy and ecstasy all at once that he's never had an orgasm to match it and he certainly doesn't want to dilute it.

And yet, he can't pull his attention away from the woman with red hair who floats above the grass at the end of her garden, looking up and listening to him so intently. And actually, far from diluting Finn's experience, it strangely seems to enhance it. He feels the intensity of her listening so deeply that it's almost as if she's touching him. It feels as if her fingers hover just above his bare skin, so he can feel the heat of her, then she strokes her fingertips along his body, unwrapping him like great swathes of silk, until she's able to reach in and take hold of his heart so it lies warm and beating in her hands.

And, as she listens, his playing takes on fresh force so that the music becomes his fingers and with every note he reaches out, very gently and very slowly slipping her clothes off, until he's caressing her, tracing his touch through the spirals of her hair, along the arc of her cheek, the slope of her neck, the swell of her breasts, the curve of her belly . . . He feels himself stroke his fingertips over every inch of her soft body, as the notes begin to wrap themselves around her, draping over her shoulders, curling tenderly around her chest, until her whole body is enveloped by his music, his touch, his spirit and his soul.

By the time Finn finally pulls himself, with paralysing reluctance, away from his violin, his skin is slick with sweat and his heart pounds against his ribs. When he drags himself away from the window, catching sight of the alarm clock and knowing he can't postpone his departure a second longer, he has to bite his lip to stop from calling out to her. He hasn't the nerve. Because he's terrified, that she'll either turn away and never return or – more likely – that she'll prove to be a transparent, floating figment of his imagination. And Finn will gladly put off that moment of disillusionment for ever – even if the woman isn't real, even if her presence is putting his job in jeopardy, he doesn't care.

Ava is giddy. Every morning she wakes before her alarm, her eyes snapping open, her bare feet already on the floorboards as she hurries towards the bathroom. Her new neighbour plays every morning as the birds start to sing and she needs to be outside to hear him so she doesn't miss a single second. She wants to soak up every note, every sound. She wants to close her eyes and let the music sink deep into her body. She wants it to flood through her, the pure tones cleansing her blood, healing her spirit, clearing all the thoughts from her head.

Ava doesn't understand the strange, hypnotic influence the music and the musician have over her but neither does she care to analyse it. She feels so brightly and suddenly alive, so sharp and so soft all at once, as if she's being born and dying in the same breath, opening her arms to embrace everything in the world while letting it all go. Listening, Ava feels entirely serene, as if she has all she could possibly want and needs absolutely nothing more. She has all the joy her heart can hold, so it overflows to her feet and dampens her toes, so it floats in the air around her, returning to her with every breath.

Perhaps the best thing about the enchanting music is that Ava carries it with her throughout the day. The rich, deep, sweet notes echo until her fingertips buzz and her lips quiver with the resonance of all that vibrant beauty so that Ava has a sublime soundtrack to backlight her life. The main result of this is that Ava no longer carries her crossword clues tucked safely and snugly into the corners of her mind, she no longer retreats behind her eyes, ferreting away for answers to cryptic questions in the nooks and crannies of her encyclopaedic knowledge. Instead, she is borne through her days on an exalted river of sound.

Now Ava smiles at the students who take out textbooks for their essays and exams, she looks at her colleagues, nodding as they chat about their lives, listening to their complaints and concerns. And, although she doesn't go so far as actually replying or responding in kind, Ava does feel a slight sense of connection with herself and the outside world beginning to ignite. And the idea of speaking with people, of allowing them to see who she is and how she feels, no longer feels quite so terrifying as it once did.

Of course, it's not simply the music that pervades Ava, but also the musician. Thoughts of him bob up and down on the river of Mozart, Vivaldi and Beethoven. She wonders where he came from, what he does every day and whether or not he has love in his life. Does he have a woman he kisses every day? Does he make love as passionately as he plays? Would she faint dead away if he ever touched her? What if she simply held herself while he held his violin, his fingers vibrating over the strings, would it be enough to give her the greatest pleasure of her life? Ava blushes at these thoughts. She's never had anything like them before. Nor such dreams.

The musician and his music visit Ava every night. And her visions of him are so vivid, the sensation of his touch so strong, the sound of his playing so sensational, the feeling of their emotions so overwhelming, that she wakes after every dream – heart hammering, skin wet with sweat, tears streaming – believing that he's there in bed with her.

Ava is astonished at how he's transformed her life, so suddenly, so completely. How can it be that, now, even her dreams are far more passionate and powerful than her days ever were before? How can it be that all her senses are heightened: sights brighter, sounds clearer, smells sharper, tastes richer, touches acuter? And, so it seems, she is feeling so many things for the very first time. She'll be stacking bookshelves and, all of a sudden, realise that her cheeks are wet with tears. She'll be checking out books and start grinning, for absolutely no reason at all but the sheer delight of sliding them across the counter. Occasionally she'll get some odd looks but, mostly, Ava just receives smiles. And, usually, now, she'll smile back.

For her part, Greer spends more time than she strictly should listening to the musician. She doesn't think about him when he's not playing – since she doesn't seem to have any type of extraneous thoughts at all, nothing that doesn't pertain to the present moment she's actually in, rather like a baby – but every morning she finds herself materialising by the ancient apple tree and watching him until he disappears. And, each time, she's mesmerised. Hours dissolve in several sweeps of the musician's bow, but time also stops as he plays. So Greer feels as if death has enveloped her again and she's suspended in infinity, only with every molecule of her spirit now resonating to the tune of his music.

When she'd suddenly found herself standing again at the bottom of her own garden, Greer had been more than a little surprised. One instant she'd been in – well, she couldn't quite recall – and the next she'd been home again. How long had it been? Again, she can't remember. How had she returned? She isn't quite sure. Why has she come back? How does she feel about it all? Greer doesn't really know. Or at least, if she does, she's unwilling to admit it, even to herself.

When Greer listens to the musician she feels as if she should be able to float right up to his window and touch a transparent finger to his chest. She feels as if she should be able to fly, swooping above the apple tree, soaring over the flowers, diving with the swallows and alighting with the blackbirds next to their nests. She can hover a few inches into the air, after all; indeed, she can't seem to touch the ground even if she tries, so why shouldn't she be able to fly? And his music seizes her spirit and lifts it upward towards the sun, so it should only make sense if her transparent body followed suit. But then, admittedly, nothing much of being dead seems to make much sense at all.

Greer imagines that she must have come back for Edward: he is – or, rather, was – her husband who, by all accounts, has been willing her to return ever since she left. Though, despite what she said to reassure him, Greer doesn't really understand why that would be now instead of any time before. And why does it feel that she was pulled from the other side by the power of the musician's music? Perhaps it's a combination of both? But, whatever it is, Greer only knows that she feels a sharp twist of guilt in her ribs every time she shimmers away from Edward's side each morning to materialise again in the garden. She feels even guiltier when he asks where she's been and she lies, saying she doesn't know, claiming that every now and then she'll disappear and reappear without remembering where she's been or gone.

'It must be part of the whole being dead thing,' Greer will suggest with a casual shrug.

'I suppose,' Edward will say. 'Still, it's strange.'

'But it's all a bit strange. This,' Greer will say. 'Don't you think?'

And Edward will admit that it is. And then Greer will change the subject.

Chapter Seven

It's the middle of the afternoon, more than three hours before closing time, but Clara can't wait that long before she takes a walk. She's been pacing up and down the shop for the past hour, willing a customer to come in and distract her from herself but, at the same time, not really wanting to see anyone.

At three o'clock – with the shop still empty – Clara realises that she just wants an excuse to leave early. And, since she's her own boss, she takes it. Slipping a little sign into the window apologising for the early closure (not that it'll disappoint too many people, clearly) Clara hurries through the crowded streets of the town centre until she reaches the bridge by Magdalene College and begins walking along the river. Twenty minutes later, having passed through parks and by trees and spotted a fair number of ducks, Clara realises she's standing outside his house. She peers, a little guiltily, into his front room. It's empty. Clara sighs. Where is he? Where is his daughter? What are they doing? It's the middle of the afternoon, she realises, so he's probably doing whatever it is he does for a living and she's probably at school. Most people aren't able to leave their place of employment on a whim. She considers waiting a while in case one of them appears at some point as, indeed, they must. But this feels too close to stalking and, since she's always been a bit sensitive on this subject, Clara decides to hurry along.

Half an hour later, wandering along a row of houses on the waterfront, she spies an old man, staring sorrowfully at his kitchen wall. He will be the next rightful recipient of a letter, someone who deserves a little love and inspiration simply because he does, and not because Clara has developed a slight obsession with him and his family.

Clara looks in at the old man a while longer, absorbing him into her subconscious, so that she can better write the letter. Though, in truth, she has no idea if this is a necessary part of the process or, indeed, how the process works at all – does she simply identify the recipients and after that she's nothing but a vessel? – but, nevertheless, Clara goes through these motions every time anyway, just in case.

She doesn't stay too long at the old man's window (staring at so much palpable sadness does wear on her heart a little) but doesn't return to the shop. Instead, she ambles back in that general direction, through the parks, along the river, contemplating the old man, the man whose name she doesn't know, his daughter, and herself and her life. She has led such a small life, such a safe life because that's how she's always preferred it. She's never wanted to travel, to explore exotic places, to meet mysterious people, to eat unknown foods. She's always been perfectly satisfied with her internal journeys and the people who've come to her. And yet . . . Very occasionally, on days like these, Clara wonders just how much of her life is a product of genuine passion, or fear.

An hour later, when she's back at the shop, sitting at the writing desk, Clara has managed to push these thoughts from her mind and focus instead on the recipient of her letter. When she puts pen to paper it is him she's thinking of. Which is why it's rather strange that – for the very first time ever – after writing a letter, Clara picks it up and reads it. What's even more strange is that she finds it's not addressed to the old man but to her.

Clara reads the letter over and over again. She still can't quite believe it's actually intended for her. But it clearly is. Even though her name isn't on it, the letter can't be meant for anyone else.

Monday 15th May '17

It's time for you to take a trip. It's time for you to be bold. It's time for you to step outside those four little walls and stride into your life. It's time for you to stop just taking care of everyone else and start taking care of yourself. And, when you return, your life will be so different, so gloriously delicious and delightful, you won't recognise it at all.

But first you need to experience what it's like to not know what's going to happen next. You need to learn to feel safe while having adventures, to feel secure living fully in each moment without being at all sure what the future will bring. You need to fall in love, head-over-toes. You need to lose love and know that that's okay too, that you will always be okay, no matter what.

Shut the shop. Run out into the world with open arms and let it knock you around a bit. Let it lift you up to its highest heights, let it drag you through the dirt, let it shake you up. Lose your balance, so you can find it. Step off the edge, jump off the cliff, throw yourself into the winds. Do the things that

scare you most of all. Discover that nothing matters, not even
death, for only then will you begin to truly live.

Clara knows it's meant for her because every time she reads it she cries. For the next few days she reads it before she goes to bed every night, when she wakes in the morning, and several times in between. It's not long before Clara has memorised every word, but she still reads the inky letters because seeing them flowing across the page reminds her that she's not making it all up, she's being told to do something and, eventually, she's going to have to act.

Deep down, or not so deep down, really, Clara knows what she needs to do. It's obvious. If she's being told to take a trip then it must be to Amsterdam. Where else? Well, she could go somewhere properly faraway and exotic, like Hong Kong or New Zealand, but those places don't hold any special significance for her. For which, quite frankly, Clara is rather grateful. She hates flying. Or, since she's never actually done it, she hates the *idea* of flying. A heavy metal tube hurtling through the sky? No, thank you. But Amsterdam is, by all accounts, beautiful and quiet and, happily, close to Cambridge. She can catch a train to London, then get the Eurostar and arrive at her destination a few hours later, unscathed.

And so, at last, Clara goes to the library. Nearly three hours after she's sat down at the infernal computer (having failed to find any available library assistants), Clara finally buys her train tickets to Amsterdam. It only takes her fifteen minutes of fumbling to purchase the damn things; the extra two hours and forty-five minutes are whittled away in worry and panic. When she stands again and stumbles out of the library, Clara is still so overwhelmed with nerves that – even though she passes by a lovely smiling librarian who's softly humming Beethoven's Ninth Symphony – Clara forgets all about checking out any books. A fact that makes her feel rather guilty when she remembers. So, when she's lying in bed that night, she divides her fretful thoughts between the terrifying subjects of European travel and the tragic decline of local libraries.

Edward's feeling odd. He knows he should be absolutely over the moon, giddy with joy, drunk with delight that his wife's come back at last – even if she is a ghost and he can't touch her – but he's not exactly. He's *happy*, very happy indeed, to see her again. He's happy to know she's okay. He's happy to be with her. But his happiness doesn't seem to be coated with desire and craving. He doesn't long to embrace her and kiss her and never let her go. Which is odd since, for years after she died he'd have traded a year of his life for just one more touch, one more kiss, one more glance . . .

Edward still loves her, certainly. He still loves her, deeply. He doesn't want her to leave again. He wants her to stay for ever. He's overjoyed to get his best friend back. But now, two weeks after the event, the shock of Greer's return has softened and settled into something almost ordinary and expected, so Edward is no longer surprised to see her floating into rooms and hovering above floorboards and materialising beside him.

Despite their talks late into the night – about everything from Tilly, architecture and heaven to cold crumpets and *Downton Abbey* – he hasn't been able to admit the true complex, conflicted nature of his feelings to Greer. He skirts around the subject but hasn't yet found the courage to settle on it. Tonight they sit (rather he sits, she hovers) in the living room by the fireplace. Edward slowly sips a scotch, with ice.

'You can't remember anything?' he asks, for perhaps the hundredth time since Greer arrived.

'I told you I can't,' she says. 'I'd tell you if I could.'

Edward raises an eyebrow. 'Would you? Or is being dead like a secret society and you're not allowed to reveal any of the particulars to the living? In which case, that's exactly what you'd say, if I asked.'

Greer laughs. 'Well then, I'm afraid you'll just have to trust me.'

As Edward looks at her he realises that he doesn't, not entirely. He suspects that there is something she's not telling him – whether it's about heaven or another matter entirely.

They've been putting off telling Tilly. First of all, because they didn't know how long Greer would stay. They reasoned that, if it was only a brief visit, it wasn't worth upsetting Tilly and possibly scarring her for life, for a momentary reunion. The potential cons outweighed the pros. But now it seems that she might actually be here to stay, it feels wrong to keep the secret any longer.

'How the hell are we going to do it, though?' Edward says, for perhaps the hundredth time in twenty-four hours.

'I have no idea,' Greer replies, which has been her standard response – sometimes coupled with a sigh, sometimes not – every single time.

'Well, we've got to think of something,' he says again. 'It's got to be subtle, so she doesn't "totally freak out" and not sleep through the night till she leaves home.'

'Yes.' Greer considers. 'Or faint and hit her head on something nasty.'

Edward nods. He has missed this; he's missed this so much. After his first wife, Tilly's mother, died he found parenting pretty challenging but since Greer died he's found it well-nigh impossible.

Being a good father to a toddler was one thing – since it mainly involved potty training and learning all the words to every nursery rhyme ever written – but being a good father to a teenager is something else entirely.

Edward smiles at Greer. She's glanced away and doesn't see but as he soaks her in suddenly he wants to hug her, to hold her close. His heart aches to know that he can't.

'I'm so glad you're back,' he says softly. 'I can't tell you how much.' When she doesn't reply, Edward returns to the topic. 'Why don't we just tell her at dinner tonight?' he suggests. 'I'll cook her favourite. We'll keep it low-key and casual. I'll just bring it up in the conversation and then you can come in. What do you think?'

Greer shrugs. 'It's as good a plan as any, I suppose.' She smiles. 'I can't wait for her to see me. I wish I could . . .'

Edward sighs. 'I wish I could hold you too.'

Greer floats over to her husband and hovers close to him. She lifts her hand close to his cheek and he closes his eyes. Her almost-touch is surprisingly warm and sends pricks of sensation along his skin. Edward's heart begins to beat a little faster and he can feel the stirring of something he hasn't felt in a very long time. He opens his eyes and looks up at her. Suddenly he wants to kiss her. He wants to kiss her so much he can feel his lips tingling as if he'd just eaten chillies. He wants it. All at once, he wants it more than anything in the world.

'Are you still my wife?' he asks softly.

Greer nods. 'Yes, I suppose I must be.' She should say something else. She should mention her feelings about the musician. She should be honest and open. But she can't face the thought of breaking his heart all over again. First cancer, then an unfaithful heart. How much cruelty can one person be expected to bear? So instead she leans forward and places her lips against his.

Edward gasps, then quickly pulls away, touching his fingers to his lips.

'Oh, shit, I'm sorry,' Greer says. 'Did I hurt you? I didn't mean – I didn't know what it'd be like, I just . . .'

Edward shakes his head. He feels it now. He feels everything he felt before. It's all come rushing back, surging through his body: love, adoration, desire, longing, tumbling over each other in a gluttonous flood of emotions. 'No, no, it's okay,' he says, 'please, don't worry. It wasn't . . . It was a bit like getting an electric shock, that's all.'

Greer looks stricken. 'Oh dear, how awful.'

'No, no, just a tiny one,' Edward reassures her. 'I was just surprised, that's all. Now I know, it's okay. We can try again. Next time it'll be fine, I'm sure.'

Greer nods. 'As long as I didn't hurt you.'

'You didn't, I promise, you didn't.'

Greer sighs, tension leaving her body in little sparks.

Next time. The words hang in the air between them. *When?* From his chair, Edward gazes up at his wife. She gives him a small, reassuring smile, then glances out of the window and into the garden.

'What's going on, Dad? You're being weird.'

Edward frowns. 'I am not "being weird", I'm being perfectly normal.'

'You are not.'

Edward sighs and looks down at his plate. He's meant to be creating an atmosphere of relaxed calm and then, when the mood is right, he's meant to introduce – carefully and gently – the subject

68

of Tilly's deceased stepmother and her strange but welcome return to this earth. Unfortunately, actually doing this is as awkward and difficult as it sounds. Finally, after procrastinating by poking his fork into a slice of pizza for a few minutes, Edward decides, since he's clearly failing so spectacularly at the delicate approach, to plunge in head first.

'Till?'

'Yeah?' Tilly picks the fresh basil off her pizza.

'What would you say if I told you, if I told you . . . ?'

'What?' She says, still not looking up.

'That your—that Greer has, um, well . . . come back as a ghost.'

Tilly looks up. 'I'd say that you should probably see a therapist or stay off the drugs – like you're always telling me to.'

Edward glances around the room. 'Greer! It's time, I've told her!'

Tilly looks at her father as if he's just declared a lifelong desire to dress up as a drag queen and take to the stage.

And then Greer materialises in the kitchen, a few feet from Tilly.

Tilly screams, then plants her hands over her mouth, then lets them drop to her lap. 'What the fuck?!'

'Tilly!' Edward and Greer exclaim in unison. They both stare at Tilly, who just stares at Greer.

'Although,' Edward admits into the ensuing silence, 'if ever there was a time for swearing, I suppose now would be very much it.'

Tilly says nothing. So they both continue to watch her, waiting.

Tilly just stares at Greer, incredulous.

Greer and Edward stare at Tilly, nervous.

'Till, are you . . . okay?' Edward ventures.

And then Tilly bursts into tears. Sobbing, she reaches out to Greer.

'Mum . . . Mummy,' she gasps. 'You've come back.'

And then Edward feels his heart shatter. He'd forgotten that his daughter had called Greer that in the last few months before she died. And the sorrow and joy in Tilly's voice is almost more than he can bear. He wants to take them both in his arms and hold them so tight that no more misery can ever touch these two women he loves more than life itself. In that moment Edward vows that, no matter what, he will move heaven and earth to be certain that Greer never leaves them again.

Chapter Eight

There is a reason that Ava doesn't socialise. As there should be, since – on the surface – she's the sort of person most people find easy to approach and engage in conversational chit-chat. Except that Ava isn't very good at chit-chat. It's not that she's particularly philosophical, ardently political or uninterested in casual topics. It's simply that she can see the saddest events in people's lives – those that have been and those that are to come – and, quite apart from the pain this causes her, she also sometimes finds herself blurting out decidedly unwanted and unasked-for information.

Unsurprisingly, most people don't want to know the exact date and circumstances of their deaths, they certainly don't want to know about any horrific events that might be looming on the horizon and they usually don't want to discuss the most painful events of their pasts, things they've tried hard to bury and forget. As a child, Ava was fairly quick to learn this, though not before she gave the class bullies sufficient ammunition to make her school years quite unbearable.

And so, when it came to choosing a profession, Ava picked librarian, since it was a job that seemed to require, nay demand, silence and so it was perfect. Her first thought, aged sixteen, was clairvoyant or fortune-teller, since she clearly had the credentials, but she quickly reconsidered, on the basis that her clients would probably want to hear mostly positive prophecies about their futures, or at least a balance of good and bad, not unremittingly depressing divinations that would make them want to give up on life right there and then.

However, in choosing her profession, Ava hadn't counted on the possibility that staff and students might try to converse with her. And, as she soon discovered, her fellow colleagues seemed to want to talk, connect, share and gossip at any available opportunity. Indeed, though Ava couldn't understand why, many of them preferred it to shelving books or doing data entry. Although, perhaps if you're not cursed with a serious conversational tic then having a friendly natter over the water cooler – or, in the case of the Cambridgeshire Central Library, a cup of weak tea in the tiny grotty kitchen next to the loo – is a rather more appealing prospect.

Of course, as is so often the case in magic and in life, Ava's particular powers of perception only seem to work on other people and not on herself which, in this case, is a great relief rather than a frustration. So she's never been able to see her own terrible events in advance, she hasn't had an inkling, not even a moment before. She wishes she hadn't been able to see the terrible events of those she's loved most in the world but, sadly, she hadn't been able not to. She'd seen her sister's death, from leukaemia, aged twelve. Fortunately, Ava's life following that devastating incident has been quite uneventful. Which is exactly the way she intends to keep it.

Ava recalls then the woman in the letter writing shop, the owner of the quaint and mysterious place she'd somehow stumbled into, the place she'd written that letter to Helen, the particulars of which she couldn't recall even a moment after writing it. She'd liked that woman, had wanted to befriend her, but had thought she'd better not as it would no doubt only end in tears. Now Ava tells herself that her specific affliction is the reason that she can't go and introduce herself to the musician next door. And it is one reason, but not the main one. The main reason would be her overwhelming fear of being rejected, dismissed, spurned, rebuffed, disdained, scorned, refused. Not that she was thinking of declaring her undying love and affection. She simply wants to tell him just how much his music means, how it has lit up her life, how it has changed the way she feels about everything. Though, naturally, Ava is a little worried that some avowals of adoration might slip out, unbidden, while she's gushing about Mozart and Vivaldi. And so, to preserve the dignity and composure of all concerned, Ava is staying put.

Finn has made a decision. He's going to approach the ghost at the end of his garden. This is absolute madness, he knows, since it'll shatter the electrifying illusions he's been basking in for the past few weeks. But he just can't stand it any longer. He has to know if she's real. Of course she won't be, she'll vanish the moment he sets foot on the grass, or she'll evaporate at his touch, or she'll disappear as soon as he stops playing, never to return again. He shouldn't upset the status quo, Finn knows this. He shouldn't be greedy by wanting more than he already has – it'll only lead to misery, disappointment and dejection. And yet his curiosity and desire has finally become too overwhelming to contain. The ghost has become a particularly beautiful and enchanting version of Pandora's Box and Bluebeard's Cupboard. Finn has to know. Even if it'll ruin everything, he simply has to know.

And so, the next morning, instead of standing at his window Finn dresses early and takes his violin down to the garden. It's pre-dawn and chilly and the ghost is nowhere to be seen. Perhaps she knew he was coming so hasn't appeared. Finn feels his heart contract, his stomach drop, his skin prick with sweat, all the colour drain from his face. It was a mistake. A dreadful, totally misjudged mistake. He wants to take it back. He wants to turn and run into the house and up to his bedroom window again.

He'll choose to be content with just seeing her every morning, with watching her, playing to her and having her listen to him. Finn holds his violin to his hollow chest and glances back at the house, about to turn on his heel, when Greer appears.

Finn's breath catches in his throat. He stands still, unable to step forward. Greer doesn't move either. They stand a few metres apart. They watch each other. Very slowly, Finn exhales. He's scared that if he disturbs the air even a fraction, she'll dissolve into unsettled molecules. Now that he's closer to her, Finn can see just how beautiful and absolutely transparent she is. He could reach his hand right through her. But he longs to touch her long red curls, to gaze into her big green eyes, to press his cheek against her lips, to entwine their fingers together.

From his very limited knowledge of fashion and style, it seems to Finn that the ghost has come from the 1950s. She's voluptuous, beautifully fleshy and rounded in all the places Finn would particularly love to squeeze. And she's wearing a tight moss-green silk shirt that reflects her eyes and a long light-blue skirt that puffs out to settle just below her knees. Her feet are bare.

Suddenly, the ghost is standing just a few feet in front of him. Finn freezes.

'Hello,' she says.

It feels like an eternity before he finds his voice. 'Hello.'

'I'm Greer.'

Silence.

'Finn.'

'I love to hear you play.'

'Thank you. I . . . I love playing for you.'

She smiles, eyes lighting up, the lines in her face deepening. She must be in her mid to late forties, Finn guesses. Or, at least, she was.

'I wasn't certain if you were playing to me or not,' Greer says. 'I hoped you were, but I wasn't certain.'

Finn nods. 'You listen so . . . deeply, so completely. I've never . . .' he smiles. 'Not even my mother listened to me like that.'

'Oh?' Greer asks. 'How can you be so sure?'

For a moment, Finn recalls the intensity of Greer's listening, almost as if she were touching him, the heat of her fingers on his bare skin, until she was unwrapping him and holding his beating heart in her hands.

'Because I feel it.'

'Oh, okay.'

Slowly, she floats towards him, only stopping when they are nearly nose to nose. Finn exhales in rapid, stifled puffs. Greer doesn't breathe at all. Instead, she closes her eyes.

She knows she shouldn't be doing this. Just last night she kissed her husband, sort of, as much as she was able, anyway. Her husband. She hasn't forgotten him; she still loves him. But she *wants* Finn. She can't help it, she can't control it, she can't stop it.

75

Greer has never felt such desperate, deep longing in all her life – or death. With Edward love was easy, safe and sweet. She stepped into their life together as one might step into a warm bubble bath, sinking into the water with a glass of wine and a great book. Their days together were lovely, playful and kind. The sex was delightful too, though it didn't keep them up at night, even in the beginning. They didn't find themselves overcome with lust, sparks firing off their fingertips at the smallest touch, they didn't lose themselves in infinite, eternal kisses. And this, Greer is quite certain, is how it would be with Finn. Although, of course, how will she ever know? And perhaps that is simply it. Perhaps she only craves Finn so much because she can never truly have him. Isn't it ever thus?

Greer opens her eyes, chastising herself. She's clearly come back to earth in order to be a wife and a mother once more. She's not here to indulge in fantasies, she's not here to experiment and explore, she's not here for personal gratification but to continue the life she'd left so abruptly before.

Finn is gazing at Greer with great longing. Greer bites her lip. She really should nip this in the bud. She should return to her husband's house. She should soothe her spirit by watching Edward and Tilly sleep. Greer takes a step back, quite intending to do everything she'd just planned. But instead she seems to fold her legs under her skirt then float down to the grass.

'Play for me,' she says, her voice a betrayal, her heart snatching control from her mind. 'Please.'

Without saying anything, Finn nods. He brings his violin up to his chin and rests his thin, delicate fingers on the strings. He takes his bow and begins to play. As the notes seep slowly into the air, Finn closes his eyes. As the music gradually fills the space between them, Greer watches Finn's face soften and sink into the sounds, she watches his fingers shift and dart, she watches his body absorb every note and sway, ever so gently, in time to the music. And she longs not only to hold, to touch, to consume the musician, but also to step inside him so that she is the one creating the music, so that she too can feel the way he is feeling now.

Chapter Nine

Clara stands on the platform at St Pancras. She clutches her heavy cloth bag so tightly her knuckles are white and her fingernails dig into her skin. It's the first time she's left England and she's going to a country where she knows no one and doesn't even speak the language. She's booked a B&B and has a map and phrase book. But, having already tried to practise, Clara quickly discovered that Dutch was rather tricky. It didn't flow off the tongue like French or Italian, it stuck in the throat. Every sentence seemed to employ vast amounts of guttural consonants that twisted and tangled in Clara's voice box leaving her speechless.

Someone next to Clara coughs. She glances across her shoulder to catch an older man looking at her.

'Excuse me, but are you quite all right? You seem a bit . . .'

'Terrified,' Clara supplies. 'Yes, I suppose I am a bit.'

'You've never been to Europe before?'

Clara shakes her head.

The older man – short and stout with a cloud of white

hair, a reassuringly ancient face that speaks of wisdom and experience – smiles. 'Isn't the mind a funny thing? Some people cherish the known and are terrified of the unknown while others are quite the opposite way, scared of routine and craving what's new and untested.'

'Yes, I suppose so,' Clara says. 'Though I don't really have much knowledge of anyone else's mind other than my own.'

'Wait till you're my age,' the old man offers, as the train doors slide open and passengers begin filing on, 'then you'll know so much you'll keep forgetting it all.'

Clara gives a little snort of laughter. 'I doubt that.'

Joining the lines of people boarding the train, Clara hesitates at the step, then takes a quick, deep breath and walks through the doors.

'Oh, I don't know,' he says, following her on. 'It seems to me you're widening your world already.'

Clara nods, glancing around for her seat – she's memorised the number, 56D, and has hopefully alighted on the correct carriage – and dearly hoping that the old man will be seated close by. Unfortunately, among the bustle of people and bags, she loses sight of him and finds her seat next to a suited businessman with his bespectacled face buried in the *Financial Times*. Clara sighs softly. Usually she'd relish not having to converse but, in her nervous state, she'd rather welcome the distraction. As a chatty travelling companion he doesn't look promising.

Sure enough, he doesn't say a word during the two-and-a-half-hour trip to Brussels. But, at the station, when Clara undergoes a minor nervous breakdown while trying to find the correct platform to transfer trains, he proves to be kind and helpful. Clara thanks him profusely and surprises them both by squeezing the businessman's hand then dashing off towards the train bound for Amsterdam.

'I'm so glad you're back, Mum.'

Greer looks at Tilly and smiles. 'Me too, dearest, me too.'

They're sitting on the sofa (Tilly sitting, Greer hovering just above it) not really watching *Thelma and Louise*. They've seen the film nearly a hundred times and know virtually every line but still never tire of it – especially not of Brad Pitt. When Greer was very sick, in the final stages, Tilly would sit by her bed for endless hours while they watched (Greer drifting in and out of consciousness) their favourite films.

Often, in the last few weeks of her life, Greer would pretend to sleep but slowly turn her head towards Tilly, open one eye and gaze at her. She no longer had the energy to be furious at the fact that Tilly was being robbed of two mothers in one short lifetime; instead it just made her melancholy, the pain spilling out in tears that fell down her nose and soaked the pillow, before she tumbled back into true sleep again.

Now Greer again glances surreptitiously at Tilly, emotions once more threatening to overwhelm her, not sadness this time but joy. How could she have forgotten all of this life, all of this love? Death is a strange thing. The absence, the detachment, the serene emptiness of it. And she's still finding settling back into the world, where everything seems dictated by desire, to be a rather difficult experience. It's not helped, of course, that now her deepest desire seems to be for the musician.

When she was alive, Greer was overwhelmingly attached to Tilly. She'd put her to bed every night. She'd never missed a single night, not once. And every night, after she'd tucked Tilly in, after

81

she'd switched on the bedside lamp, after she'd turned off the light, after she'd said 'goodnight' half a dozen times, Greer would whisper thanks to the woman who'd died, leaving a mother-shaped space for someone to step into and be charged with taking care of her daughter. Every night Greer thanked her stars that she was that woman.

Greer had been pregnant once in her life, as a teenager. At first she'd been scared and had hoped that ignoring the situation might make it go away. But the first time she'd felt her baby move she'd started wanting it to stay. As the months passed, Greer's attachment had grown and when she at last went into labour her excitement – before the searing pain kicked in – fizzed over into bubbles of joy that burst open in the hospital corridors, making the nurses giggle.

But, thirteen and a half hours later, when her baby finally slid into the world, the sterile room wasn't pierced with infant cries. And Greer had been too stunned by pain to do anything but wait while medical staff darted about. She didn't know to be worried. She'd never experienced birth before, so she didn't know what normal procedure was. And so, when they finally placed her daughter, wrapped in a thin pink cotton blanket, in her arms and started to explain, Greer wasn't listening. She was staring at her baby girl, so achingly small, so heart-contractingly beautiful: big fluttering green eyes that didn't focus, bump of a nose, tiny bow mouth, dusting of dark red hair and minute fingers that wrapped themselves tightly around hers and held on as long as they could.

Now Greer reaches for Tilly across the sofa. But, of course, her transparent fingers slip right through her stepdaughter's solid hand and Greer sighs. Or she would have, if she had the breath to do so.

Instead the strain of a sigh rises up and shakes through her spirit. The inability to touch is difficult. It's funny, really, what the living take for granted – their five senses – while Greer is left with only three. She can't taste, since she doesn't eat, and she can't touch. Naturally, she couldn't miss this while dead but now that she's back in a world dominated by senses she misses them both enormously. Touch, most of all, but taste too. Greer was always an eater. She adored food and had looked forward to the moments when it would punctuate her day. Now she watches listlessly while Tilly and Edward eat dinner (decidedly sub-par compared to the meals she'd always cooked, though she's tactful enough not to comment on this) wishing she could have a bite of buttered toast or baked potato. Perhaps it's a good thing that Edward's culinary skills are pretty basic then, since his offerings don't infuse Greer with the depth of longing more splendid fare might.

'Hey, girls,' Edward says, poking his head around the living-room door. 'What are you up to?'

Greer looks up but Tilly doesn't take her eyes off the TV.

'Haven't you seen this a thousand times?' he asks, without waiting for an answer.

Greer nods, smiling apologetically. In the past she would have made a joke about the infinite allure of Pitt, but now guilt – exacerbated by the fact that she actually is lusting after another man – silences her.

'Brad Pitt is totally gorgeous, Dad,' Tilly says. 'You just don't get it.'

Amused, Edward catches Greer's eyes and rolls his own.

'I'm so glad you're here,' he says, 'to help me navigate the turbulent waters of the teenage years.' He steps across the room to the sofa and bends down to kiss the air above her head. 'And, of course, because I missed you like hell.'

Greer looks up at him, smiling again, more lovingly this time.

'Me too,' she says, because it's true. She just wishes it was the whole truth.

Clara stands on tiptoes, looking out of the little attic window at the rain. It's pouring down in thick sheets, promising to soak to the bone anyone who dares to venture outside. Clara finds this oddly comforting: not only does the weather remind her of home but it's a little like an invisibility cloak. People don't stop and chat in the rain, they barely even look at each other, hurrying face-to-the-ground to their destinations. It's in sunshine that you have to meet people's eyes and return their smiles and slow down to appreciate your surroundings. Clara isn't such a fan of summers – though, fortunately, in England it rains for most of the summer months too.

Clara glances back at the bed where the thick folder of letters sits atop the patchwork quilt. The room is very small, with just enough space for a single bed, a tiny table and chair, but Clara takes comfort in its smallness – snug and close like a hug. Today she has an appointment at The Amsterdam Archive of Paperphilia, one of the curators having promised to take a look at her letters, and she doesn't want to be late. Fortunately, she's brought a raincoat and umbrella and an oversize oilcloth handbag in which to house her letters. So she slips her city map into the bag, along with her purse, room key and, finally, very carefully, reverently, the folder of letters.

Stepping onto the slick paving stones of the street, Clara walks slowly, umbrella in one hand, map in the other, bag slung tightly across her chest. She plans on walking all the way, not trusting her abilities to navigate public transport without ending up somewhere else entirely. She's worked out that it'll probably take about an hour to reach her destination, taking into account the careful stepping necessitated by the heavy rain.

In fact, it takes Clara nearly two hours to find the Archive, having taken several wrong turns and wandered down a few too many streets more than once before realising what she's done. Unfortunately, the street names – Helmersstraat, Herengracht, Honthorststraat, Hobbemastraat – don't make navigation the simplest of tasks, especially with the downpour of rain. And, by the time she finally reaches the steps of the Archive, Clara is nearly weeping with relief. Fortunately, she's not late, having planned on arriving an hour before she needed to, so she's now exactly on time. And absolutely soaking wet.

Hurrying up the stone steps as safely as she can without slipping, Clara shakes off her sodden umbrella and wraps it up, still dripping, and tucks it under her left arm. Then she shakes herself, like a dog who's just clambered out of a river, sending raindrops scattering. Finally, as dry as she can possibly make herself in a minute, without the aid of any towels, Clara pushes through the thick glass doors and into the dark foyer.

After announcing herself at the check-in desk (trying to ignore the slightly scathing look of the receptionist, clearly unhappy at the puddles collecting under Clara's feet) she sits on a wooden bench a few feet away. Just as soon as she's sat, Clara stands as a gentleman, probably in his early fifties, wearing a corduroy suit and gold eyeglasses balanced atop his long nose, strides towards her, arm outstretched and smiling.

'Ms Cohen, what a pleasure.' His voice is soft and low and warm. 'I'm Mr Akkersijk, and don't worry, I don't expect you to attempt pronunciation.'

Clara swallows a smile. 'Thank you,' she says, shaking his hand. 'I'm sure I would butcher it dreadfully. But it's a pleasure to meet you, anyway. Thank you so much for agreeing to see me.'

'Not at all, not at all,' he says. 'Anything of an epistolary nature fascinates me, especially that which is historical. Please, follow me.'

Mr Akkersijk turns and his long, thin legs take him quickly through a door and down a corridor. Clara hurries after him. When they reach his office he gestures for her to sit in the only other chair apart from his, then slides behind his desk.

'So, Ms Cohen, what do you have for me?'

He sits forward, his voice keen as a schoolboy's and Clara sees that he wasn't exaggerating his passion for letters. She opens her bag slowly, partly to prolong her enjoyment of his endearing eagerness and partly to postpone the possible disappointment if her letters don't meet his expectations.

Carefully, she slides the folder across his desk as Mr Akkersijk leans forward to claim it. She watches Mr Akkersijk as he reads the first, then the second letter. She's strangely charmed by him, by his total absorption, how he mouths the words as his eyes follow the sentences, the way his fingers twitch, as if unable to contain his energy, his excitement.

As he continues to read, turning the pages precisely and delicately, not once looking up, Clara is surprised to find herself begin to feel something else – charm and interest are slowly threading together to form a tentative, incomplete attraction. Clara frowns. Mr Akkersijk is possibly a decade older than she and not exactly handsome. And yet . . . He has a quality about him she's never seen before. It's so unusual, in fact, that it takes her a little while to make sense of it, a way of being usually only seen in young children and canines: an unreserved delight for life.

Finally, Mr Akkersijk looks up.

Quickly, Clara flicks her glance from his face to the letters.

'Well, Ms Cohen,' he says, his voice now quite giddy with glee. 'I do believe you have some very special letters here.'

Chapter Ten

Ava holds a plate of blueberry scones out in front of her. Though she's still ever-so-slightly terrified of rejection, and rather scared of blurting out the saddest events of his life, she's been unable to resist meeting her new neighbour any longer. And, to soften the potential blow, Ava's decided to hide behind baked goods.

She taps on the door and waits. After a full minute, realising she hadn't knocked loudly enough, Ava does so again. Three minutes after that, she knocks again. The door opens immediately. He looks dazed and confused.

'Oh.' Finn pauses. 'Hello.'

Ava's grip on the plate tightens. She can see he was hoping it'd be someone else. She wants to turn and scamper back to her own doorstep. But that would be rude and, more importantly, embarrassing. So, given that she might be living next door to him for a while (she's certainly planning on staying put for the rest of her life) it's important to maintain a modicum of cool.

'Hi, um . . .' Ava thrusts the plate forward. 'I brought you these.'

Her neighbour looks at the plate, perplexed, as if trying to fathom what the small lumps of baked dough might be.

'They're scones,' Ava explains.

'Ah.'

'You don't like them? That's okay.' She withdraws the plate, pulling it back to her chest. 'I just, I just wanted to welcome . . .'

As she trails off, Finn looks suddenly mortified.

'Oh, God.' He runs his long, thin fingers through his hair. 'I'm so sorry, I'm being completely—I thought . . . I just . . . Never mind . . .' He steps aside. 'Please, come in.'

Ava considers making an excuse, saying she has an appointment, somewhere else to be, a vital and important place. She shouldn't risk the high probability of making a total fool of herself, of saying something extremely unorthodox, of exposing herself as not entirely normal and thus alienating her beautiful neighbour for ever. But of course, no matter the risk, Ava can't resist stepping forward and into Finn's house.

She follows him along the hallway, through the living room and into the kitchen. His home is narrow and dark, just like hers. But, while every inch of Ava's home is crowded with books (she could open her own large-sized library) her neighbour's is almost entirely empty. Perhaps it's just because he's only recently moved in, although Ava's surreptitious glances don't glean any piles of boxes or swathes of bubble wrap, nothing that promises any amount of hidden belongings.

Finn hovers next to the kettle, drawing his finger delicately up and down the wooden kitchen counter. Ava watches, hiding her gaze behind her plate of blueberry scones, feeling a fluttering in her chest as she starts to imagine his fingers opening the buttons on her crisp white shirt, gently slipping the cotton over her shoulder blades, and . . . Ava lets out a little gasp and Finn glances up.

'What?'

Quickly, she shakes her head. 'Nothing, nothing.'

'Okay. Well, um, would you like a cup of tea?'

Even as he asks Ava senses that he doesn't really want to. He'd rather be somewhere else, doing something else. She should say 'no'. She should just excuse herself and leave.

Ava nods. 'Yes, please. That'd be lovely.'

'All right.' Finn nods. He opens the cupboard above his head. It's empty – except for a small box of tea bags. 'Is Earl Grey okay? It's all I've got.'

'Perfect,' Ava says.

As Finn boils the kettle and roots around for cups, Ava wracks her befuddled brain for some new words, preferably ones that might dazzle and intrigue him. But what can she possibly say to someone who plays the most exquisite music she's ever heard? Does he even talk about normal things, or is it that he only cares about lofty concepts, philosophical and esoteric ideas – thoughts that soar above everyday chatter, in the same way his music does, beyond the trees and far, far out of her reach?

She could talk about books, or cryptic crosswords. She still has a few clues knocking about in a mind otherwise overflowing with sonatas, concertos, symphonies and canons. *Hey, Finn, how about: A mad girl's composition (8)? A rider is all for a recess (5)? Turned on the epidural! (4-6)? Oh, you think I'm a little strange? You've changed your mind about the tea, after all? You think I should leave your house, right now, sharpish. Okay.*

This fantasy scenario wraps itself so firmly around Ava that she actually pushes her chair away from the table, and is about to stand, before realising that the conversation only took place in her head. She looks up to see Finn still staring at the kettle, waiting for it to boil.

Ava wonders what type of books she could discuss. Novels or non-fiction? What might Finn be more interested in? Since he has no clues in his house – at least from what she can see so far – it's a little hard to tell. She could pick something *learned*, something deep and clever, something to prove her worthiness as a life partner. Shakespeare? Too cliché. Woolf or Eliot? Too feminine. Turgenev or Dostoyevsky? Too risky. Ava chews on her lip, considering her options. Slowly, she scrolls the bibliography in her brain, letting each author and title roll past until she settles then discards, settles then discards . . .

Perhaps she should just ask him who his favourite authors are. It'd be a lot simpler. But less like kismet. Ava opens her mouth, then shuts it again. Perhaps she should talk about music instead? About Mozart, Mahler and Monteverdi, Beethoven, Bach and Brahms, Schubert, Stravinsky and Strauss, Purcell, Puccini and Pergolesi, Rachmaninoff, Ravel and Rossini. Surely Finn would love that. It'd be fabulous. A perfect plan. Except for the small fact that Ava knows nothing about any of these musicians other than their names, dates of birth and major compositions. Six years ago she read the blurb of a dense book entitled *The 100 Greatest Classical Composers* and, being blessed with a photographic memory, Ava can now recall every name on the list. It's a shame she didn't read the actual book.

Finn slides a cup of tea onto the table. Ava looks up.

'Milk?' he asks.

She shakes her head. Now she needs non-milk-related words. Great, perceptive, witty, profound, dazzling words. But what can she possibly offer him in verbal brilliance that could match the glory of his music?

Finn sits at the table and takes a sip of tea. Then he lets out one long, deep sigh.

'I think I'm in love with a ghost,' he says.

Next door Greer, standing in the kitchen and instructing Edward on the correct way to prepare chicken, stops. She feels a shift in the air, though she can't say exactly what it is or what it means. She glances over at Edward to see if he feels it too, but he's staring intently at the lump of raw meat on the chopping board in front of him, poking it suspiciously with a knife, as if it might suddenly sprout feathered wings and fly away.

'Why don't I buy a hot one from the supermarket?'

Greer smiles, still wondering at the warm breeze that just brushed against her cheek and shivered through her whole body.

'Now, what would be the fun in that?'

'Fun?' Edward looks up at her, stricken. 'This is supposed to be fun?'

Greer shrugs apologetically. 'If I could do it, I would. Sadly . . .' She flaps her transparent hands in front of him. 'And, at this rate, our daughter's going to end up malnourished and the size of a stick.'

Edward sighs. 'I know,' he says. 'It's hopeless.'

Greer is surprised to realise that the absence of the brief, warm breeze has left her feeling cold. She hadn't noticed this before – her ability to feel physical sensation – when did it develop? Why? Greer feels a sudden flash of hope. Does this mean something? Is it possible that she's slowly becoming a flesh-and-blood woman again? The very idea seems ludicrous. How would that work? And why on earth would *she*, of all the people who've ever died, be given the gift of life again? It makes absolutely no sense at all. And yet, now that the hope has risen up – unbidden – she cannot quash it down again.

* * *

Now Ava is truly speechless. Conflicting emotions explode like fireworks and ricochet through her body. Shock. Sorrow. Disappointment. Devastation. Curiosity. That he's already in love with someone else shouldn't, of course, be a surprise. She'd have been surprised, in fact, if he wasn't. Though she'd hoped somehow, she'd hoped – is hope a frightful thing sometimes? Does it turn disappointment into devastation? – that perhaps he might be free. But here it is. Declared. Unable to undo, to unsay, to let the words curl up once more and return to his mouth.

'A ghost?' Ava says at last, when the storm of devastation has finally settled enough so the light of curiosity can peek through. 'You're in—you . . . with a ghost?'

Now that she looks at him, Ava sees Finn's face is marked with his own sorrow and shock. He nods.

'I'm sorry. I don't know why I said that – I don't even know . . . You probably think I'm absolutely mad now, don't you? Well, of course – what sort of man blurts out confessions of devotion for the deceased,' he blathers on, seemingly unable to stop. 'But, don't worry, I'm not talking about a corpse. I'm not a necro—whatever those people are called who have sex with dead bodies. Oh dear, now you probably think that's exactly what . . . You think you're living next door to a total lunatic.'

Ava watches Finn chatter on, rather touched by his total unmooring. It's somehow comforting to see someone she thought so completely perfect slowly unravelling, thus bringing the pedestal she'd put him on down by a notch or two. It seems, now, that in fact he's not quite so different from her. He may be able to play the violin in a way that is sublimely other-worldly, but when it comes to love he's just as crazy as anyone else.

Ava smiles, grateful that the tables have suddenly turned, that

94

the attention is on him instead of her. It makes sublimating her devastation so much easier.

'Oh, no,' she says, magnanimously. 'I don't think you're a total lunatic. Well, no more than I am, anyway. Though I must confess, I'm curious about the ghost.'

Finn sighs. 'I'm not seeing things. I mean, I don't know if anyone else can see her, or not. But I've been . . . close, and she is real, I'm quite sure of it.'

Ava considers this. 'How do you know she's a ghost?'

Finn frowns. 'Because I can see right through her.'

Ava's smile, and her gratitude, deepens. 'I take it you're not speaking metaphorically.'

Despite his furrowed brow, Finn lets escape a small smile. 'No, I'm not.'

'Ah, well then,' Ava says. 'Perhaps I'll have to rethink my hasty judgement on your not being a lunatic – I'm kidding!' she exclaims, seeing his stricken look return. 'That was a joke. An attempt to lighten the mood. But I see I've failed miserably. I shall refrain from jokes in future.'

Ava grins, unable to believe how much fun she's suddenly having. The morning hasn't exactly turned out as she'd hoped – having realised all her worst fears of rejection and humiliation – and she couldn't possibly have imagined this particular turn. But, despite the fact that Finn is either in love with another woman or is, in fact, certifiably insane, Ava is making jokes, she's speaking effortlessly, she's free and easy, she's not worried about saying the wrong thing – blurting out a hideous premonition – or unable to say anything at all because she's trying so hard to make a good impression.

Ava can't remember the last time she was so relaxed, so

unrestricted, released from all the stifling, crippling thoughts that normally tether her tight. She had no idea it felt so glorious to be so free.

And then, suddenly, she sees it: the worst event of Finn's life to come. For a moment, Ava can't move. Then she pushes her chair away from the table.

'I'm sorry,' Ava says, already standing. 'I—I've got to go.'

Chapter Eleven

Clara sits forward in her chair, her glance shifting between Mr Akkersijk's excited, twitching fingers and the letters he's grasping tightly between them.

'How?' she asks. 'How are they special?'

Mr Akkersijk takes a deep breath, smoothing the papers with a slow, soft, rhythmic circling of his palm. 'Well, I will need to get them authenticated, of course, but I believe – from the content – that they were written during the Second World War, during the Nazi occupation of Amsterdam.'

Clara puts her own hand to her mouth. 'Oh.'

He nods, eyes alight with excitement. 'Do you know much about the author of the letters?'

Dropping her hand back to her lap, Clara shakes her head. 'Not much. Marthe was my great-grandmother. She raised my grandfather in Amsterdam before the family moved to England in the 1960s. She died long before I was born. I only found the letters a few weeks ago in the attic. My granddad left a note, but he didn't explain anything. I'm not sure he knew. But he wanted me to find out. That's why I'm here.'

'Ah,' Mr Akkersijk considers this. 'That's very interesting. Well, often Holocaust survivors never spoke – quite understandably – of what they went through.'

Clara feels her hands go clammy in her lap. She squeezes them together.

'Holocaust?'

'Well, I can't be certain, of course, until I've read them all,' Mr Akkersijk says. 'But, even though they aren't dated, and even though they seem to be simply love letters, a few references are made that lead me to believe—'

'—love letters?'

Mr Akkersijk nods, with the flicker of a smile. 'Yes, they are really quite passionate.'

Clara sits forward again. 'They are?'

'Oh, yes.' He nods again and points to the first letter atop the little pile. 'Would you like me to translate some of them?'

A shiver of something: anticipation, excitement, nerves, panic, flushes through Clara. 'Well, yes, that would be . . . lovely. Thank you.'

Mr Akkersijk nods once more and bends his head over the letter.

'*My dearest, darling Otto,*' he begins. '*How I—*'

'Otto?' Clara interrupts. 'Who's Otto?'

Mr Akkersijk smiles. 'I rather hoped you might know that. You certainly have a better chance of knowing than I do.'

'Yes, of course,' Clara says. 'Sorry, I just didn't realise, I mean, I didn't know who the letters were for.'

'He wasn't your great-grandfather?'

'No,' Clara says. 'I'm pretty sure he was called Lucas, like my granddad.'

'Ah, well then it would seem that Marthe had another love, this Otto, before she married Lucas.'

'Yes,' Clara agrees. 'So it would seem.'

'Shall I go on?'

Clara nods, a little more vigorously than she expected to. 'Please.'

Mr Akkersijk returns to the letter.

My dearest, darling Otto,

How I miss you. I never imagined life could feel like this, full of shadows, memories, empty pockets of longing I stumble into every few minutes or so . . . How long do you think we are to be parted? I cannot imagine it will be too long. I pray not too long. Dare I hope it will be not more than a few weeks? Of course, we must be careful. I know I can't leave to post these to you. But still, I will write & one day soon, when we are curled up together in our marriage bed, I will read them aloud, so you can know that I was thinking of you all this time, always.

I will write as often as I can – though I must ration the paper, for I don't know when I'll have more. Know then, my love, that I am thinking of you every minute, that each word I write represents a hundred thousand thoughts I have of you. While I am locked away in this room I remember us running down the Rozengracht, hand in hand, bent over in laughter. I let memories of every kiss we've shared comfort me at night – my favourite at the moment: the Oosterpark, under the birch tree when you pulled me to you so quick and tight that I gasped in surprise. I can only hope that it won't be so very long before you will hold me again.

Until that moment,

Marthe

When Mr Akkersijk reaches the end of the letter, he looks up at Clara. Not quite catching his eye, she glances quickly down at her still-clammy hands clasped in her lap. She hadn't taken her eyes off him while he read – the words ribboning from his mouth to curl around and tug at her heart – but suddenly she's embarrassed for him to see her staring, in case he can tell on her face the way she's feeling.

At thirty-three years old she's never known love as it's written in Marthe's letter. She's never known love *unlike* it either, because she's never known true love at all. To hear Mr Akkersijk speak such love aloud, even though, of course, he's not actually addressing his words to *her*, causes Clara's body to react in strange blushing ways, as if he's touching her, as if his voice is blowing softly on her bare skin, as if he's whispering into her ear, little puffs of air brushing past her hair.

Clara coughs. When, at last, she glances up Mr Akkersijk is looking right at her.

'It is beautiful, no?'

Clara nods.

'From what I've read so far, I believe she was writing during the war, most probably to a lover she was separated from.'

'A soldier?'

Mr Akkersijk gives a slight shrug of his thin shoulders. 'I cannot tell. I hope to gain that information when I have a chance to read all the letters in detail.' His eyes glint with excitement and the silver edge of glee coats his voice.

Clara wants to ask: *Have you ever been in love like that? Are you still? Tell me, tell me how it feels.* But, of course, she doesn't.

Mr Akkersijk stands. He presses one hand next to the pile of letters, fingers just touching the paper edges. He reaches out his other hand across the table. Tentatively, Clara takes it.

'Thank you for bringing me these letters. I will take great care of them,' he promises.

'Thank *you*,' Clara says. 'I'm very grateful for, for . . . .'

Gently, he releases her hand.

'When I've read them, how shall I contact you?' he asks. 'You'll be returning home soon, I imagine?'

Clara wishes she wasn't. She wants to say 'no', to say that she'll be staying, that she'll wait until he's ready to see her again, that she'll stroll the streets of Amsterdam for the next few weeks – or however long the translating will take – and return to the steps of The Amsterdam Archive of Paperphilia the moment he calls. But, of course, she can't. She must return to the shop; she must leave on a ticket already purchased for the day after tomorrow. But Clara doesn't want to leave. Since the moment she set foot on the first cobblestone, Clara has felt a strange sort of claim on this place. As if it were hers to explore, as if it would unfurl slowly to reveal all its secrets, its nooks and crannies, its places of darkness and light.

'I'll give you my phone number,' Clara says, conceding to the duller reality of practicalities. 'And, again, thank you so much for helping me.'

Mr Akkersijk nods. 'Not at all, Ms Cohen. I'm sure it will be a very illuminating experience for me too. It's always a thrill to find historical correspondence such as this. I thank you for bringing it to me.' He gives a little bow and Clara realises that, much as she might like to stay, this is her cue to leave.

Edward sits happily at the kitchen table, devouring his chicken dinner – rather pleased that it's actually edible – and still utterly thrilled to be sitting between his wife and his daughter. He wonders if the experience will ever become commonplace again. He hopes not, just as he hopes it will last for ever.

Swallowing a slice of potato – only slightly burnt – he turns to his wife. 'Have you been outside the house yet?'

An odd glimmer of guilt flits across Greer's face. 'Wh—no, why do you ask?'

'Oh, no reason,' he says, chewing on a piece of chicken – admittedly a little too dry. 'I was just wondering if you're able to?'

Greer shakes her head.

'I don't think Mum can go out, Dad,' Tilly says sagely, pushing a forkful of peas across her plate. 'I think she's trapped by some sort of spiritual force field and can only remain manifest in the house.'

Both her parents turn to face her.

'Remain manifest?' They echo, almost in unison. 'Spiritual force field?'

Tilly gives a self-satisfied nod. 'I've been doing research. You can find out everything on the Internet.'

'Clearly,' Edward says, swallowing another potato. 'Though how accurate is, I imagine, another matter.'

Tilly regards her father with a look he's become sadly familiar with lately, the look that says: *Oh, what do you know?*

Edward returns to his wife. 'Well, force fields aside, I was just wondering if you'd seen that new atrocity they've erected in the city centre?' He grimaces, plunging back in without waiting for an answer. 'It's nearly as awful as the Queen Anne multi-storey car park . . .'

Tilly gives a dramatic sigh. 'Oh, here we go again.'

'Well, it *is* hideous,' he snaps. 'There aren't enough expletives in the English language to adequately describe that monstrosity. I swear, every time I drive past it I get hives. And, if you're

102

ever forced to park there, you can feel how angry the architect who built it was – I bet he was pissed off not to get a greater commission, just a car park, he was ranting, *just a bloody car park*! – the parking places are far too small, too many pillars, too many twists, too many kerbs to trip and fall off. I bet, when he finished, the architect gave a self-satisfied "fuck you!" to the city council. Who, probably, couldn't have cared less—'

'Dad!'

'Oh, yes, sorry, I didn't mean . . . But still, I meant every word, except the swear words, of course.'

Greer smiles.

'But, seriously, can you blame me?' Edward storms on. 'I mean, the city of Cambridge is one of the most beautiful in the world, elevated to the sublime by nine-hundred-year-old colleges, by the intricate carvings of King's College Chapel and the like, by buildings so beautiful they bring tears to my eyes, and then the council let total idiots shit on all that splendour with buildings that look like they've been chucked together by children. Except that your average three-year-old could do a much better job building that parking lot, I'm—' Edward regards his wife. 'You're getting that look again.'

Greer sits up, defensive. 'What look?'

'That glazed look you get when I talk about architecture.'

'I do not,' Greer protests.

Tilly shuffles in her chair. 'May I be excused?'

Greer shifts her gaze to Tilly's plate. 'Are you sure you've finished?' She dips her head meaningfully to indicate the chicken breast that has been cut up but barely consumed, the potatoes and peas pushed around the plate collecting congealed gravy. 'It doesn't look like you ever started.'

Tilly nods. 'Maybe we could go back to getting takeaway tomorrow night.' She raises her eyebrows in Edward's direction. 'Sorry, Dad, but cooking isn't really your forte.'

'Cheeky monkey,' he says, then shrugs. 'But, yeah, I suppose you've got a point.'

'Perhaps you should leave chickens alone,' Tilly suggests, 'and just stick to buildings. Maybe you should ask the city council if you can design the next available car park – show them how it should be done.'

Greer laughs.

And, despite these harsh criticisms of his culinary prowess, Edward still can't imagine ever being happier than he is right now.

'Yeah,' he says. 'Well, maybe I will.'

Chapter Twelve

How strange it is, Ava thinks, that you can be perfectly decided upon a course of action, certain that it will bring your greatest happiness, and discover instead something even greater – joy you couldn't possibly have conceived – springing from the exact opposite outcome from the one you wanted.

Ava had never before, at least not to her memory, experienced herself in the way she had with Finn – the freedom of self-expression, the delight in her own self – and it hadn't come from love but, really, from an absence of love. But, why? And, how? Could it be because, after Finn had told her he was in love with a ghost, she had – with the shock – suddenly stopped caring what he thought, given up trying to seduce him, realised that it didn't matter how she acted any more. The experience was, Ava thinks, rather like being drunk or on drugs. Not that she's ever actually experienced these things personally, but she's read about them in books . . .

'I'm looking for *Tractarians and the Condition of England.*'

Ava looks up to see a tall, blonde, beautiful young woman standing in front of the desk. She has a breezy, effortless air. Ava imagines that this is a woman who always experiences the freedom of self-expression and delight in herself, who's never known anything else. But perhaps she is wrong; perhaps appearances are deceptive.

Do you ever swallow your words because you're afraid people won't like you? Ava wants to ask. *Do you ever just nod and smile during conversations when you really want to shake your head and scream?*

'Certainly,' she says instead, 'you just need to fill out an order slip and it'll be collected on the next trip to the stacks in twenty minutes.'

'Thank you,' the student says. And then, much to Ava's surprise: 'You know, you really do have the most beautiful eyes.'

Ava blinks. This statement is so surprising, so unexpected, that it leaves her quite unbalanced. 'Oh,' she mumbles. 'Oh, I . . .'

Ava grapples for the right response, the best thing to say next but, as she begins to form a disclaimer in her mind, the beautiful student turns away and is gone.

'I . . . I . . .' Ava echoes, 'I . . . I . . .' Then she shuts her mouth before she starts attracting speculative glances. A sense of slight panic sweeps through her. She searches the nooks and crannies of her mind for a few unanswered cryptic questions she can focus on. Ava's stomach turns as she realises she'd forgotten – for the first time in forever – to read *The Times* cryptic crossword puzzle that morning. So she has nothing else to focus on except the discomfort rising in her chest, which she'd really rather not do.

Ava sits behind her desk, praying she's not pounced upon by any other generously expressive students, while wishing she wasn't afflicted with such a cruel 'gift'. If she hadn't seen the worst event of Finn's life, she'd still be able to visit him, to experience again the delight and joy of speaking without censorship, of just being

106

herself without any effort or extra energy. Now, of course, she can't see him again since the risk of just blurting it out over coffee is too great. And then he'd hate her and she'd hate herself into the bargain.

Finn wakes at dawn. He yanks aside his curtains and peers out, bleary-eyed, into the milky grey light. It isn't raining. With a half-smile he stands, pulls his long, thin fingers through his hair, patting down the stray black curls, then tugs on a T-shirt and pyjama bottoms. Finn picks up his violin and bow and walks quickly across the room.

Five minutes later he's standing underneath the apple tree in his garden, warming up the wood with a few scales. And, as he begins working his way through Vivaldi's *Four Seasons*, Finn's breathing quickly falls into time with the music so each note draws each breath, pulling it from his lungs and into the air. He is quite lost to the soaring ebbs and flows of spring when Greer appears above the grass beside him. But, with eyes closed, fingers darting up and down the strings, every cell of his body vibrating with sound, he's still quite oblivious to everything substantial around him – not that Greer is particularly substantial.

She coughs. Finn's fingers freeze and he smiles before his eyes open.

'No, please don't stop on my account.'

'I won't,' he says. 'Since I came to play for you.'

Greer smiles. 'Thank you.'

Finn nods, basking in delight that she's returned to him, before settling his violin upon his shoulder again.

'How does it feel?' Greer asks suddenly. 'When you play? I watch you and it seems, it seems . . . like the most heavenly thing on earth.'

Finn smiles. 'Well, I've not experienced much else to compare it with but, yes, I believe it is for me.'

Greer sighs. 'I wish I could feel it.'

Finn considers this. 'Well, perhaps it's possible you can.'

'How?'

'I'm not sure. But,' he nods towards her, 'given your . . . transparent state, maybe – I imagine all sorts of things are available to you that aren't available to everyone else.'

'I suppose,' Greer says.

'Perhaps . . .'

'What?'

'Well, can you disappear into things?'

Greer frowns. 'What do you mean?'

'I mean,' Finn says, 'can you walk through walls, that sort of thing?'

Greer shrugs. 'I don't know.'

'You don't know?'

'I've never tried.'

'You've—well, why don't you give it a go?'

Greer wrinkles her nose. 'I'm not sure. What if I get stuck? What if I can't come out? I'm not sure I want to risk . . .'

Finn considers. 'I doubt you'd get stuck, I mean – you're like smoke or mist or . . . clouds. I think you'd pass right through.' He nods at the tree. 'Why don't you try it now?'

Greer looks a little shocked.

Finn laughs. 'I've not seen that prim side of you before.'

'I am not prim!' Greer snaps.

Finn just looks at her, still smiling.

Greer shrugs. 'Well, maybe just a little.'

'Go on, then,' he goads her. 'Be brave, be bold . . .'

Greer hesitates. Then she glances at the violin Finn now holds against his chest.

'All right, then,' she says. 'Keep your fingers crossed.'

Finn does so, holding up his hand to show her.

Greer drifts across the grass, but wavers as she's about to touch the trunk of the tree.

'Go for it!' Finn calls.

And so she does.

Finn holds his breath, praying he was right in his assumption that she'll float straight through. The next ten seconds seem to stretch into the length of an entire opera. And then she emerges, his beautiful ghost, completely unharmed and looking exactly like herself: red curls falling over her shoulders, green eyes sparkling with delight.

'I did it!' Greer exclaims. 'I did it!'

The leaves of the tree all flutter at once, as if blown by a breeze, as if breaking into applause. Finn uncrosses his fingers, tucks his violin and bow under his arm and joins in, clapping, cheering and grinning.

Greer drifts back to him. 'You were right,' she says, still beaming. 'So now what, what's the second part of your plan?'

My dearest Otto,

It has been less than a week since we've been separated – a week! Such a trifling amount of time. Ridiculous to complain about it, I know. And, usually, under ordinary circumstances, I could have borne it quite easily. But these circumstances are hardly ordinary, are they? They are the worst of all things. I can hardly believe that our beautiful world, the one that led us to each other, that held us in its hands, that witnessed our love and

109

the love of so many, is the very same world in which people kill each other, in which people – members of the very same human race – hunt and shoot women and children in the streets. I am so scared that we'll be found. And yet so grateful to those, to Mr & Mrs X who hide me, to their nephew who keeps our secret. And, of course, to whoever hides you.

How is it, again I wonder, that the world can hold within it such great good and such great evil all at once? I can only pray that, ultimately, soon, good will triumph and people will be safe and we shall be together again.

I don't think that I shall be able to get these letters to you. So you must wait for me, you must stay safe for me. Until I can give them to you, until I can whisper in your ear, until I can hold you again. Will you write to me? Are you writing to me, right now? I feel that you will, that you are. Despite the fact that we didn't say we would, that we never had a chance to say goodbye, I believe that you're writing to me. Every night, as I close my eyes and imagine that I am looking up at a black sky full of bright stars, I believe I can feel your words floating up from the page, from wherever you are hiding, the little black letters drifting through the air and into the sky, touching the stars, then tumbling back to me, falling into my open hands.

And I imagine you whispering your sweet words into my ear, your soft breath on my skin and I shiver and I smile. And then I long to hold you. My body yearns for you so deeply it aches. I press my hands to my chest and I cry, softly, silently, and I pray we will soon be together again.

Ever Yours,
Marthe

* * *

Clara spends her last night in Amsterdam walking the streets. Although she has nothing particular to do and no one to meet, she wants to get to know her newly, momentarily adopted city as best she can before she has to leave. She should visit the Anne Frank house, the Van Gogh Museum, all those significant, important sites. But Clara finds she doesn't have the inclination to do so. All she wants to do is walk and see everything else she'd miss if she were indoors or hurrying from place to place.

Because she can't help it, Clara glances into people's windows as she walks past their houses, looking out for the lonely and sorrowful ones. Of course, it's to no purpose, as she's without her special papers and pens and the all-important writing desk. If Clara was to pick a recipient now, then go back to her B&B and try to write a letter with borrowed pen and paper on the rickety wooden desk in her attic room, she's quite sure the results would be disastrous, certainly entirely without insight or inspiration.

As it is, Clara doesn't see anyone so is unable to test her theory. Lights are on in most of the windows of the tall, thin houses she passes, and in some of the houseboats floating on the canals, but she rarely sees a single person sitting behind these windows. At first Clara is disappointed, since spying on strangers is not only a profession but also a passion, but then she reasons it's probably for the best. Perhaps she should take a little break.

One thing Clara notices is how incredibly neat, elegant and stylish each house is – quite unlike English homes in their particular monochrome beauty. Clearly, the Dutch leave their lights on, even when they're out, so they can show off their glorious homes to curious tourists, nosey neighbours and – in her case – strange spies. And Clara would do the same, if her house resembled the interior of *Homes & Gardens*, instead of an eccentric, eclectic clash of design and style.

As she crosses another bridge, Clara thinks of the man and his daughter and wonders what they're doing now. Playing? Reading? Eating dinner? She sighs. And then she looks up to find that she is standing outside The Amsterdam Archive of Paperphilia. She smiles, thinking she's been drawn there like a homing pigeon, and wonders if Mr Akkersijk is still inside. She imagines him sitting at his desk, bent over her letters, his lips moving slightly as he reads. But, of course, he won't. It's far too late. He'll be at home, probably eating a delicious meal cooked by his loving wife while entertaining their three beautiful and impeccably behaved children with stories of his day. With an even deeper sigh, Clara walks on.

She ambles across another bridge and wanders along three more pebbled streets, under avenues of trees and past rows of bikes, until she stops in shock. For there, lit by the soft light of a lamp, and almost entirely hidden behind a pair of thick velvet curtains, sits Mr Akkersijk in a deep-red leather chair. And he is, indeed, reading her letters. Now, Clara can't be entirely certain that they are *her* letters he reads, but they certainly might be. They probably are. And he is alone. No beautiful wife, no impeccable children. Though perhaps they are off playing, hidden in other rooms. Clara stands on tiptoes to get a better look, peering through the crack in the curtains. From what she can make out, she's quite sure this is the home of a man who lives entirely alone.

Clara, given her habit of spying on strangers and writing them unbidden, unasked-for letters, has developed a good sense for people's homes and is able to tell a great deal from very little. In the case of Mr Akkersijk, however, it'd be easy for even the untrained eye to ascertain that he's a bachelor. His living room is sparse in terms of furniture – containing only the red leather chair, a small round table and a bookcase – and extremely overcrowded in terms of papers. Stacks of paper are piled upon every surface and across virtually every inch of the floor. A small pathway is carved out between the manuscript mountains, snaking from Mr Akkersijk's chair to the closed door.

Clara smiles. Mr Akkersijk is clearly something of a Dutch aberration, at least in terms of elegance and style. No wonder, unlike the rest of his countrymen, he hides behind his curtains. And, at least in terms of paper, they couldn't be more perfectly suited. And the way that he read that letter, the way his voice curled around the sentences, weaving tapestries of words that shone and then disappeared, the way it felt as if, as he spoke, he was blowing softly onto her bare skin . . . A shiver of self-conscious pleasure passes through Clara at the memory. And it – this memory – Clara tells herself later, is the reason for the emboldened and distinctly out-of-character move she makes next.

Clara reaches up and taps on the window. Lightly. Three times. Mr Akkersijk looks up.

When he sees her, she suddenly wants to run. Instead she stands completely still, a deer caught in headlights. Frowning, Mr Akkersijk stands, places the letter carefully atop a pile of papers beside him, and makes his way slowly along the path to the door.

Clara waits, anxiously attempting to conjure up credible and un-embarrassing reasons for doing what she just did. Why is she here? *How* is she here? How did she find him? How will she prove she isn't stalking him? What urgent thing could she have to tell him before she left?

When Mr Akkersijk opens his front door, Clara just stares at him, stupefied. When it's clear she's not going to break the silence, he's forced to speak first.

'It's . . . It's nice to see you again, Ms Cohen.'

Clara nods. 'Yes, thank you, you too. I was just passing and I saw—'

'You were just passing?' He interrupts. 'But, I thought you were going home?'

'Not till tomorrow,' Clara explains. 'I was just taking a walk through the city and I . . . I found myself here.'

'Oh,' he says. 'Well, it's cold now – I suppose you should come in for some tea.'

'Ah,' Clara echoes, stalling, sensing that, in all politeness, she really ought to decline the half-hearted invitation. But being in a foreign city makes her feel like a bolder, more dream-like version of herself, so she does just the opposite. 'Thank you,' Clara says. 'That would be lovely.'

Chapter Thirteen

Finn considers Greer's question.

'It's a bit silly,' he admits, suddenly thinking that what he's about to propose is too rash and too soon. He can't risk scaring her off, he really ought to wait, so he stalls. 'It probably won't work . . .'

'Well, it worked with the tree, so we may as well try.'

Finn smiles at her sudden boldness. Perhaps it's not too soon, perhaps she's ready and he, in turn, wouldn't want to lose the possibility, to let it slip from his hands because he waited too long. Perhaps he should simply seize the moment.

'All right then, if you insist,' Finn says, crossing his fingers and praying he's about to make the right choice. 'So, my theory is, that if I start to play and, while I'm playing, you step inside me—'

'Step inside you?!' She shouldn't be surprised, of course, given what's just happened, she should have foreseen it. But she's shocked. It's her prim nature, perhaps, but Greer feels this would be a betrayal of Edward – the circumstances are particularly strange, no doubt, but somehow it feels rather too close to adultery to be either proper or right.

Finn stares at her, desperately wishing he could unwind the last minute of time and take a different choice. But he can't and, as he sees it, his only choice now is to press on and try to salvage something.

'Well . . . why not?' he says softly, pleading. 'After all, as you said, it worked with the tree so there's no reason it wouldn't work with me.'

'Yes, but . . .'

Finn takes a deep breath and prays.

Greer dips her head to gaze at the grass. 'It's so, so . . . intimate.'

Finn wants to gobble up his words, swallow them down as if they've never been said. Of course, he's desperately curious to experience the sensation of Greer stepping into him. Perhaps it'll be painful, being invaded in such a way, but Finn doubts it. He imagines it might be like making love. Something he's wanted to do with Greer since the first moment he saw her, though he never thought it'd be possible. In truth, Finn would be content to simply be near to Greer for the rest of his life – to look at her, to play to her, to talk with her – but if he can have more than that, then . . . But her reticence scares him. If the only woman who's ever stirred his heart disappears he'll be truly bereft. It doesn't matter if he can't touch her, he doesn't care either way. All Finn cares about is that, for the first time in his life, he's starting to feel about another human being (or ghost) the way he feels about music. And Finn never thought that would happen. Not ever.

'It's okay,' he says. 'You don't have to, if you're scared . . . Try it another time or don't do it at all – whatever you want, I don't—'

'No,' Greer protests, 'I'm not scared. It's just, I-I . . .'

What happens next happens so quickly that it takes a little while for everyone involved to make sense of it.

The sound of giggles lifts the air; then Tilly pokes her head over the fence.

'Mum! There you are – what are you doing? Dad says you're late for breakfast. He's made something yucky again, you're so lucky you don't have to eat it.' Then she notices Finn. 'Oh, hello. Are you our new neighbour?'

Finn just stares at the girl, unable to form words. His fingers clutch his violin and bow so tightly his knuckles turn white. Slowly, he forces himself to turn to Greer, who looks utterly mortified.

'You . . . You're—you have a family?' Finn whispers.

Greer gives him the slightest of nods.

'But . . . I don't understand,' Finn mumbles, 'you never, you never . . .'

And then Edward appears. He comes up behind Tilly, smiling, saying something that's lost on the breeze as soon as he sees his wife standing in front of a stranger. He looks from one to the other.

'Greer?'

'Ed. Till.' She smiles at them and, with one last glance back at Finn, Greer drifts towards her husband and daughter and is gone.

'What was *that*?' Edward hisses, as soon as Tilly has left the table and they can hear her bounding upstairs to her room. 'What's going on?'

Breakfast had been a strained affair. And, unfortunately, the dubious standard of Edward's cooking meant that its consumption wasn't quick.

Greer looks at her husband. She knows what she's meant to be feeling: guilt, contrition, sorrow and regret. But she can recall these feelings only very vaguely, in the deep recesses of history – she can pull on threads of memory and just touch the edges of the

117

sensations with her fingertips. And yet now, in her current state, Greer can't actually feel anything, she simply *wants* to.

When she was properly alive – with a beating heart and breath – Greer experienced every range of emotion and, had she been forced to admit it, she'd say that she danced more often in the winds of the dramatic, darker emotions than the lighter. In her previous life, as she now thinks of it, it would have been unusual for a day to go by without a minor meltdown over the ripped seam of a dress or a tray of burnt brownies. But, since returning to this world, Greer has been upset by nothing. Even the act of rebirth itself, which admittedly came as a bit of a shock, didn't sway her, didn't elicit any physical rush or overspill of panic. Although it's not as if Greer hasn't felt *anything*. Indeed, she's been suffused with a glorious sense of wonder, stepping newly into a beautiful, bright bubble of sights and sounds where everything elicits a fresh sense of sublime awe. Those delightful feelings haven't yet subsided and they infuse her so fully that they haven't left much room for anything else.

'Greer. Greer?'

She blinks to see Edward staring at her, his eyes brimming with tears.

'Oh, gosh, I'm sorry,' she says. 'I didn't mean to drift off. I just, I was thinking. What were you saying?'

'That I didn't even . . . I wasn't sure if . . .'

'If what?'

'If anyone else could see you but us, Tilly and me, I mean. I hoped . . . But now a total stranger . . .'

'Oh, sweetheart,' Greer says, 'I understand. But that doesn't mean anything. It's okay, it's—'

Edward sighs. 'I thought you came back just for us.'

Greer's spirits sink. This conversation is going to be harder than she thought and she suspects Edward doesn't even sense the worst of it yet.

'Is . . . Is something . . .' Edward's face crumples and he can barely get out the words. 'Is something going on between—with you and . . . ?'

Greer is silent.

Edward takes a deep breath as tears slip down his cheeks. 'Do you still love me? Or don't you feel anything any more, after all this time. Is that it?'

'No!' Greer exclaims. 'I love you. I adore you. I cherish you. I couldn't possibly love you any more than I do. Oh, my darling, you mustn't doubt that. Not for a second.'

'But . . . But . . . So then why didn't you tell me about *him*?' Edward takes a deep breath and a look of pure sorrow passes over his face. 'I saw . . . the way you looked at him. It's . . . It's the same way you look at me.'

'Oh, sweetheart.' Greer holds her palm close to his cheek, so he can feel her warmth. She considers, for a moment, doing what Finn had suggested and attempting to enter her husband as she'd entered the tree. She wants to bring him comfort, solace and, if possible, a little joy. But something holds her back.

Edward looks at her with glassy eyes. 'Are you having an affair?' His voice is soft, anger flattened into sadness. 'Please tell me, if you are. Don't drag me out into misery. I've had quite enough of it for a lifetime, I honestly don't think I could bear any more.'

'I'm sorry,' Greer says softly, 'I'm really, really sorry.'

'So, then you are,' Edward says, barely audible. 'I didn't . . . I hoped . . .'

It's a minute before Greer speaks, not because she wants to

make Edward suffer but because she truly doesn't know what to say, doesn't know how to explain.

'We're . . . It's not anything like . . . I just feel, I feel drawn to him, in a way I can't . . . He plays the violin and it's the most . . . magnificent music you've ever heard . . .' Greer trails off, realising such effusions probably aren't helping. 'I listen to him, that's all really and . . .'

Edward is quiet for a long time.

'So, I was right,' he says at last. 'You don't love me any more.'

'No!' Greer says. 'That's not right, not at all. I love you just the same, as much as I always did.'

Edward shrugs. 'Well, it can't be enough any more, if you're' – he injects the word with great venom – '*drawn* to him.'

Greer sighs. 'I don't know how to explain it,' she laments. 'I don't seem to have the same emotions I had before – I don't feel sadness or jealousy or . . . attachments.'

Edward wipes his eyes. He gazes at her, incredulous. 'What?'

'Well . . . It's hard to say – it's different. I feel very different, since . . .' Greer trails off. 'When I came back I came with my mind and my memory but without all that other "human" stuff: possessiveness, needs, demands – and I suppose it affects the way I love. It's absolute and complete and total but it's also not . . . exclusive.'

'Not *exclusive*?' Edward asks, desperately. 'What does that mean? What are you talking about? Free love? An open marriage?'

Greer feels a bubble of laughter rising up and, sensibly, stifles it. 'No, that's not what I mean. It's not about sex and lust and all that – I simply don't feel *attached* to you in the way I did before, like we own the right to each other. So, I feel drawn to other people and things . . . but it in no way lessens my love for you. I know it probably sounds hurtful . . . but, I'm afraid . . . I can't seem to change myself and I have tried.' Greer decides not to go into detail here, not to mention that she hasn't tried particularly hard, since she's rather reluctant to return to a state of being shaped by mercurial emotions. A constant state of delightfully detached contentment has a lot to recommend it.

'You've *tried*?' Edward's eyes fill again. 'I didn't think you'd have to try, I thought you'd love me, just me, like in a normal marriage . . .'

'But I'm not normal, am I?' Greer says softly. 'I don't feel anger and pain and jealousy – you could call me a whore right now, anything you like, but I wouldn't be hurt. I'd simply understand that you're hurting and that's how you're expressing it.'

Edward opens his mouth, seemingly contemplating a few choice words at her suggestion. Then he shuts his mouth and sighs and rests his head in his hands.

'So, where does that leave us?'

'I don't know, my love,' Greer says. 'I think that's up to you.'

121

Chapter Fourteen

My Otto,

Do you remember the very first time you took me out to dinner? Do you remember what we ate? You had beef with potatoes and I had trout with sautéed broccoli and green peas. For dessert we shared a slice of chocolate cake. My trout was so tender and full of flavour; I can still taste it on my tongue. The cake was rich and moist, with three layers of buttercream filling. If I close my eyes and think back through the days, tumbling through time until I'm sitting again in that cafe on the Rozengracht, before we were banned from such places, I'm holding your hand again and my mouth is full of chocolate.

I miss you. I miss your touch. I miss your voice. I miss your . . . everything.

I miss food. In twenty-three days I've only eaten bread, a few pieces of meat and as many vegetables as Mrs X can manage to spare. Of course, I'm extremely grateful for all that they give me. They are depriving themselves so that I may eat, so that I may live. Of course, I will never complain nor ask for

more. And yet, I cannot help but miss the tastes I used to know.
Sometimes I dream of sugar, of those boiled sour cherry sweets
you used to buy me. And when I wake my mouth is moist and
my pillow is wet.

Isn't that a silly thing? When all this madness is going on
around us, so much devastation and death, and I am dreaming
of sugar. I would not admit this to anyone but you. Because I
know you won't judge me, you'll just laugh at your little Mattie
and tease me.

What are you doing now? I wonder this every day, so many
times. Where are you living? What are you eating? Where are
you sleeping? Do you have company? Today you ate a tiny slice
of roast beef for lunch, along with a single potato – with butter!
And, as you swallowed your food, you remembered the time we
ate together, when we held hands, when we were free.

Ever Yours,
Marthe

'I'm very sorry for the, um . . .' Mr Akkersijk trails off, clearly unable to refer to any of his precious papers as 'mess'.

'No, please,' Clara stops him. 'I can't imagine anything more beautiful than all this.' She gestures, the sweep of her fingers encompassing every manuscript mountain in the living room.

'Thank you. I'm grateful you don't judge me.' A rare, bright smile lights Mr Akkersijk's face. 'Although, I'm afraid, I realise, I don't have anywhere for you to sit in here. I, um, I don't get many visitors.'

Clara feels a flush of shame. She shouldn't have intruded. She should have left him alone, respected his personal space and let him be.

'We could take tea in the kitchen,' Mr Akkersijk suggests. 'It's not particularly comfortable, but I have two small wooden chairs . . .'

Clara nods, grateful she won't be putting him out too much. 'That's—thank you.'

'Okay.' He nods. 'Follow me.'

Clara follows him down a dark, narrow passage. The floor here is clear of papers but, Clara suspects, only because it would otherwise pose a rather serious health and safety problem. Mr Akkersijk would risk life and limb every time he went to and from the front door.

The kitchen, however, is not bereft of papers. Little piles (not so tall as the mountains in the living room) are scattered across the black-and-white linoleum tiles, stacked up on the tiny wooden table, on both chairs and across the counter. Clara has never seen anything like it. Upon entering, without meaning to, she lets out a laugh.

Mr Akkersijk, who has stepped carefully, intuitively, through the little paper heaps to reach the kettle on the counter, turns.

'Oh, gosh,' he says, 'I really shouldn't have let you . . . I should have cleaned up first, what was I thinking? How can you possibly take me seriously now, I—'

'Oh, no,' Clara blurts out, horrified that he would think this. 'No, not at all, I shouldn't have laughed – I'm just nervous, that's all. I didn't expect . . . I didn't expect to be here, and – this is exactly what my house would be like if I let it be . . .'

'Ah,' Mr Akkersijk says, 'but you don't, I suspect. Unlike me you are tidy and self-disciplined.'

Clara gives an apologetic shrug. 'Only to avoid the complaints of my mother, who would have a verbal heart attack every time she visited.'

Mr Akkersijk turns back to the kettle, switches it on. He takes a large china teapot from the cupboard, along with two cups. 'Yes, well, I would no doubt do the same, were my mother still alive. She had piercing opinions and always voiced them with a razor-sharp tongue.'

'Then I think our mothers would have been perfect friends.' Clara gives a little grin. 'Or perhaps not.'

Mr Akkersijk returns her smile. 'It sounds as if they might have sliced each other's throats.' As the water boils he pours the contents of a small bag of herbs into the teapot. 'I'm sorry, I don't have any English tea. No milk and sugar, no Earl Grey.'

'Oh, please, don't apologise. I'm getting quite used to Dutch tea. I had orange and cardamom at a cafe yesterday,' she says, reluctant to admit that she does, indeed, miss Earl Grey. 'It was quite delicious. Very . . . calming.' She nods towards the mounds of paper settled on each chair. 'May I?'

'Oh, of course,' Mr Akkersijk says. 'Thank you.'

Tentatively, Clara lifts each stack off the chair and places them, one by one, on the floor. Then she sits.

'This is a mixture of herbs, I forget what exactly, but it's one of my favourites.' Mr Akkersijk hands Clara her cup of tea and sits himself.

They sit in silence and sip. As he drinks, Mr Akkersijk seems to soften somewhat. His shoulders relax and the slightly steely gaze lifts, so Clara can see the suggestion of sweetness in his eyes.

He leans back in his chair, still holding his cup. 'I've been reading more of your letters. They're really quite beautiful.'

Clara sits up, placing her cup on the table. 'Oh?' she says, hoping to appear quite casual but unable to keep the delight out of her voice.

Mr Akkersijk nods thoughtfully. 'Yes, quite beautiful.'

Then, all of a sudden, he stands, spilling drops of tea down his shirt but not seeming to notice. 'Would you like me to read you a few? To translate, I mean – I just finished one that gives us some quite exciting news.'

'Oh, yes, please,' Clara exclaims.

'Okay, I'll get them,' he says, before rushing off.

Clara waits, listening to Mr Akkersijk hurrying through the house and hoping he doesn't slip or trip over any of his hundreds of heaps of papers. Fortunately, he returns a few minutes later, all in one piece and letters in hand.

'Perhaps I could begin with the last one I read,' he suggests as he sits. 'That's the one with the—anyway, you can hear for yourself.'

Clara nods as Mr Akkersijk begins to read.

My dearest Otto,
I know now that I won't see you for quite some time. Too long, far too long. I can't tell you how I miss you, how I love you. Of all the words I know, none are brilliant or bright enough to reflect the true nature of my feelings. I've been thinking often about this, actually – since I have far too much time available for such pursuits – and I believe that only music, the sort written by Mozart and Vivaldi, can come close to mirroring the human spirit and soul. Last night Mrs X was singing, while she scrubbed the floorboards of the parlour, and her voice rose up to reach us. It was The Marriage of Figaro *and the notes were so sweet, so high, so pure that – for a few moments – everything in this dark world was suddenly illuminated by stars. I closed my eyes and I was in your arms again, as you kissed my cheeks and stroked my hair. My heart flushed so full of happiness that it bubbled over, like the hot syrup in a peach*

pie, and I—I felt the same as I did the first time you kissed me.

But I've been putting off my news. I've been hoping it away yet it will not be hoped away. And I'm left wondering how can something be a sorrow and a miracle all at once? I would have wished, of course, that this hadn't happened before we were free to be together again. And yet, now I cannot wish it away. He (for I am convinced it is a 'he' – I just know, though I can't explain it) grows too fast and I don't know what shall be done when he's ready . . .

Oh, my darling Otto, how I wish you were here, to hold me in your arms again, to promise me everything will be all right.

Ever Yours,

Marthe

Mr Akkersijk doesn't look up at Clara this time but keeps his eyes on the page. Clara wants to ask him to read it twice over again, so she can warm her hands on the heat of the words, so she can be quite certain of the meaning. But she's too shy to ask such a thing, for this extra favour, from a virtual stranger. Instead, Clara filters the facts silently in her head.

'My great-grandmother was pregnant,' she says. 'With Otto's child. So, if the baby survived – I might have a grand-uncle or aunt . . .'

Mr Akkersijk is silent before he says, 'Yes, indeed you might.'

And they sit, neither looking at the other, in the quiet kitchen, everything said and unsaid curling and uncurling like the steam from their teacups in the air between them.

She's lost the cost of the ticket home, but Clara doesn't really care. She simply can't leave Amsterdam now, knowing that she might still have relatives here.

Last night Mr Akkersijk promised to read the rest of the letters as soon as he could, in order to glean any extra information about the child – if, in fact he was born and if he survived. While she waits, Clara walks across bridges and along cobbled streets, learning to stop still when she hears the ding of a bicycle bell instead of trying to dodge it and risk both her and the cyclist ending up in the river. Clara contemplates hiring a bike, since every single person in Amsterdam seems to own one. She'd see a lot more of this beautiful city that way and a lot sooner. But Clara dismisses the thought almost as soon as she has it. Cambridge is also a city of cyclists but, despite having lived there all her life, Clara has always preferred to walk. Indeed, she's never *learnt* and has always been quite scared at the prospect of doing so. There's so much to miss while whizzing along and she's always liked to keep an eye out for the little delights of life that most other people neglect: a cluster of fresh blackberries on a bush, a sweetly scented rose, a tiny, fat dormouse disappearing under a hedge, a soft white feather drifting down from the sky – a gift from a watchful angel.

Clara is so lost in thought that it's a few moments before she realises the sound of the ringing phone is coming from her own bag. Startled, she rummages around until she finds it, dispersing half the contents of the bag across the cobbled pavement in the process. She doesn't recognise the number.

'Hello?'

'Ms Cohen?'

She smiles at the sound of his voice. 'Speaking.' She scrambles about on the pavement picking up her belongings.

'It's Mr Akkersijk,' he says.

Yes, she almost replies, *I know*. But it seems too intimate, somehow.

129

'Are you free to come to my office, now?' he asks.

'Yes, of course,' Clara says, caught by the excitement in his voice. She leans against the iron railing of the bridge, gazing down at the shifting, shimmering water below.

'I've just finished translating another letter,' Mr Akkersijk explains. 'I confess I've neglected the day's work in the process. But it's been worth it. I have his name – the name of the child.'

'Oh,' Clara says, nearly dropping her phone into the canal. 'That's . . . I'm on my way.'

Chapter Fifteen

A wife? *A wife and a mother?!* Finn paces across his living room. He hasn't left his house in three days, for fear of bumping into his neighbours. Any or all of them. He hasn't been able to play his violin again since the last time he saw Greer, though he hasn't put it down either. Instead, Finn clings to it like a safety blanket, like he did as a little boy. The bow sits on the mantelpiece, untouched, though his eye is drawn to it every time he passes by the fireplace.

Finn freezes, mid pace. What if he's never able to play again? What if he's given his spark, his flare, his entire desire to this woman and, without her, he'll never get it back? It's exactly this fear that has caused him to hold back in the past, that has cautioned him against playing truly – opening up and pouring every fibre and beat of his heart into his music – for any woman. He has, quite wisely it seems now, never done so before. But with Greer he had no choice. For her, he couldn't play any other way. Finn wipes his eyes with the back of his hand. When Greer listened, he could only respond by giving her every piece and breath of himself. He couldn't hold anything back: his whole self, his soul flowed into each note. He laid himself bare for her.

When Finn was a little boy, his mother would tell him stories of how his father broke her heart and, at the end of them, she would make him promise not to let anyone ever do the same to him. 'You can love a woman,' she'd say, 'but don't give her everything, don't give her your whole heart – always save something just for yourself – that way you will be sure to survive.' Finn would nod, reassuring, though for many years he didn't really understand what she meant. Then, when puberty kicked in and he began yearning for girls, Finn knew and he did just what his mother had told him to do. And he did it for the rest of his life. Until Greer.

Unfortunately, his mother never told him what to do if he failed. She never told him, in the event that he did give his heart away, how he might get it back. So Finn is adrift on a sea of unknowing. A wild, wind-blown, stormy sea and – with only his unplucked violin to cling to – he's feeling himself begin to drown.

Every few minutes his resolve not to leave the house crumbles and Finn is overcome with the need to run into the garden, to run next door and find her, to throw himself at her feet and beg her to come back. But something of his mother's advice must have survived since, every time it arises, Finn always manages to stop himself from acting on that particular urge. So far.

And so he continues to pace. Time passes; the hours wear on slowly. And, as the sun sets on the third day and she still hasn't come to him, Finn begins to feel the skin of his chest softly tug and twitch as his heart starts to harden, thin ice gradually forming over the lake of blood and pain.

* * *

Edward doesn't know what to do. He can't really make sense of what his wife has told him. His wife. *Wife.* Surely this means she shouldn't want to be with another man, even if she is a ghost. Though, of course, Edward has to acknowledge he has absolutely no idea how she feels or what it's like to be her – not that that really helps stabilise the turbulence of his emotions right now.

Greer has promised not to see Finn again until Edward decides what to do. And he's asked her not to see him at all, not even to explain what's going on, because Edward isn't above poking the man he currently hates hard in the ribs. And he finds that imagining his neighbour suffering does bring a small measure of relief to his own. For the past three days Edward has spent a fair amount of time torturing himself with thoughts of his wife with this other man. This much younger, horribly sexy musician, whose hideously sublime playing has been serenading his breakfast every morning for the past few weeks. And, although Edward resents the fact greatly, he can understand why she'd choose such a man over him: an ageing architect who hasn't created anything new in years. He has no spark any more, no spirit, he'd be the first to admit, and who would want to be with someone like that?

Except that Greer hasn't said she doesn't want to be with him, simply that she wants to be with *him* as well. But how does she expect that to work? He isn't a ghost and nor is the next-door neighbour. How can they be expected to happily share her? At least sex won't be involved, thank God. That, surely, would be too hard for any human to happily manage. A ghost, perhaps, but not a living, breathing person who clings to physical, material things, who believes in the exclusivity and possessiveness of romantic love, who doesn't have the ultimate perspective an afterlife clearly affords.

Tonight, having drunk his third cup of coffee – with Tilly at a sleepover and Greer drifting about upstairs – Edward paces up and down the cold kitchen floor. His fingers twitch and he bites his lip. Can he do this? Can he possibly do this? Perhaps. Perhaps he can control his jealousy, perhaps he can learn to be a more evolved person, or perhaps he will lose his mind.

'I've been thinking . . .'

Edward looks up to see Greer in the doorway.

'Yeah, me too,' he says. 'I've been thinking about nothing else. But you said you wouldn't rush me.'

Greer floats into the kitchen. 'I've not come to rush you. I just had a realisation – a question.'

Edward waits.

'So . . .' She's tentative and he's suspicious. 'When . . . When you fell in love with me did you stop loving your first wife? Did your love for me eclipse your love for her?'

Edward regards her warily. 'I think I know where you're going with this.'

Greer shakes her head. 'No, really, it's a genuine question. When we met, the last man I'd loved had proved himself to be a complete bastard – so I was delighted to replace him. I was so incredibly grateful for you.'

Edward smiles. 'Me too.'

'Yes, but your wife had died,' Greer says. 'You didn't let her go because you wanted to, you had to. And I always wondered where that love went, since I doubt it just disappeared.'

'No, it didn't,' Edward admits. 'I didn't stop loving Amelia when I loved you. I don't really know how it worked exactly, I never really thought about it . . .'

'And, what would you do, if she came back?'

Edward looks at his wife, eyes wide. 'What do you mean? Is she . . . ?' He glances up at the ceiling. 'Do you know something . . . ? Have you heard . . . ?'

Greer looks momentarily alarmed. 'Oh, no, I'm sorry, I didn't mean to get your . . . I don't know anything. I don't have a direct connection to . . . I'm as clueless about this whole situation as you are. I don't know why I came back and she didn't. But' – something else occurs to her – 'do you . . . Do you wish she had? Do you wish she was here instead of me?'

Edward sighs. 'No – well, I don't know.' He sighs again. 'I don't know anything; I don't understand anything. This whole crazy situation is a complete mystery to me.'

'Me too,' Greer says softly. 'And I'm sorry if I'm making it harder . . .'

Edward gives her a wry smile. '*If?*'

Greer smiles. 'Okay, I know, I know. But I wouldn't, if I could help it, if I could be any different—'

'But, can't you?' Edward pleads. 'Can't you just try?'

Greer floats towards him, her hand outstretched. 'Oh, sweetheart.' Edward takes a step back.

'Look, I want to let you be whatever . . . whoever you are,' he says. 'But it's bloody hard, what you're asking – you know that, right?'

Greer nods.

'And I get what you're saying, I do, about the fact that, technically, I have two loves in my life too – but not at the same time, not really, so . . .'

'What about when you're dead too?' Greer says. 'And we're all – wherever we are – together. You won't be able to choose between us then, will you? We'll all be together and it'll be okay.'

Edward holds up his hand. 'Okay, look – so I don't know what they get up to in the afterlife, perhaps it's all free and universal love and all that crap. But down here, on earth, we tend to go with the whole one man, one woman deal. Or' – he thinks of his sister – 'one woman, one woman thing or, whatever. Anyway, my point is, I'm sorry. I'm still human. I'm a child and I don't want to share my toys, okay?' He sighs. 'Sorry, that sounded horribly misogynistic. I didn't mean it like that, but I can't do this, okay? Okay?'

Greer is by his side, her hand against his cheek. 'Yes, yes, it's all right. Don't cry, please, you know I could never bear to see you cry.'

Edward puts his own hand up to his cheek, surprised to find his skin wet.

'We can make this work, just the two of us, don't you think?' he asks, his voice cracking. 'I've been missing you for three years and now you're back and I don't want to let you go again – don't you see?'

Greer nods. 'Of course,' she says softly. 'I won't see him again, I promise. Okay? And yes, we can. I know we can . . .'

And she dearly hopes, for both their sakes, that she's right.

As she sits at her desk Ava thinks, as she often does, about her next-door neighbour and what she saw. It brings tears to her eyes, so much beauty and love and sorrow all wrapped up together. She is jealous of him, even with the sorrow, because it's so much experience, so much feeling, so much living! Which, Ava realises, is what she's been missing her whole life. How can one be alive but not really *alive*? It's a strange thing, she thinks, but true. So, even though Ava sees how much Finn will ultimately suffer, far in the

136

future, she still envies him his suffering, envies him his life.

Ava half-heartedly ponders a few stray cryptic crossword clues secreted somewhere in the folds of her mind, before her attention soon drifts. She's not in the mood to hide any more. And yet, Ava isn't certain about the best way to go about reaching out to people. Even though she's recovered from the shock of seeing Finn and would dearly love to visit him again, she can't for fear of blurting out what she saw. She can't risk hurting him like that, in exchange for her own enjoyment at his company, it simply wouldn't be fair. And yet she misses him, too much. More than that, she misses *her*, who she is when she's with him. Or, rather, who she was.

Ava stands, pushing her chair back and glancing around the library, at all the students with their heads bowed over their books. She gazes at them for a while, totally and utterly absorbed in the pursuit of their futures. It's then that she realises something else. She, in her own wanting, is being too passive. She can't expect life to hand her happiness on a plate. She has to go out herself and seek it. She has to find it and seize it and hold it captive. Or woo it and seduce it and nurture it. Whatever one does, whatever is best in the pursuit of happiness. Ava has no idea, but she's now determined to find out.

As she's looking out at the students, Ava's sight snags on a pinboard behind the Victorian Fiction section. It's dotted with adverts for every kind of thing one could possibly imagine wanting to do, a thousand classes of every fashion and sort: opera, salsa, calligraphy, Japanese, French cooking, wine appreciation . . . Without thinking, she darts out from behind her counter, her skirt snagging on the edge of the desk, catching on a stray splinter. When Ava tugs at the stiff tweed she hears the tear of a thread and looks down to see half an inch of dark-blue wool sticking out from her skirt. Instead of annoyance, Ava finds herself smiling. It is, she thinks, as she hurries across the faded carpet towards the pinboard, the first thread of her old life beginning to unravel.

Chapter Sixteen

My Otto,

I nearly died today. The Gestapo came. We thought someone had betrayed us. I thought Mr & Mrs X, and their nephew, who lives with them, would be shot on the steps of their own house. All I wanted to do was disappear, evaporate. I'd have killed myself, even with our child inside me, if it would have saved them. But I knew, too, that it wouldn't. So there was nothing for me to do but wait. I never thought it would be possible to be so entirely consumed with fear – for our child, for Mr & Mrs X, who would each die, if they died, because of me. I had no fear for myself, strangely, as I do on most other days. As, to save them, the two who risk their lives every day for me, I would have run out onto the street to be shot.

Of course, once our child is born, once he is out of my body I know my greatest fear shall be for him, even above our protectors, though that feels rather unfair. But I'm afraid I shan't be able to help it. I would surrender myself in a heartbeat for him, of course, but I would surrender them too. Not that I'd

*have the right and though it would be a great wrong indeed to
do so. I wonder if they will guess at this, once he is born and if
they will cast us out.*

*When at last I told Mrs X of my condition, I believe she
talked with Mr X about doing just that. I don't blame them
for this. When they agreed to hide me, they didn't expect to be
hiding a baby too. He might cry out too often and too loudly;
he might be heard, we might be betrayed. And, even though
it would make sense, since to be discovered would kill us all, I
could not smother him, I simply could not. I will fight for him,
I promise you, I will protect our son until I can do no more.*

Ever Yours,

Marthe

'But, how? It doesn't make sense.'

'I'm afraid I can't explain it. I am not a historian. I can only
give you the facts.'

Clara stands behind the counter of the Office of Records on
Haarlemmerdijk, 102. Having already waited three days and four
hours for the information she applied for, Clara is now feeling
more than a little agitated at not being given it.

'So, you're saying that there's no record of an Otto Josef Garritt
van Dijk being born in Amsterdam, *ever*?'

'No, Miss Cohen,' the short, spidery woman says. 'I'm saying
we've no record of an Otto Josef Garritt' – she slides from her
precise, perfect English to give extra, particular emphasis to the
pronunciation of the surname, highlighting Clara's mangled
attempt – 'van Dijk being born between 1939 and 1949. Those
were the dates you gave for us to check. Correct?'

Clara sighs and nods. 'But I don't understand. I have his name here, written down by his mother.' She slides the letter onto the counter.

The woman purses her thin lips. 'Yes, you've already shown me it several times. As I told you before—'

'But look,' Clara taps the paper, feeling the panic rise in her chest. 'She gives his exact name. It can't have been that common. I mean, it's unlikely there was another boy born with the very same name, so . . .'

The woman's eyes narrow. 'Yes, clearly that is correct, or we would have found record of one. However, as I've already explained, if the mother – as you believe – was a Jew being hidden by a Dutch gentile family during the war, then that explains why she never registered the baby. It's very simple. It makes perfect sense.'

'Yes, I understand,' Clara says, trying very hard not to raise her voice, 'which is why I asked you to check the marriage and death records too. I mean, even if his birth wasn't registered during the war, it might have been afterwards, to make him legitimate – don't you think? And, if he got married or had children, there would be no reason not to register that, don't you think?'

'I am not paid to think about such things, young lady,' the woman retorts. 'My job is simply to check the records. A job you have been preventing me from doing for the last' – she glances at her watch – 'fourteen and a half minutes. So, if you don't object, I really ought to get back to it.' Without waiting for a reply, the woman turns from Clara and ensconces herself firmly behind a computer screen, immediately tapping her skinny fingers rapidly against the keys.

For a few moments Clara remains, reluctant to let go of her only chance of finding her unknown relative. Still, she holds on to the one piece of good news: there was no record of Otto Josef

Garritt van Dijk's death. Which might, just *might*, mean that he's still alive. And thus she somehow, if only she can figure out how, still has a chance of finding him.

'You should return to England,' Mr Akkersijk says. 'You'll probably find records of him there. After all, your grandfather left Amsterdam as a teenager, yes? So it's possible his older brother went with him.'

'But, why do I know nothing about this brother?' Clara asks. 'Why did Granddad never mention him? If he was still alive, wouldn't he have told me all about him? It doesn't make sense.'

Mr Akkersijk sips his tea. 'I'm afraid many families don't make sense. Especially those of older generations. My father was taken to Auschwitz in 1944, three months before the end of the war, before that camp was liberated. He was fourteen years old. He never spoke about it. Not a word. Not as long as he lived. I asked him a few times, especially when we started learning about the war at school, but he'd just shake his head and mutter something I couldn't understand and my mother would tell me not to bother him.'

Clara sits in silence, clutching her teacup, not knowing how to respond to such a grand, grave admission. She glances at his kitchen floor, anchoring her gaze to a pile of letters. 'I'm sorry,' she says softly.

'It's okay,' he says, though his voice has a raw edge, like the underbelly of a wounded creature. 'It's a long time ago now.'

'Still . . .'

He shrugs. And Clara suddenly wants to reach out and touch him, to press her face against his chest.

'How old are you?' she blurts out, before instantly regretting it. 'Sorry, I—'

Mr Akkersijk smiles. 'That's all right. I'm fifty-four. You?'

142

It's fortunate that Clara wasn't sipping her tea at the time of this revelation, or she'd surely have spat it out across the table. 'Fifty-four?! Really? You're *twenty-one* years older than me? I didn't, I didn't – you're so, so . . . You're still . . .'

Mr Akkersijk's smile deepens. 'Alive? Walking without a stick? Able to remember my own name? You young people are so funny, how you perceive the ageing process, when you really have no idea.'

'No,' Clara huffs. 'Actually, it wasn't that at all. I wasn't thinking anything like that, I was thinking, I was just . . .'

Something in the air shifts as Clara trails off, as if her unspoken words have strung themselves together in a taut wire suspended across the table. When Mr Akkersijk looks at her now there's a dash of mischief in his gaze.

'What were you thinking?'

'Well, I, um . . .' Clara's own gaze slips quickly back to the floor, to the safety of the papers, their curling, crisp edges, the scratch of black ink across their creamy surface. 'Nothing.'

Mr Akkersijk inhales deeply, then picks up the teapot on the table between them. 'More tea?'

Clara looks up. 'No, thank you. I'm fine.'

He nods at the plate of speculaas between them. 'Biscuit?'

Clara shakes her head.

'Will you,' she ventures, 'will you read me the letter again, about the baby?'

Mr Akkersijk looks surprised, but nods. 'Yes, of course.'

'Thank you,' Clara says. She sets down her teacup and opens her bag – hanging on the back of the chair – and pulls out the letter. 'I want . . . I've never, never—'

'Yes,' Mr Akkersijk says softly, 'I've never experienced anything like it either.'

'You haven't?' Clara asks, without looking him in the eye. 'Oh, I—'

'Thought I would have,' Mr Akkersijk finishes. 'Given my grand old age of one hundred and three.'

Clara giggles. 'Yes, I suppose so.'

'Well, I haven't,' he says. 'Their feelings are quite incredible, aren't they? And – it's comforting, in a way, to know that love like this survived, even amid all the tragedy.'

'Yes.' Clara slides the letter across the table, letting her hand rest atop it for an extra moment, so their fingers touch when Mr Akkersijk picks it up.

My dearest Otto,

He's a boy, just as I promised he would be. He's beautiful. So beautiful. Just like his father, though even now, I'm so sorry to say that your face is fading in my memory – I used to know every line, every freckle, every eyelash, every curl of hair. As I squeeze my own eyes shut now, to put you in focus you come back to me, though still as a watercolour rather than a photograph. His eyes are blue, just as yours, though I hear they can change up to two years after birth. I hope they won't. I dearly hope they will be just as yours are, for ever.

How I wish I could get this letter to you. None of the others before this matter, only this. I wish that somehow I can get word to you. I would ask Mr & Mrs X to deliver this to you, or word alone, but I cannot. They are doing so much for me, risking their lives every day just by my being here. And now, little Otto is here too and we are praying that he will continue to be as quiet as he has been thus far. I sleep with him at my breast so he never wants for food or comfort. I swaddle him in

144

blankets, his only clothes so far, but I shall sew him more.

Mrs X brings me extra bread and soup, to keep my milk plentiful, and she even slips me an extra piece of meat now and then. I know she's taking it off her own plate and I'm so grateful but cannot say because she would deny it. Even her nephew sneaks down here now and then to bring us little extras, for which I am deeply grateful. He stays to talk sometimes, too, and provides some welcome distraction, though, given that you are of similar ages, I cannot help but wish he was you.

What do you do every day, in your hiding place? Are you as well cared for as I? I do dearly hope so. How much longer will we have to wait? Will we live? We must. We must survive to raise our son and love him and show him a world that is bright and beautiful, not this wild, terrible world we hide from now. I will write to you every day, telling you news of your son. I shall pray for us all; I shall pray that this madness will soon be over.

Ever Yours,
Marthe & Otto Josef Garritt van Dijk

Chapter Seventeen

At first, Edward is happy. He has everything he's been longing for. He has his wife back. They sit up late at night and talk. She continues teaching him how to cook – with mixed results. His daughter's giggles fill the house again. They watch films together in the evening, Edward and Tilly sharing a bowl of overly buttered, slightly burnt popcorn. He and Greer can't make love, of course, but Edward has so much and feels so blessed that he doesn't mind forgoing that particular pleasure. He's so happy, in fact, that he begins applying for architecture jobs again.

'I was thinking, since it seems you're here to stay, that we could invite my little sister over for dinner,' he suggests to Greer one night. 'What do you think?'

Greer gives him a wry smile. 'So long as it's your younger sister and not your older one.'

Edward, who always attempts to be diplomatic about his family, winces slightly. 'Well, yes, I wasn't thinking of inviting Charlotte. I don't think she'd, um, respond very well to our particular situation.'

Greer laughs. 'You can say that again. Plus, she's a total bitch.'

'Sweetheart,' Edward admonishes. 'That's a bit, well, that's to say, I don't think . . .'

Greer raises an eyebrow. 'Oh, just admit it. She's absolutely awful.'

Edward remains tight-lipped.

'Come on,' Greer teases. 'She hated me too, you can't say she didn't.'

Edward allows himself the flicker of a smile. 'Well, okay, but Charlotte hates everyone, so you can't take that personally. Anyway, Alba will be thrilled to see you. Zoë too.'

'You don't think they'll be a little shocked?'

Edward shrugs. 'Of course, at first. But they'll get used to it and then they'll be as thrilled as I am.'

Greer smiles again. 'Um, maybe not *quite* as thrilled as you are.'

'Well, okay,' Edward admits, 'maybe not quite. But then I doubt anyone is quite as thrilled as I am right now.'

Greer's smile fades, though she tries to keep it in place. She'd like to disagree, to argue that she's just as happy as he but, unfortunately, as the days pass without the musician that's becoming less and less true.

'We have news,' Alba announces, after everyone has finally put down their knives and forks.

'So do we,' Edward says, beaming, delighted both by the revelation he's about to share and the fact that his dinner – nut roast – actually went rather well, for once. He's so excited, in fact, that he forgets to let his sister go first. He takes his glass of white wine, half filled, and holds it aloft. Greer had argued that they introduce the delicate subject of her return in a subtler way at a subtler occasion, but Edward insisted that such glorious news demanded proper ceremony.

Now he stands, wipes his free hand on his jeans and glances up at the ceiling. The crack he'd fixed seems to be snaking out from underneath the new plaster, stretching its fingers out to grasp what it can. He'll have to fix it again.

'Oh, come on, Dad,' Tilly groans. 'I've got things to do – homework and stuff.'

Edward darts his daughter a suspicious look. Alba and Zoë glance at each other. 'Okay, okay,' he says. 'I was just waiting for the right moment. I wanted to introduce the topic with the deserving amount of solemnity. I thought—'

'Dad!'

'Okay, okay.' Edward waves his daughter down, then regards his sister with an enormous grin. 'Greer has come back.'

Tilly slouches back in her chair, arms folded. Alba and Zoë look confused.

'I don't understand,' Alba says slowly, glancing around the kitchen. 'What do you mean?'

In reply, Edward walks over to the door, opens it and sticks his head into the hallway. 'Darling, I just told them,' he calls. 'Where are you? They're starting to think I'm insane.'

At that, Greer materialises beside the kitchen table. Alba gawps and Zoë emits a small shriek. Edward gives a start.

'No need to shock them like that,' he protests. 'It's enough of a shock already.'

'You can say that again,' Zoë mumbles, once she's found her voice.

Alba laughs. 'Why all the cloak-and-dagger stuff, Ed? You know I met Aunt Stella the same way.' Then she jumps up from her chair and is, in the next moment, standing at Greer's side. 'I wish I could hug you.'

Her transparent sister-in-law smiles. 'Me too.'

Zoë sighs. 'Well, this makes our news seem a little passé.'

Tilly sits up. 'What's your news, Aunt Zo?' She throws a look at her father. 'I want to know, even if no one else cares.'

'Till!' Greer reprimands. 'Of course we want to know the news too.'

'Yes, of course we do, Till,' Edward says, though admittedly he'd totally forgotten the fact of his sister's news. 'Don't be silly.'

Alba and Zoë hold hands.

'You're pregnant!' Tilly exclaims, pointing at Zoë.

Zoë looks shocked. 'How did you—?'

Edward, nearly dropping his wine glass, looks startled. 'You *are*?'

'Oh my goodness,' Greer exclaims. 'Congratulations!'

Despite his shock, Edward can still hear the edge of disquiet in his wife's voice just as, though he pretends even to himself that he doesn't, he notices that her own edges are becoming, very gradually, almost imperceptibly, less defined as the days pass.

'Woo-hoo!' Tilly cries, hugging a still-bemused Zoë before hopping over to her Aunt Alba and giving her a huge hug too. 'A baby! A baby! You're going to have a baby!' She turns back to Zoë. 'Is it a boy or a girl?'

Zoë smiles. 'We don't know yet. We'll find out in a few months.'

'Ooooh, I really hope it's a girl,' Tilly coos. 'Then I can dress her up in pretty dresses and play with her and, and . . .' She sighs.

Edward frowns. 'I never knew you liked babies so much, Till.'

Tilly shrugs. 'I guess I wanted a sister, but, you know . . . Anyway, it doesn't matter any more, cos now I'm sort of going to have one anyway – a cousin's the next best thing, isn't it? I can babysit all the time, right?' She appeals to Alba and Zoë. 'And you'll bring her round all the time, won't you?'

'Will you still be so enthusiastic if it's a boy?' Alba asks with a smile.

'Yeah, of course!' Tilly says. 'Anyway, when he's a baby I can still dress him up in pretty stuff, can't I? He won't know, so it doesn't matter, does it?'

Alba glances at Zoë, who shrugs happily. Alba nods at Edward and addresses Tilly. 'Well, funnily enough, I believe your dad used to dress up in your Aunt Charlotte's school uniform when he was a kid and, sometimes, even in Mum's ballgowns though they were, of course, a little big for him at the time.'

'Al!' Edward exclaims. 'I most certainly did not.'

'Oh, don't be embarrassed,' Alba says. 'Why shouldn't boys get to dress up in girls' clothes when girls get to dress in boys' clothes and no one thinks anything of it? It's all social convention, anyway. Two hundred years ago, the sight of a woman in trousers would have been outrageous. Hopefully, before too long, a man could wear a dress without being judged for it—'

'I do *not* want to wear dresses,' Edward protests, as Tilly and Greer both giggle. 'I don't care about social convention, I . . .'

Alba shrugs. 'I'm just saying.'

Tilly smiles. 'So long as we're all okay with dressing up the baby, it's fine with me.'

'Do . . . Did you really want a sister so much, Till?' Edward turns to his daughter and lowers his voice. 'Are you sad that you didn't have one?'

Tilly glances at Greer, who gives her a reassuring smile.

'Well, yeah, I guess so,' Tilly admits. 'I mean, didn't you want another kid? If Gr—if you could have had one.'

'No,' Edward says, too quickly. 'You're quite enough of a handful, thank you. God knows I couldn't cope with another one.' But, as he speaks he fixes his gaze on his wine glass instead of his wife.

Ava stands at the bottom of the long stone staircase, feeling as if she's standing at the bottom of Everest, staring up at a three-thousand-mile climb. She takes a deep breath, her fourth in as many seconds. She's rapidly starting to hyperventilate. *Get a grip*, she snaps silently at herself. *Get a bloody grip*.

With one more deep breath, Ava sets her foot on the first step. It's only a dance class, for goodness' sake. A few steps of salsa. How hard can it be? It doesn't matter that she's never danced before in her life. The flyer had insisted that this was a class for 'complete beginners'. Thank God. She desperately hopes that everyone else will be as utterly inept as she. Thus somewhat lessening the potential for total, earth-shattering humiliation. But only somewhat. Ava takes another step. Halfway up the stairs she stops to collect and congratulate herself.

'Hey, lassie, are you comin' or going?'

Ava glances behind her, in the direction of the voice, but the owner of said voice is already bounding past her on the stairs so she's forced to look up at him.

'I . . . I . . .'

The man stops at the top and looks down at her with a grin. 'Well, if you're comin', then you'd better get a wee move on, or we'll be starting without ye.' And, with that, he bounds off, disappearing through the double doors in a flurry of Scottish flair.

Ava doesn't move. She presses her left hand against the wall to steady herself. The encounter doesn't inspire her to keep climbing the mountain. She should probably go home. Taking a tentative step out of your comfort zone is one thing, salsa dancing out of it is quite another. What *is* she thinking?

And yet. Ava wants to change her life. She wants to feel again the way she felt with Finn. She wants to experience liberation and fun and delight. And the only way she can touch upon these things is to do something different, something she's never done before. Salsa certainly falls into that category. So she keeps walking, until she reaches the door. Then she pushes it open and walks inside.

A small circle of men and women stand in the centre of a large room. The floor is scratched wood and the walls faded white. A line of plastic chairs – most of them draped in coats, bags and other outdoor paraphernalia – are pushed up against one wall. Ava notices the Scottish man standing in the corner of the room, bending over a battered black stereo, fiddling with its buttons and muttering. A few heavily accented curse words float across the floor.

'Are you staying for one class or two?'

Ava realises she's standing in front of a table and a bespectacled, skinny young man is looking up at her with a serious expression.

'Oh, right, sorry,' she says, fumbling in her bag for her purse. 'Just one, please.' There's no need to push her luck. It'll be a miracle if she survives one class, let alone two.

'Are you a member?'

Ava shakes her head. 'No, no, thank you.'

'Okay. That's six pounds, then.'

Ava nods and pays him. Then she slowly takes off her coat and places it, along with her bag, upon the only empty chair. Then she shuffles across the floor to join the circle.

'Okay!' Ross shouts, as he abandons the stereo and strides across the floor. 'Okay, you wee bunch of swing beginners, we gonna have fun, so let's get on with it!'

153

Ava stiffens. *Swing?* She dips her head in the direction of a timid man standing to her left.

'Isn't this a salsa class?' she asks, under her breath.

Without looking at her, he shakes his head.

'What's that, lassie?' Ross bellows, as he stops in the middle of the circle. 'If ye've got a question, you'll have to speak up. Be bold! Ye canna dance swing if ye're gonna be too scared to speak.'

Despite herself, Ava smiles. There's something about this strange, explosive man that makes him hard to dislike, much as she might want to.

'I think I'm in the wrong class,' she says.

'Nonsense!' Ross declares. 'Come here.'

For three seconds Ava is absolutely horrified. Then, Ross snatches her up in his arms and starts flinging her about the dance floor. At least, that's how Ava feels, for the first few moments. And then, somehow she feels as if she's gliding on ice, as if she's floating on air, as if she's the most elegant, graceful creature in the entire world. She is, all of a sudden, someone else entirely; someone she's always *dreamt* of being. Ava feels his large fingers lightly cupping hers, his other hand pressed lightly against her back and she never, ever wants him to let go.

An hour later, after the beginner's class has ended and the advanced class has begun, Ava leaves the room with the scratched wooden floors and the faded white walls with greater reluctance than she imagined possible. She has danced. Danced! For the first time in her life Ava has danced and, for the most part, she loved every single second. She had a few hiccups, of course. And dancing with the other beginners hadn't been anywhere near as glorious as when the teacher had scooped her up and twirled her around the floor. But glorious moments were had, echoes of grace and elegance and joy. Moments that made Ava smile deep into her soul.

As she pushes the door open again, Ava glances back at the new group of students standing in a bigger circle. 'Zoot Suit Riot' fills the room and the students begin to move, each grabbing a partner and starting to dance. They dip and jump and leap together and Ava stops to watch, entirely lost in the astonishing beauty of it all.

Ross McKinney has a gift, a gift with women, and for them. He was six years old when he first found it, though he had no idea at the time what he was doing. He kissed the cheek of Frieda Fyfe (the shortest, skinniest girl in school, who wore broken glasses fixed with Sellotape and clothes made from curtains) and turned her into the most popular girl in school. By the time he reached secondary school, and after a few more kisses, Ross started to realise what it was he could do. And so he made a mission of it. He sought out every girl who was shy, scared, sad or riddled with self-doubt. And, one by one, he inspired them. He helped them find their courage, he helped them realise who they really were, and just how amazing they were capable of being.

Ross McKinney's gift is in revealing to women their own brilliance, being a mirror to their potential, making them see what they're really and truly capable of, if only they decide to do it. When women see themselves through Ross's eyes, when they see themselves the way he sees them, then all the world opens up and they can do anything they set their minds and hearts to doing. So this is what Ross has dedicated his life to doing, this is what he does better than anyone else.

Ross loves what he does. And he falls in love – at least a little bit – with every woman who finds him. And yet, though they've only shared a single dance, Ava already intrigues him more than most he's met. She seems so timid, withheld and full of fear. But, underneath all that, he senses something special: fire, passion and true joie de vivre. And, if he can help her release it all, if he can help her unleash the great glory he sees residing within, well then she'll be simply magnificent.

Chapter Eighteen

My Otto,

One day, when we are together again, I will read all these letters to you. I will wait, of course, a few days, then you will lay next to me and I shall read you all the words I wrote while we were apart. And, in the reading, the past will be brought into the present and merge with it, so that we will never have been apart at all and we will always be together again. Is that madness? If so, I don't really care.

I want to read you what I've written for you, because I've always believed that a letter isn't complete until it's read, just like a book. If you talk to someone and they don't listen, if your words fall into the air unheard, you feel invisible, unimportant, alone. And it is much worse than simply being alone. To feel alone while with another person is, I think, the loneliest we'll ever feel. I'm so fortunate to have never felt that with you.

But, I digress. I meant to talk about letters. I think that it's even more important for letters to be read than books, because

*letters are written to a specific someone, they are a conversation
and, if they go unread, it's as if the person who wrote them went
unheard. And I want you to hear me. I want to speak with you
again, as much as I want to touch you and hold you and never,
ever let go again.*

Ever Yours,
Marthe

There is no longer any reason for Clara to see Mr Akkersijk.
He's translated all the letters and the search for Otto has been
met with only dead ends. It's time for her to leave Amsterdam
and return to England. She has responsibilities; she has people
who need her. Lately, Clara has been dreaming about the shop,
about the inhabitants of Cambridge who are waiting, though
they don't know it, for her letters. She wakes in her B&B in
the middle of the night, sitting up sharply, nearly banging her
head on the sloped attic ceiling, sticky with sweat and out of
breath. Her mother has been leaving ever-increasing numbers
of messages on her phone. Clara should catch the next train
home. But she won't. There's something she must do first.
Though she has absolutely no idea how she's going to manage
it, or if, indeed, it is even possible. Yet her longing – unexpected
and inexplicable – for Mr Akkersijk has reached such heights
that it will not leave her alone and, so Clara imagines, the
only way to overcome her desire is to feed it, fulfil it, to sate
and satisfy it. Then she can return to Cambridge unburdened,
without regret.

So she finds the most appealing dress she owns among her
luggage – she's been washing everything by hand in her bedroom
sink, having in the first instance only brought enough clothes for

a few days – and buys a bottle of very expensive red wine and sets off for the Amsterdam Archive of Paperphilia. She can't rightly say why she doesn't wait until the evening and go to Mr Akkersijk's home instead, except that she's worried then her intentions might seem too obvious.

Clara carries the bottle in her right hand and a letter in her left. The previous night she dreamt about the man she saw through the window of number ten Riverside Drive, with his daughter, looking so sad. And, when she woke, she knew she had to write to him again. It no longer mattered that she didn't have the writing desk, or any special pen or papers. She didn't know exactly what to say, or if it would make any sense, or matter anyway. But Clara knew that wasn't the point. She had to follow her instinct. And so she'd sat at the tiny desk of her B&B and begun. And, when she'd finished, she asked at the front desk for an envelope and they'd kindly given her a stamp along with it.

Clara posts the letter on the corner of Sint Luciënsteeg, where she's drawn into a shop rather like her own. Its tiny dark door is set a little back from the street and she almost walks past without seeing it. But the sight of letters in the window stops her. She glances up at the inscription in oak above the door: *De Posthumuswinkel – 1865*. As she steps inside, Clara sighs happily. The shop is a cross between a glorious stationery stash – monogrammed, personalised, embossed in every colour and style – and a museum of letters. One of the walls, bereft of dark wood shelves and drawers, is enveloped in antique letters, the scratches of ink and scrawl of words barely visible on some but bold on others. Among the letters are photographs of ancient printing machines and the streets and canals of Amsterdam. Glass wax stamps line shelves along with hand-printing supplies, beautiful papers, envelopes and a hundred small glass jars containing a hundred different colours of ink.

Clara takes a deep breath as she stands in the centre of the shop, allowing the scent of paper and ink to sink into her skin. With a sharp, sudden stab of longing she misses home and, for a moment, wants to be back sitting at her own writing desk more than anything. And yet, in the next moment, she wonders if she couldn't relocate. Could Amsterdam support two very special stationery shops? Possibly. Perhaps. Why not?

This rather exciting thought keeps Clara company, buoying her steps as if she were bobbing along the canal in a longboat, until she comes to the Archive of Paperphilia and steps inside. When she approaches the counter, Clara slips the bottle of wine behind her back. The beautiful, voluptuous woman guarding the gates to Mr Akkersijk's kingdom sits to attention before Clara reaches her.

'May I help you?' she asks, in perfectly accented English.

'I was hoping to see Mr Akkersijk,' Clara says, while thinking it is fortunate that Dutch people speak English so well. It would certainly make relocation that much easier, should she take such a bold leap. 'Is he in?'

'Do you have an appointment?'

'No,' Clara admits. 'But he knows me. If you might call through and ask . . .'

The beautiful woman raises a perfectly manicured eyebrow. 'I am afraid I couldn't possibly do that, he's in a meeting.'

Clara frowns. For some reason she feels as if she's stepped into a boxing ring without realising it. So she takes a step back.

'Okay, then, I'll wait.'

The beautiful woman shrugs her sculptured shoulders and says nothing. She simply nods towards a single chair next to the doors.

'Thank you,' Clara says, turning and walking to the chair with as much dignity as she can muster.

It's nearly dinner time, two and a half hours later, before she sees him. Or rather, before he sees her, since Clara is staring out into space – thinking how incredible it is that she can even *entertain* a thought as radical as actually moving to Amsterdam, when only a week or so ago she was virtually petrified at the thought of even visiting the place – so doesn't notice Mr Akkersijk walking towards her.

'Clara?' he's surprised, clearly, but not, visibly, displeased. 'Did we have an arrangement?'

'Oh!' she turns, brightening at the sight of his face. 'No, I just . . . I really ought to leave tomorrow and I wanted to say goodbye and thank you.' She holds out the bottle of expensive wine as explanation.

'Oh, goodness, you certainly didn't have to do that,' he says, taking the bottle and admiring it. 'Though, I can't say I'm sorry you did – you have very good taste.'

Clara smiles. 'Thank you . . .' Realising she hasn't really thought her plan through in sufficient detail, she doesn't know what to say next. She'd rather hoped it might all happen naturally or come to her in a flash of inspiration on the spur of the moment. She stands. 'May I take you out to dinner?'

Mr Akkersijk glances down at the bottle he holds. 'As well as the wine? I couldn't possibly, it's far too much.'

'Oh,' Clara's spirits sink and she understands that she'll have to return to England with this particular wish unfulfilled after all.

'But I would love to take *you* to dinner.'

Clara looks up – hearing a muffled splutter of disgust from behind the counter.

'Really? How lovely, thank you.' She stands and smiles, instantly flush with happiness, so she feels able to be silly. 'But, since we're in Amsterdam, perhaps we could go Dutch.'

Mr Akkersijk laughs as they walk together out through the double doors.

'Where shall we go?' Clara asks, as they walk along a canal, bicycles weaving elegantly in and out of their path.

'I know a place,' Mr Akkersijk says.

'Okay,' Clara says, wondering if he's taken many women there before.

'I've never been,' he says. 'But I've walked past it a thousand times. I've always wanted to step inside.'

Clara smiles. 'Then why haven't you?'

He shrugs. 'I've never had occasion to take someone.'

'I can't believe that.' She wants to put her arm through his but they are folded together through his woollen coat and she doesn't dare ask.

Mr Akkersijk shrugs again. 'It's true.'

'Really? Well, that gorgeous woman who works at the Archive, I have the feeling she'd say "yes" if you invited her.'

'Greta?' Mr Akkersijk exclaims. 'No. She's far too . . . That's absurd.'

Clara turns so she's facing him, playful. 'Too what?'

He smiles. 'Well, too young and beautiful for such an old man as I. Wouldn't you agree?'

'I certainly would not.' Clara says, emboldened by his coy smile. 'So, are you saying I'm old and ugly enough for you?'

'For me?' Mr Akkersijk asks. 'Is this a date? I hadn't realised. I thought we were simply two colleagues together celebrating . . .'

Clara eyes him, unsure whether or not he means it. Then, all of a sudden, to the shock of them both, she steps quickly across the distance between them, stands up on tiptoes and kisses him. At the last moment, she misses his mouth but her lips land smooth and soft on his cheek. Mr Akkersijk stares at Clara as she sets down on the pavement again. For a second she thinks he's going to kiss her back, properly. But he doesn't.

'Well, Mr Akkersijk,' she says, regaining her composure, unsure whether he deflected her on purpose, or she just hadn't been accurate in her aim. She decides to believe it was the latter. 'I think it's only right that I should know your first name now, don't you?'

He nods, a little dazed. 'Pieter.'

'Ah,' she says.

'It's like your "Peter",' he explains. 'We just say it slightly differently.'

Clara smiles, touched by his nervousness. 'Yes,' she says, 'I think I got that.'

'Okay, right, well then . . .' Pieter unfolds his arms and sticks his hands firmly in his pockets. He begins walking again, then stops. 'Please . . .' He sticks his right arm out, offering her the crook.

Clara slips her arm through his and they walk on, a little lopsided, to the restaurant.

* * *

'So you write to them but they don't know who you are?'

Clara nods, chewing her exquisitely soft salmon. It's the first time she's ever told anyone, other than her grandfather, her secret. She didn't plan to, she hadn't even been thinking of it, but it simply slipped out, after her very first bite of fish. She finds, strangely, that she feels safe telling him anything.

Pieter sits forward, putting down his knife and fork. 'And you never see them afterwards?'

Clara shakes her head, still chewing. 'Not usually.'

'But you're not curious, about how the letters might affect them? You don't want to visit the houses again and take a peek inside?'

Clara swallows and gives a little shrug. She thinks of the letter she posted a few hours before – a rare instance of writing to the same person twice and the only letter she's ever written without the help of her writing desk. But, since it's such a fresh, new, strange experience that she can't quite explain, Clara decides not to try.

'Well, perhaps I see people I've written to, now and then, if I happen to wander down the same streets again,' she says. 'But I don't really think . . . Well, it's not—*I'm* not really writing the letters. I don't think about what to say, I just write and after I've finished I've no idea what I've written.'

'Oh,' Pieter says. 'How intriguing.'

Clara slides another piece of salmon onto her fork, along with a slice of dauphinoise potatoes and a leaf of curly kale. 'This restaurant really is delicious,' she says. 'I don't think I've ever had food like this before.'

Pieter smiles. 'I have a confession,' he says softly.

Clara looks up, still chewing, expectant.

His voice drops to a whisper and he stares down at his plate. 'I wanted . . . I've wanted to . . .'

Clara swallows. 'To what?'

Pieter glances up, but still doesn't catch her eye. And then, finally, he looks at her. 'Perhaps it's the letters . . . but, I . . . Well, when I read you the first one . . .'

'Yes?' Clara asks, while hoping she already knows the answer.

'I wanted, afterwards, I wanted to . . . to . . .'

'To kiss you,' Clara finishes.

Pieter frowns. 'You?'

Clara blushes. 'Me? No, I was just saying, if that's what you were going to say – you seemed to have a little trouble getting to the words – well, I wanted to say that I wanted to kiss you too.' Clara sets down her knife and fork, suddenly extremely nervous. 'Oh, God. But now you're going to tell me that wasn't what you were going to say at all, that in fact you wanted something else entirely.'

'No,' he says, glancing down at his plate again. 'That's exactly what I wanted, I just, I just . . . I couldn't say so. Then, or now, it seems.'

Clara smiles, utterly relieved. 'You have no idea of your effect on women, do you?'

Pieter Akkersijk frowns.

'Seriously?'

He shrugs.

'How long has the woman I saw been working in your office?' Clara asks, suddenly keen to shift the conversation away from their kissing.

'Greta?'

'Yes.'

'I don't know – about six years.'

'Six years?' Clara raises her eyebrows. 'And in all that time, you've never asked her on a date?'

Pieter shakes his head.

'No wonder she hates me, then.'

Pieter, who'd been taking a sip of red wine, splutters. He dabs his napkin to his chin. 'I'm sorry?'

'Well, um, here I am,' Clara says, 'pushing my way in, when she's been waiting six years for you to proposition her.'

'What?' he exclaims. 'She has not.'

'Oh, trust me,' Clara says, 'she has. You might be oblivious to women's signs, but I know our ways. And she wants you, she's wanted you for a long time.'

'Gosh,' Pieter says. 'You really think so? I had no idea. No idea at all.'

'I know. That's part of what makes you so attractive,' Clara says, while slightly unable to believe she actually has. Perhaps she's a little drunk.

'Oh?' Now Pieter smiles, taking another, bigger, sip of red wine. 'And what are the other parts?' he asks, blushing even as he says the words. 'I'm sorry, was that too much? I confess, flirting isn't my forte.'

Clara smiles. 'Mine neither. But maybe that's why I find it easier with you.'

'Why? Because I'm so dreadfully bad at it you feel like a positive Casanova next to me?'

Clara laughs. 'Perhaps. Or whomever the female equivalent is. But that's another part of it – you're not slick, you're not practised and glib. You're real and true. You don't seem, anyway, to hide yourself behind cute lines and witty responses, you reveal yourself when you speak. It's very . . .'

'I hide behind other people's letters,' Pieter says, putting down his glass. 'I hide behind other people's declarations of love. Another confession: I've never written a single letter in my life.' His voice drops to a whisper again. 'Isn't that awful?'

'No,' Clara says, simply, though she is rather surprised. 'But why – why haven't you?'

'I don't know,' he says.

'Oh.'

Pieter sighs. 'No, that's not true. It's because, perhaps having read such a great many beautiful letters – exquisite, moving, touching, sometimes heartbreaking letters – I've always felt too intimidated. I couldn't bear to attempt to write so beautifully and fail so miserably.'

Clara grins. 'But not all letters are like that. You've obviously just been reading the cream of the crop. Loads of them are mundane and boring and utterly prosaic.'

'Perhaps,' Pieter admits. 'But I don't want to write those kinds of letters. If I wrote, I'd want to be as witty as Austen, as passionate as Anaïs Nin and Henry Miller, as profound as de Beauvoir and Sartre, as literary as Virginia Woolf . . .'

'Oh, so you keep your expectations nice and low, then.' Clara smiles. 'I think we've got more in common than just the letters.'

'How?'

'Well, when I was a little girl, my grandfather gave me a pen, in fact he made it—'

'He *made* it?'

'Yes, that was his profession, before he opened the stationery shop. But he never stopped making them – his pens were famous. He made, maybe, one a year and sold them for a fortune.' She smiles, proud. 'I have three of his pens in my shop: one that John Lennon used to write *Imagine*, one that Daphne du Maurier used to write *Rebecca*, another Quentin Blake used to illustrate *Matilda*.'

Pieter stares at her, open-mouthed. 'How incredible. That is to . . . What's his name?'

'Lucas Janssen. He died nearly ten years ago. He—'

'Lucas *Janssen*?' Pieter exclaims. 'Goodness! I've always wanted to hold one of his pens, but it's impossible. I've never even seen one. There are, what? Perhaps a dozen in circulation and they sell for about half a million euros each.' Pieter sighs. 'I was in London once and one of his pens was at auction in Sotheby's. I almost went, but I couldn't bear to torture myself. To be so close, yet so far from something I wanted so much.'

'Really?' Clara says, deeply touched. 'I had no idea you were such a fan.'

'And I had no idea you were the granddaughter of Lucas Janssen.'

'Then I'm glad I didn't tell you until now.' She smiles, still rather surprised by how relaxed she feels. 'Or I'd never have known if you really liked me, or just wanted me for my pens.'

Pieter returns her smile. 'Well, yes. And now I can't rightly say . . . If someone were to offer me one of your grandfather's pens in exchange for you, I don't know what decision I would make.'

'Cheeky bugger!' Clara pretends to whip him with her napkin across the table. 'I'll have you know—'

'—ah,' Pieter interrupts, 'but don't worry, in the end I would, of course, choose the pen.'

Clara laughs. 'I shan't be inviting you home, then, or you'll be making off with all my most prized possessions.'

Pieter considers this and is suddenly serious. 'Well, in that case,' he says. 'If you won't invite me to your home,' he says, 'may I invite you to mine?'

Chapter Nineteen

'I can't believe I'm going to be an uncle,' Edward says, with a happy sigh. 'And you're going to be an aunt – isn't that wonderful?'

Greer nods.

'Do you think Al and Zo will let us help choose names?' Tilly asks. 'I've already got a list of some beautiful girls' names: Lily, Lilac, Lotus, Iris, Sage, Ivy, Heather, Holly, Poppy, Rosemary, Olive, Blossom, Fern, Jasmine . . .'

Edward smiles. 'Do you have any that aren't flowers or herbs?'

Tilly sniffs. 'They're very fashionable right now, actually, Dad. You'd know that if you weren't so totally ancient.'

'Oh, I'm sorry,' Edward says. 'Yes, I admit, I don't have my finger on the pulse of the "youf" of today.'

Tilly frowns at him. 'See, that's exactly what I mean. I have no idea what you're talking about. Mum?'

Greer shrugs.

'Yes, well, fortunately youth isn't a quality coveted in my profession,' Edward says. 'And, since I do have a job interview today, I really ought to focus on that.'

'That's cool, Dad,' Tilly says, actually sounding like she means it. 'You should get out of the house more.'

Now Edward frowns. 'What do you mean?'

Tilly shrugs. 'Well, I mean, Mum has to stay in, right? Cos she'll scare people if she goes out. But you're alive and everything, but you still stay in as much as you did when Mum died. And now she's back, so . . . I figured it meant you wouldn't have to any more.'

Edward glances at Greer, who doesn't take her gaze off her daughter. A touch of sorrow brushes across his face. He shakes it off.

'Yes, well, I will be getting out more, if I get this job, won't I? I'll be out from eight till six every day. You'll be begging me to be home then; you'll be moaning that I'm never here.'

Tilly raises her eyes to the ceiling. 'Yeah, okay, Dad. I'm sure Mum and I will get really lonely without you. And we'll really miss your delicious dinners.'

'Oh, very funny,' Edward says, though he can't help but wonder what Greer might do while he's out. When she'd encouraged him to go back to work he believed she had his best interests at heart. But, still, he can't help but wonder, and worry.

'I'm going to teach Till how to cook,' Greer says softly. 'Just basic stuff. So we'll be okay.'

Edward frowns, wishing his wife sounded a bit happier, that he couldn't feel her sorrow from where she sat, that he knew how to make it all better, make it all work, make it all perfect. But he doesn't and he can't. 'You're all talking like I've got the job already,' he says, trying to sound upbeat. 'I haven't even had the interview yet.'

'Oh, you'll get it, Dad,' Tilly says. 'You may be ancient,

decrepit and out of touch, but you're a total genius when it comes to building stuff and everyone knows it.'

Edward smiles gratefully at his daughter. He's desperately grateful for how relaxed and content she's been since Greer's return and really, everything else aside, his daughter's happiness is enough. He will focus on this. And this, he tells himself, will be sufficient to call the current status quo a success.

The thin ice that had crept over Finn's heart has now hardened, like a pie left too long in the freezer, to a thick, concrete crust. He can almost hear it rattling around in his chest as he walks, weighing it down so he has a slight stoop. However, the benefit is that he can play his violin again. Sadly, the sound of his music is not so deep and rich and moving as it was when his audience was Greer. And this irks Finn a great deal more than he'd care to admit. But still, the fact of being able to play at all is quite something and the relief takes the edge off his disappointment.

He understands why she hasn't come back. Actually, he doesn't blame her. He's guessed what must have happened. Of course, her husband gave her an ultimatum and, of course, she acceded to his request. Truthfully, he wouldn't have wanted her not to. Being raised by a mother whose heart was shattered by infidelity has left Finn with a strong moral code on that count. He would never, ever knowingly have an affair with a married woman and he'd certainly end it as soon as he found out. He just wishes he'd known about the husband and child, then he'd never have let himself get involved with Greer in the first place. But he did and now he can't undo it.

Finn even considers going next door, to visit the sweet – if slightly odd – woman who brought him the cakes. Or what did she call them? He can't remember. In all honesty, he couldn't tell the difference at a push. Finn might be able to identify Mozart's Sixth Concerto or Vivaldi's Spring Quartet from the first few notes, but food has never been something that interested him very much. He never understands why women complain about the size of their thighs (he once had a fling with a woman who wouldn't make love with the lights on, so self-conscious was she about this particular area – although he'd caught a lucky glimpse of the supposedly enormous thighs once and found them perfectly lovely) since surely just eating less would solve the problem without fuss. Finn has the opposite problem since, especially when he's practising a new piece, he often forgets to eat altogether. At least Greer would never worry about her weight, having virtually none of it to speak of at all.

Stop! Finn admonishes himself. *Stop thinking about her. It's over. It's not happening. Just let it go.* And yet, regardless of how many times he tells himself this, Greer keeps snapping back into his mind, suddenly appearing centre stage like a reappearing magician's assistant. And there doesn't seem to be much he can do to make her disappear again. No matter how hard he tries. Sometimes, he doesn't even bother trying, he just lets her hover at the edges of his vision, waiting in the wings, waving at him. It's easier that way – when he includes her she seems content to be a constant part of the background. But when he tries to banish her, she'll leap unexpectedly into the midst of an unrelated thought and scare the bejesus out of him.

Truthfully, Finn knows that any attempt to truly forget Greer, or try to replace her with another woman, is futile. She has marked him, she has claimed her stake and while some men can erase such things, can move on without even a scar, he cannot. Despite the

174

fact that this has never happened before to Finn, and despite the fact that it's only been a week and he can't really judge so soon, he just knows, somehow he just knows. And so, eventually, he stops telling himself to stop and simply resigns himself to his fate.

Both letters arrive on the same morning, three days later. Edward picks up the thick cream envelope first. He sees the internal postage frank and knows what it is without even opening it. A&B Associates are writing with their formal offer of a position at their firm. They'd suggested as much after the interview, so Edward isn't surprised, nor is he particularly delighted. And, before he opens the second letter, he decides to turn it down. He'll simply tell Greer and Tilly that he didn't get the job after all. He knows he'll have to find something soon, but not yet, not quite yet. He needs to stabilise his family first; he needs to be sure that it'll be safe to leave them when he does. And he isn't at all certain of that right now.

And then, as this runaway train of thoughts is hurtling through his head, Edward begins to open the second letter. He doesn't know whom this one is from. The stamp is foreign, from Europe, though he doesn't know exactly where, not understanding the language on the postmark. The envelope doesn't bear his name, it simply says: *To the Householder*, followed by the address. It's only when he's torn open the envelope and is pulling out the single sheet of paper that he recognises the handwriting. It's from the same person who sent him that first anonymous letter, the one he received before Greer returned, the one he read so many times he ended up having to Sellotape it back together along the seams. He never thought he'd get another, though he dearly wished he would. And here, at last, it is.

Edward steps back to sit on the staircase. If this letter is anything

175

like its predecessor, he'll want to be sitting down when he reads it. He takes a deep breath, before smoothing out the page on his knees and beginning to read. As before, the letter isn't addressed to anyone. But, as before, Edward hasn't a single doubt in his mind that it's meant for anyone else but him.

Please forgive me for writing to you again like this. I wasn't intending to. I cannot explain what moved me to do so, nor can I know if what I say will be right or, indeed, make any sense to you at all. If not, I apologise. And, if so, I do hope you will find comfort and understanding in these words.

Last night I dreamt about you. I think of you quite often, though I don't even know your name – I probably shouldn't mention that, but don't worry I'm not a stalker, just a letter writer – and, though I can't explain it, I felt your sorrow, how it's seeping out of you, though you're trying desperately to contain it, to be strong and seeming normal so as not to hurt those you love.

Speaking of love, when I woke, I remembered this poem, a Shakespearian sonnet – does it have a title? I'm not sure. Sadly I can't recall it all, but I think I have the most important lines here, the ones that say what I wanted to say to you:

Love is not love
Which alters when it alteration finds,
Or bends with the remover to remove:
O no! It is an ever-fixed mark,
That looks on tempests, and is never shaken;

Now, I can't explain why I had to tell you this. I hope you will know. I hope it will make sense to you. No doubt you know this poem, but I'm guessing you'd forgotten it, I'm guessing you had forgotten how to love. I think (and of course I could be entirely wrong, though I believe this poem backs me up) that true love means allowing a person to be exactly as they are — exactly — not trying to tinker with the wiring or adjust a few fundamentals here and there. It means wholehearted embracing, not simply enduring the bits you don't like, or trying to change them.

And, I believe, though I've admittedly never experienced it for myself, that there may be great liberation in true love. It means that you fully know who and what you want. If you say 'yes' to everything a person is, if you welcome their whole self into your heart then, and only then, can you really know if that's the person you want to spend your days with. You know then if something is missing — something you in fact want and need — but something you were glossing over in the hopes that it would change, or you could change it. But you can't change another person and, if you try, they will only hate you for it and, what's worse, you'll hate yourself while trying.

True, unconditional love — as opposed to romantic love, the sort that everyone believes is unconditional, until they discover it's not — is the only sort that fills you, body and soul. It swells your spirit and opens your heart so you feel gratitude and joy to be in this bright bubble of life. It's all-encompassing and non-exclusive. It does not fix its mark upon one person and insist that one is the only one who must meet your every desire. It simply loves everything as it is and does not seize upon a single soul and try to

alter and tinker and tweak until it's satisfied – that type of love
is always edged with pain and suffering. No, it opens its arms to
embrace everyone exactly as they are and it trusts that, one day, it
will find its perfect match.

When he's finished reading, Edward wants to scrunch the letter up and burn it. He wants to unread it. He wants to pretend he never opened it in the first place. But, of course, he can't. Once the words have been released, he can't squish them back into the bottle. And he can't pretend he doesn't know exactly what the letter writer means. If only. Although, how on earth does she – for he believes, unequivocally that it's a woman – know what's in his heart and in his life? Could it be his sister? Alba has always been acutely perceptive and no doubt she picked up on all manner of undercurrents when she and Zoë came to dinner. And yet, the tone and language of the letter makes Edward think otherwise. He doesn't know the writer of this letter, he might not know much about much, but he's absolutely certain of that. And so *how* does she know him so well?

Edward sighs. He may be a little clueless and self-deluded, but he knows why he'd rather sit on the bottom of the stairs and wonder about the origins of the letter, rather than act on its decrees. Slowly, he stands and folds both letters and stuffs them in his back pocket. Then he climbs the stairs to go and find his wife.

Edward finds Greer on the second floor of the house, gazing out of the window into the garden. She's so faded now that he can barely make out her edges in the light. She doesn't turn when he walks into the living room, perhaps because he's too quiet, perhaps because she's looking for someone else. Edward suspects the latter.

'I got the job,' he says, because he can't bear to say the other thing just yet. He wants it all to remain the same, if only for a few moments longer.

She turns to him then, a half-smile on her lips. 'Congratulations. I knew you would.'

'Thank you.' Then, with another deep breath, he crosses the floor to reach her. 'Are you happy?' he asks.

Greer nods. 'Of course.'

'Bless you for lying,' Edward says. 'but I don't think I've ever seen you so unhappy.' He sighs. 'When you came back you were . . . radiant, sparkling, effervescent . . .' He can't help but smile at the memory of it. 'I thought, as you said, that's how you were now, that's how you'd always be, in this . . . particular state.'

'Yes,' Greer agrees. 'That's what I thought too.'

'But you're not any more, are you?'

Slowly, reluctantly, Greer shakes her head.

'Is it . . . Is it because of him?'

Greer looks up at her husband, surprised at his directness. It emboldens her in return. 'Actually, no – I don't think so. It's hard to tell, of course, since I have no frame of reference.' She gives a weak smile. 'I haven't been like . . . this for very long, so I don't really know how it goes. But . . .'

'What?'

'But, much as I miss . . . him, and I do,' Greer admits, 'it's not simply that – it feels, it feels more as if I'm trying to go against the nature of who I am now, trying to be a way I am not meant to be . . .' She falls quiet for a while. 'Do you see?'

Though he'd rather go down fighting, Edward nods.

'It's as if . . .' she continues, 'As if I'm a river flowing into an ocean, that's my natural state, the state in which I'm truly myself, truly happy, perfect – but instead I'm a river that's stopped flowing, a still, stagnant pool of water slowly filling with algae and bugs and—'

'Okay, okay,' Edward says, unable to hear any more. 'I understand.'

Greer looks at him, slightly incredulous. 'You do?'

'Yes, I do. I've been keeping you stagnant, trapped, forcing you to try and be a way that you can't possibly be. And I, I . . .' He bites his teeth together and takes a deep breath. 'And having you here like this is, well, it's worse than not having you here at all.'

Hope fills Greer's eyes and Edward finds it almost unbearable to see. He's been her captor, her jailer and now she's on the edge of being free.

'You can do what you want,' he says softly, 'be the way you need to be. No rules, regulations, no expectations.'

'Are you sure?' Greer asks. 'Are you really sure you're okay with that?'

'No. I don't know.' Edward shrugs. 'It doesn't matter. I'll get used to it. Since it can't really be any other way now, can it?'

'But I don't want you to suffer, simply so I don't,' Greer says. 'That's hardly fair, is it? Anyway, I couldn't, I—'

'I'll be fine,' Edward says, 'don't worry about me.'

'But I do.'

'I know, and I love you for it. But I also know that this is the only way we can be together,' Edward says. 'If you're able to be yourself, otherwise, what's the point?'

'How will it work? What will we do? What . . . ?'

Edward shrugs again 'I don't know; I've not thought that far. I suppose we'll talk it over with Tilly and try to explain and then . . . Then we'll just try to figure it out as we go along.'

'Are you sure?' Greer asks again.

'I believe,' Edward says, 'at least I want to believe, that this is the best way to be and the only way to love. And, after that, we'll just have to see how it works out.'

'Thank you.' Greer holds her hand up to Edward's cheek and he closes his eyes. He wonders if his heart will ever recover. He wonders that for a long time. Long after she's disappeared.

Chapter Twenty

'Oh, dear,' Clara says, 'Greta is really going to hate me now.'

Pieter runs a finger along her bare arm. 'I'm starting to get a little jealous of your obsession with Greta. Are you certain that seducing me wasn't just a way of getting to her?'

'Um,' Clara pretends to consider it. 'Er . . . yes, quite certain.'

'Then I have absolutely no idea what your ulterior motive is. You've got me stumped.'

Clara turns onto her side, letting the sheet slip from her shoulders. 'Is it not possible that I just wanted you?'

Pieter shakes his head. 'You're saying that I was the final objective in your plan? No, I'm afraid I can't possibly believe that. You are, quite simply, the worst liar I've ever met.'

Clara casts her eye around the bedroom. Happily, like every other room in the house, every inch of its floor is completely covered with piles of papers. 'I get the feeling that you haven't had that many liars – or, indeed, honest people – in this room at all . . .'

Pieter smiles. 'Gosh, you women really do have your extra senses, don't you?'

Clara studies him. 'Have you ever been in love?'

'Well . . . yes, I have actually. Perhaps not in the way of Marthe and Otto, but yes, in my own way, I have.'

Clara waits.

'A woman lived in this room – well, in the whole house, of course – for about five years,' he continues, suddenly sounding sorrowful. 'She left when I was thirty-five.'

'Did she leave you because she kept slipping over all your papers?' Clara says, attempting to lighten the mood. 'Did she break her leg one too many times?'

Pieter gives her a half-smile. 'Actually, I was very tidy back then, bordering on fastidious, in fact. I only allowed myself to get like this afterwards, after I knew she wouldn't be coming back, and after I knew no one would be coming to replace her. Then I filled the spaces with my papers and . . .' He shrugs.

'So,' Clara ventures, fiddling with the edge of the sheet. 'How did you know . . . How did you know that you wouldn't, that no one would come to replace her?'

Pieter shrugs and, again, Clara waits.

'She left because she wanted a child,' he says at last. 'And I couldn't give her one. Well, no, not couldn't – although perhaps I couldn't, I don't know, we never tried – but because I wouldn't, because I didn't want one.'

'So she left?'

'She really wanted a baby. She hoped I'd change my mind. She waited five years to see if I might. And then, when I didn't – as I'd always, regretfully, promised her I wouldn't – she, regretfully, left. She was four years older than I was, so she didn't have endless amounts of time to find another man, one who wanted what she wanted.'

184

'And did she? Did she find him? Did she have her baby?'

Pieter smiles. 'Yes, she did. She came to visit me once, over a decade ago. She showed me her little boy. He was very sweet, actually. Though, of course, I couldn't permit him to enter the house. I might have found him less so, after he ran rampage over my letters. Lena was a little horrified at the sight of the house, I think. If she'd had any doubts that she'd done the right thing, when she turned up on my doorstep, that visit confirmed that she had. I'm sure she was even happier when she left than when she arrived.'

'And, why didn't you want one?'

'I don't know . . . During our final year it was all Lena wanted – to understand why I didn't want it. At least, that's what she said. I think she was just hoping, amid all the questions, all the rationalising, that I would change my mind.'

'And you didn't?' Clara asks. 'You never thought of giving her a baby anyway, because she wanted one, because you loved her?'

Pieter sighs. 'Of course I thought of it. I'd have given her a cat, even though I'm allergic. I'd have given her a dozen cats. Hell, I'd have given her a horse or an elephant, but not a baby. For a child to grow up with an unwilling father, that's a pain I wouldn't inflict on anyone.'

Clara catches his eye. 'You knew it yourself?'

He nods. 'After what he went through in the camps, my father could only survive, he had nothing left for anyone else. But, still he got married and had children because that's what everyone did then. He was never a father to me, though, not in any sense of the word.'

'I'm sorry.' Clara shifts closer and kisses him. At first it's tentative, gentle, soft, then Pieter presses his body against hers, slips his fingers though her hair and pulls her close, and the kiss is deep and passionate and long.

'You're very good,' he says softly, when they finally separate.

'Why, thank you.'

'Well, yes, at that, of course.' He smiles. 'But, I actually meant, at getting me to talk about myself. And I don't believe you've revealed one single thing about yourself yet. You never finished telling me about the pen your grandfather made for you.'

'Okay.' Clara nods. 'Fair point. But I only mentioned it because of what you said about not writing letters.'

'What did I say?' Pieter asks. 'Your kisses really are that good, I've completely forgotten anything and everything that went before them.'

Clara grins. 'You said that you haven't written a letter because you want to be as witty as Austen, as passionate as Anaïs Nin and—'

'Ah, yes, my low expectations,' Pieter agrees. 'It's all coming back to me now.'

'Well, when I was a little girl my grandfather made me a pen and—'

'I still can't believe that,' he interrupts, 'that the great Lucas Janssen is – was – your grandfather and that he made you your very own pen.'

Clara pokes Pieter gently in his arm. 'Hey, do you want to hear this story, or not?'

He grins. 'I'm sorry, I'll shut up. Tell me, please.'

'Okay. Anyway, he gave it to me on my thirteenth birthday and told me that, one day, when I was ready, I'd write a great novel with it.' She takes a deep breath. 'He told me that he'd seen it . . . in my spirit, on the day I was born . . . that it was my destiny.'

'*Fok.*'

Clara nods. 'Exactly. No pressure, right?'

He smiles. 'Ah, well, don't worry, you young people do everything on computers now, don't you? So you can just use the pen to write shopping lists. That'll take the pressure off.'

'So, did the power of my kisses also cause you to forget that I own a stationery shop?' Clara says. 'Along with the fact that I have never and will never own a computer.'

'Yes,' Pieter says. 'In my defence, those are some quite mind-blowing kisses. It's lucky you won't be staying long, or I'd soon forget my own name.'

Clara's breath catches in her throat. 'Won't I?'

Pieter frowns. 'I didn't mean . . . I only thought – you've got to get back to your shop, haven't you? I just assumed . . .'

'What? That this was a one-night stand?' Clara sits up, pulling the sheet with her to cover herself, hurt by the assumption, even though she hadn't intended to spend longer than one night with him in the first place.

Pieter shrugs softly. 'No, I didn't think about it like that – truly, I never even believed that you would ever, ever end up in my bed. It is some kind of miracle, really. But I know you're only visiting, because of the letters, and I know that you have to go home, I imagine, sometime soon . . .'

Clara sniffs. 'Yeah, okay, I know. Sorry. I just didn't want you to think I was some sort of slut or something.'

Pieter laughs. 'No danger of that.'

'Well, good.'

Pieter eyes her. 'Is this a ploy? An elaborately clever way of, once more, avoiding telling me anything about yourself?'

Clara gives him a guilty smile. 'Perhaps. Well, anyway . . . As

I was saying . . . the point is, I've never written anything longer than a letter. I've planned plenty of books and begun quite a few, but I've never even finished a first chapter. And it's been twenty years now' – she gives him a small, self-deprecating smile – 'so I'm starting to think my grandfather may have made a mistake.'

Pieter considers this. 'Or, perhaps . . . if you took the pressure off yourself, if you didn't try so hard – if you weren't trying to write a "great" novel, but just began with an "okay" one, or a really bad one, just for the sake of finishing it. Then you might find it a lot easier, perhaps . . . ?'

'Ah,' Clara says. 'Well, that is good advice. And I might be able to take you more seriously if you had' – she raises an eyebrow at him – 'I don't know, written a novel yourself, or even a single tiny little letter.'

'Oo, that's fighting dirty,' Pieter says, pulling her forward so she falls on top of him. 'And, besides, whoever let an insignificant thing like lack of experience get in the way of giving advice?' He kisses her neck. 'You're extremely beautiful, you know. Knockout beautiful, stop-and-stare-in-the-street beautiful . . .'

Clara grins. 'Is that how you get out of all sticky situations? Via the use of hyperbolic compliments?'

Pieter kisses her again, smiling. 'Is it working?'

'Not yet,' Clara says. 'But perhaps you should just keep going until it does . . .'

Clara is strolling along a cobbled street, on her way back to her B&B, when her phone rings. Her first thought is of Pieter. She smiles.

'Miss Cohen?'

Clara recognises the voice of the spidery woman instantly. She stops walking. 'Yes?'

'This is Mrs de Groot, from the—'

'Yes, I remember, is everything okay? Did you find something after all?'

'As a matter of fact, we did.'

Clara wants to ask what, but her breath is trapped in her throat.

'A colleague of mine overheard you, when you were asking, somewhat loudly, about the details of your relative. Anyway, he thought to search another archive and he found him.'

'He did, really?!'

'Yes. Would you like me to tell you over the phone, or would you prefer to come in?'

'No, no, please. I'd like to know now.'

'All right.' Clara hears the rustling of papers. 'Otto Josef Garritt van Dijk died in Herzogenbusch in 1943.'

'I'm sorry, where is that?' Clara says. 'In the Netherlands?'

'Yes.' Mrs de Groot takes a short, sharp breath. 'It was a concentration camp, Miss Cohen, in Vught. Over 30,000 people were interned there, I believe, many were transferred to other camps such as Auschwitz. But your relative died there, in December of 1943. Fortunately, if one can use such a word in this instance, the Nazis were very good at keeping records.'

Clara's eyes fill. 'But he would have been just a baby, only a few years . . .'

'Well,' the woman's voice is soft now, 'of course many children perished in the camps. But he wasn't a child, he was listed as being twenty-three years old.'

'What?' Clara frowns, pressing her fingers into her forehead. 'No, that's not possible, he was just born – in 1939 at the earliest. It must be someone else.'

189

'That's very unlikely, Miss Cohen, given the specificity of his name.'

'Then why weren't you able to find a birth certificate?'

'He clearly can't have been born in Amsterdam. I checked the records myself and there was no record of his birth, I am quite certain of that.'

'But, but . . .' Clara trails off, feeling a little desperate. 'I don't, I don't . . .'

'As I said before, Miss Cohen, I can't help you interpret the facts. But I thought you'd want to know them, nevertheless.'

'Yes, of course, thank you,' Clara mumbles. 'Thank you so much.'

'You're very welcome, Miss Cohen. Good day to you.'

'Yes, you . . .' But, before she can get the sentence out, Clara hears the phone go dead as Mrs de Groot moves on to other, more important business.

Clara walks and walks. She has to see Pieter, has to tell him about this new twist in her tale, ask him what he thinks, ask him to hold her so she can stop shaking. And then, all of a sudden, she realises. But, of course. It wasn't the baby Otto who died in Herzogenbusch. It was his father.

Chapter Twenty-One

'Hey, lassie, wait up!'

Ava turns to see her dance teacher hurrying along the street behind her. She stops, surprised, wondering if perhaps he's come to critique her, perhaps he's not seen such appalling dancing skills in all his years as a teacher. Perhaps he just didn't want to embarrass her in front of the rest of the class. In which case, Ava is deeply grateful.

'Hello,' she says as he reaches her. 'Hi.'

'You're a fast walker,' he says, a little breathless.

Ava frowns. 'I am?'

'I wanted to catch you after class, I didn't think you'd have got so far.'

An awful thought suddenly strikes Ava. 'You're not − I am allowed to keep taking your classes, aren't I? I'm not that dreadful a dancer, am I? I'm practising, I promise, I even bought a CD. I think I'll be much better quite quickly . . .'

Ross laughs. 'What are you talking about? Of course you can keep taking my classes.'

Ava realises she's been holding her breath. She exhales.

He holds out his hand. 'I'm Ross.'

Ava nods. 'I know. You introduce yourself at the beginning of your classes.'

'Aye, of course, I'd forgotten.' He smiles. 'But I've not yet introduced myself to you personally.'

'True,' Ava acknowledges. She takes his hand. 'I'm Ava.'

'Lovely name.'

'Thank you.'

'Are you from Cambridge?' Ross asks.

Ava nods again. 'Born and bred.'

'I'm from Scotland.'

Now, Ava smiles. 'I'd never have guessed.'

Ross shrugs. 'Some people think I'm Irish.'

'American people?' Ava asks.

Ross laughs. 'Aye, usually. So . . .' He shifts from foot to foot. 'I'm glad you're taking my classes.'

Ava grins. 'Me too.'

Ross points down the road. 'You going this way?'

Ava nods.

'I'll walk with you.'

'Oh, okay,' she says, wondering why, wondering what else he wants to talk about. They walk for a while, exchanging stilted sentences, until they fall into silence. Ava waits, deciding if Ross has something to say then she'll just let him say it.

At the end of the street, a skinny young woman in ripped jeans is playing the guitar and softly singing. Her voice is lovely but she swallows her words, as if half of her wants to share them but the other half doubts they're good enough.

Ross stops. 'Hang on a sec.'

Ava looks at him, increasingly confused. 'Sorry?'

'I have to say something to her.'

'Oh, okay,' Ava says.

Ross walks up to the young woman, digging into his pockets. He stands a few feet away from her, in front of her open guitar case. He drops in a five-pound note. It floats down to settle among the few scattered pennies on the black velvet. The young woman looks up, surprised.

'Never stop singing,' Ross says, 'never stop singing. You will succeed, one day you will. You have an exceptional voice. You just need to be a bit louder, a bit bolder. So, whatever happens, no matter how many times you think you should, just don't give up, okay?'

The skinny young woman stares up at him, open-mouthed, wide-eyed.

'Can you promise me that?' Ross asks.

She nods, finally finding her voice. 'Yes, I promise.'

'Grand.' Ross grins, then turns and walks back to Ava. 'Thank you.'

'What was that?' she asks as they walk on. She glances back, to see the skinny young woman staring after them with a bemused but delighted look.

'What?' Ross asks. 'With the singer?'

'Of course.' Ava laughs. 'What else?'

Ross shrugs. 'We all need a little encouragement now and then; don't you think?'

'Yes,' Ava agrees. 'But that was rather more than that.'

Ross shrugs again. 'Well, I just knew she needed to hear those words right now. When things get dark, she'll hold on to them and they'll help keep a small, flickering light on inside her.'

'Dark?' Ava frowns.

'Aye,' Ross says. 'I've got a feeling that one's going to have her faith tested.'

'How do you know that?' Ava asks, wondering if it's possible that he could be like her, if he can see the things that she can see.

'Sometimes I hear words in my head,' Ross explains, 'and I have to say them to someone, cos they need to hear them, and—'

Ava hesitates. 'You hear voices?'

'No, it's not like that.' Ross laughs. 'I'm not crazy. It's sort of . . . Heck, I guess you could say I've got a gift.'

'A gift?' Ava frowns, wondering if the Scotsman is about to declare himself to be the next Jesus. She hopes he's not crazy, since he's rather nice in an odd sort of way, and the most phenomenal dancer. She'd hate to have to give up his classes, especially on grounds of insanity. 'So, this "gift" of yours, what does it involve, exactly?'

'Okay.' Ross takes a deep breath. 'I help women realise their true potential, their innate beauty and brilliance. I enable them to see themselves through my eyes. I bring out everything that's locked up inside them, so—'

Ava raises an eyebrow. 'You're a motivational speaker?'

'Not exactly.' Ross laughs again, deep and mischievous. 'I just go about my life and, when I see someone who needs my assistance, I assist them.'

Ava regards him with suspicion. 'Is that why you're following me, then, because you think I need "assistance"?'

'Aye,' Ross says. 'You could say that. But don't say it like it's a bad thing. We all need a little help now and then.'

'Hmm.' Ava ponders this, unsure. 'So, what do you think I need?'

Ross smiles. 'Have you eaten? It's late. I'm starving. Do y' fancy a bite to eat?'

Ava and Ross sit cross-legged on the low stone wall outside King's College, the remains of a takeaway pizza in a box between them. A bottle of red wine is secreted behind the wall, and Ava and Ross each cradle a half-full plastic cup hidden within the folds of their legs, taking discreet gulps now and then between bites of pizza. They talk about this and that, and nothing in particular, until Ross gets a gleam in his eye.

'So,' he says at last, licking his fingers and reaching for another slice. 'Tell me everything.'

'Sorry?'

'Tell me *everything*. Your hopes, dreams, passions, longings, your desires . . .' Ross continues, beginning to cast his particular kind of magic, '. . . the things you've always wanted to do but have never done.'

'Oh,' Ava says, surprised. No one has ever asked her this question before. Not even her sister when they were younger, even though they'd been as close as two people could be. Or so Ava had thought. 'I don't really know. I've never really thought about it.'

'Really?' Ross asks, incredulous.

Ava considers. 'I do like dancing.'

Ross laughs. He throws his untouched slice of pizza back in the box, licks his fingers again then takes a gulp of wine. 'Aye, of course, everyone loves dancing. Unless they're so uptight they don't even like sex.'

Ava stares at him. *Is this a date? Is he suggesting something? Is she so naïve that she hadn't even contemplated that before?* Ava says nothing.

'Do you like sex?' Ross asks.

'What?' Ava splutters. She reaches for her plastic cup and takes a big gulp of wine. If this evening is going to develop in any sort of sexual direction, then she's going to need the assistance of alcohol. A *lot* of alcohol.

'You should have a fling.'

Ava chokes on her wine. 'With you?' she asks, when she's got her breath back.

Ross smiles, placing his hand gently on her knee. Ava glances down at his hand, then back at his face, his mouth, his lips . . . And, suddenly, she's so overcome with desire that it terrifies her.

'No, not me, lassie. I don't sleep with anyone I'm assisting. It's not part of the service and it just ends up complicating and confusing things. Trust me, you'd regret it.'

'Oh,' Ava says softly, trying to hide her disappointment. 'Okay.'

'Aye, but I do think ye need a fling. Not a relationship – not yet. Nothing serious, all right? Promise me that. Fun is what you need. Dancing and sex. Sex and dancing. All right?'

Ava looks at him, incredulous. 'I'm sorry, I don't mean to sound rude,' she says, still feeling the sting of rejection, 'but I don't even know you. Why on earth should I take your advice?'

Ross smiles. 'Because I know what I'm talking about. This is what I do. I see into women's souls and I tell them what they need to do to be happy. And this is what I'm telling you.'

Ava scowls. 'And how do you know I'm not already happy?'

Ross gives her a look.

'Okay, okay.' Ava scowls. 'But sex and dancing? Really?'

Ross nods. 'Aye.'

Ava frowns.

'Stop being so cynical,' he says, still smiling. 'You know – deep down, you know I'm right.'

And Ava's scowl intensifies, because she does.

When Finn opens his curtains she is the first thing he sees. He blinks, but when he opens his eyes she's still there. Finn closes the curtains.

Fuck. He can't do this. He won't. He won't step into someone else's marriage. Even if she's willing to, he will not be a party to it. No matter how deeply, no matter how desperately he wants her, he *will* do the right thing.

Finn opens the curtains a crack and peers through. Greer seems to be leaning against the tree, though of course that's impossible, since surely she'd slip right through. He steps back and waits. A few minutes later he peeks again. Greer hasn't moved.

The following morning, having kept his curtains closed for the whole day previously, Finn pulls himself out of bed and takes another peek. Greer is still standing by the tree. He wonders if she's come and gone, once or a few times, or if she's actually been there, unmoving, since the day before. It shouldn't matter. It doesn't matter. Either way, he won't go to her.

Three hours later, after he's practised and showered, Finn is in the kitchen forcing himself to eat toast. He forgets to butter it and the slightly burnt bread scrapes against the roof of his mouth. He has to go into the school today, he has eager (or, more often, reluctant) students waiting to be imbued with the joys of Mozart and Beethoven. Finn glances out of the window overlooking the garden. She's still there.

Six hours later, after a rather trying day of attempting to

persuade the young of the enlightening glories of classical music, Finn slams his front door and slumps onto his sofa. He tells himself he won't look. He'll practise, he'll eat dinner, he'll fall into bed and he'll sleep. That's what he'll do. He won't look out of his windows, he won't draw back any curtains. He'll focus. He'll be good.

Ten minutes later, after more of this self-talk, Finn wanders into the kitchen for, ostensibly, a glass of water. He stares at the glasses, the taps, the fridge. And then, just as he'd promised himself he wouldn't do, Finn sneaks a glance out of the back window. She's gone. Despite the thick, concrete crust over his heart, he can still feel it contract. Disappointment washes through his blood, sorrow. He pushes himself up against the fridge, struggling to breathe.

And then, all of a sudden, she's there again. In just the same place as before, unmoving. It was simply the light, a trick of the fickle, flickering late afternoon sunlight shining through the leaves of the tree. Finn gasps and, before he can stop himself, before he even realises what he's doing, he's yanking open the back door and is running through the grass until he reaches her.

'I'm sorry,' Greer says, before Finn can speak. 'I'm sorry I left without explaining, without coming back. I know—'

'You're married.'

'Well, yes, but—'

Finn frowns and this time, though he can hardly bear it, his hardened heart rises with hope. 'What do you . . . ?'

'I tried to be, again. I tried to be as I was before,' Greer says. 'But I'm not, I'm not the same – I don't love in the way I used to, when I was alive.'

'I don't understand.'

'I love my husband. I do. But I love you. And I, I . . . want to be with you, if it's possible, in the way you thought it might be.'

Finn swallows. His chest aches as he feels the crust on his heart start to crack, the ice begin to thaw. 'Do you want to be with him, like that, too?'

'Perhaps. I don't know. It's hard to explain – I feel deep affection for Edward, I'm sure I always will. And, at first, I thought I came back to be with him, just him, again. But now I don't think I did, at least, I don't think I can.'

'Have you told him all this?' Finn asks.

Greer nods.

'And he's okay with it?'

Greer glances at the grass. 'Well, it's a lot to ask, he's human, after all. But he understands. At least, he's trying. He's being pretty amazing, actually. And if you're not okay with it, I understand too. I know it's a lot to ask – to love without attachment. It's not something humans do very well.'

Finn nods, thinking back over the past week. 'No,' he admits, 'I guess it's not. And, I confess, I feel more attached to you, more desirous of you, than I've ever felt for anyone in my life.'

Greer is silent for a while. 'I'm sorry,' she says. 'But the way I feel about Edward is . . . It's part of the way I feel about everything. I want to see him every day, I want to be affectionate with him, I want to be allowed to keep loving him – but I won't be with you if that'll cause you pain.'

'Oh, no,' Finn exclaims, suddenly feeling her slipping away again. 'No, I didn't mean—that doesn't mean . . . I'm not insisting on keeping you all for myself. You can come and go as you please,' Finn says, slightly surprised to find himself saying the words but, at the same time, knowing that he means them absolutely. 'I don't need to own you . . . As long as you come back to me, as long as you're here from time to time, that would be . . . bliss.'

'Really?' Greer asks. 'You could do that?'

Finn nods. 'This is a very strange situation, but yes, I think so.'

Greer smiles. 'I know.'

'It's certainly not one I ever expected to find myself in.'

Greer glances down at her transparent self. 'Me neither.'

'No,' Finn admits, 'I suppose not.'

They stand in silence for a while until Greer finally speaks.

'So . . .' she ventures. 'What do you think?'

'I think I love you,' Finn says. 'I even love the fact that you love your husband, as strange as that sounds. I think I want to be with you, whenever possible. I think that I don't care about anything else.'

Chapter Twenty-Two

Our Otto,

It's hard to believe, to understand, that your son is here and you can't see him – more than that, you don't even know of his existence. You will be so happy, so overjoyed, I know, when we are at last together again and you will have more than just me, you will have him, little Otto, as well. Do you mind that I have given him your name? When we spoke of children, I know you preferred other names than your own: Jaap, Johannes, Bastiaan, Mathijs, Vincent . . . But, I'm sorry, I couldn't give him any other name but yours. When I first looked into his eyes, he was so completely you. And, of course, saying his name keeps me more connected to you, which I'm afraid, I couldn't resist. I hope you'll forgive me, I hope you'll understand, I am fairly certain you will, given these strange and crazy circumstances. Besides, he is only our first. We will have many more children. You wanted five, though I confess, after the birth I did not feel willing to go through it again so many times. Can we compromise on three? Although, as the days pass and the pain fades . . . perhaps I will be able to do it again and again. We shall see.

Yesterday he looked at me, right at me, right into me, for the very first time. It was . . . I confess, I cried. Quietly, of course. But, before I knew it, tears were running down my cheeks and I couldn't stop them. I had spent every hour, every day caring for him: feeding him, rocking him to sleep, holding him – but, even though he needed me, he didn't seem to know I was there, me, myself, a person separate – and then, suddenly, he did. One day he will see you, his father, too. I hope that day is soon.

Ever Yours,
Marthe

'He died in Herzogenbusch. He was twenty-three years old.'

'I'm sorry,' Pieter says.

'It means, of course, that he wasn't my great-grandfather. Though I still don't understand what happened to Baby Otto. I think he must have died, after all, before my great-grandmother had Granddad,' Clara considers. 'And, of course, it means that he never read the letters, doesn't it?'

Pieter briefly closes his eyes and nods. 'Which, I imagine, is why your grandfather had them in his possession in the first place.'

'Yes, of course.'

Clara reaches for Pieter's hand and he clasps hers in his. It's a sunny Saturday afternoon and they're walking back from lunch in a pavement cafe and a visit to *De Posthumuswinkel*, where Clara bought a selection of papers and her own wax seal embossed with the image of a sealed envelope, along with gold and silver wax. As she shuffled around the tiny shop, feeling as if she were in a church among ancient spiritual relics, Clara slipped into her dream of opening *Letters* in Amsterdam, of living in this beautiful city that already felt like home. She watched Pieter as he picked up different papers, holding each with tentative reverence before placing it back into its drawer or onto its shelf. And she wondered how he would react if she were to share her dream with him. Though she can't, she won't. Not yet.

'I want to go there,' Clara says. 'I want to visit the place where he died. I want to read him the letters. Does that sound stupid?'

'No,' Pieter says. 'It doesn't, not at all.'

'I don't know where it is, I don't know how to get there, I don't even know if it still exists, the site of the camp. Maybe they've built on it. Maybe nothing's left. But still, I need to go . . . I can't explain . . .'

Pieter squeezes her hand tighter. 'You don't have to. And anyway, it makes perfect sense to me. And I'm sure it's still there. Most of the camps have been memorialised to commemorate the dead, to allow for visitors. You may even find his name there. You may learn how he died.'

Clara nods. The thought of this traps the words in her throat. She bites her lip and blinks hard to clear her cloudy eyes.

'It's not far from here, perhaps less than a hundred kilometres,' Pieter says. 'I can take you there, if you wish.'

Clara stops walking. 'You'd come with me?'

'Of course. It'll be a hard thing to do alone. I visited Auschwitz-Birkenau about twenty years ago, after my father died. It was perhaps the hardest thing I've ever done in my life.' He takes a deep breath and drops her hand. 'I've never, I can't think on it still, without . . .'

A gust of sorrow sweeps off him and Clara shivers. She fixes her gaze on the pavement, not wanting to intrude on his memories, not knowing how to comfort him if he cries now. She'd find it hard, she realises, to be in the full force of his sorrow and not try to kiss it away, to stop it, but just to let him feel, to let him crumple and hold him and let him be.

'I'd like to come with you,' he says softly. 'I'd like to be there so you don't have to be there alone.'

'Thank you,' Clara whispers. 'I'd like that too, very much.'

They walk on along the canal, occasionally dodging bicycles zipping past, brushing each other's shoulders as they step but not holding hands again, keeping their space, curled up in their own thoughts.

'I've always believed, like Marthe did, that letters aren't complete until they're read,' Clara says. 'And I hate to think of Marthe's letters never reaching Otto . . . That she put all her love, all her heart into that writing, and he never heard her words.'

Pieter nods towards a turn in the road, a side street, and they take it. They brush together and he envelops her hand again.

'Will you read them all?'

Clara nods.

'Would you like me to?'

Clara looks up at him. 'Sorry?'

'Well, they're in Dutch. I imagine you might struggle a little, both with deciphering Marthe's handwriting and with our rather, how do I say, elaborate pronunciation.' He smiles.

'You'd do that for me?' Clara asks.

'Of course.'

'That's so incredibly . . . Thank you.' She's so deeply touched by his offer that the desire to declare love rises up within her. The declaration is on her tongue, ready, but it's too much, too soon and she swallows it back. 'Though, I don't know . . . Somehow, I think

I should be the one to read the letters.' She smiles. 'Even if it'll take me a hundred years.'

'Okay,' Pieter says, 'but I'll be there, if you change your mind.'

Clara reaches for his hand, brings it to her mouth and kisses his fingers. 'Thank you,' she says again, then drops her voice to a whisper, pulls him to a stop. 'And I must say that I'm rather overcome with the sudden urge to . . .'

Pieter looks a little shocked. 'Right now? Here?'

Clara grins, basking in the lighter mood that encircles them. 'No, I wasn't thinking of a public display, but we're not too far from your house, are we?'

'No,' Pieter says, his surprise now swirled with delight, 'it's about a twenty-minute walk.'

'Okay, then,' Clara says, already starting to move, pulling him after her, 'let's run.'

'I've got you a gift.'

'You have?'

They sit in Pieter's kitchen drinking tea. Despite her initial reluctance, Clara is becoming used to the herbs of the Dutch tea. She still misses the comfort of hot milk, a thing that every time returns her to childhood, but she does enjoy the scent of the dried leaves and petals as they steep, finding that just the smell starts to soothe her before she's even taken a sip.

'What is it?' Clara asks, when Pieter is still silent.

'When you've finished your tea, I'll show you.'

'Really?' Clara gulps down the rest of her tea, wincing slightly at the strength of the final gulp. 'Okay, I'm done.'

Pieter smiles as he sips. 'You're not a person of great patience, are you?'

Clara laughs. 'I used to be, before . . . I suppose, in my life back then,' Clara muses, her voice dropping as she remembers what now feels like a hundred days, a hundred lifetimes ago, 'when I didn't really—when, when I wasn't excited by anything. Back then I was slow and I had all the patience in the world.'

For a moment Clara seems sad, swept back to the past in a sharp tug of melancholy. And then she jumps up from her chair and claps. 'Okay, drink up old man, let's go!'

Now Pieter laughs. He stands and follows her out of the kitchen. 'You'll have to get fully dressed first, it's outside.'

Clara bounds down the steps and stands on the pavement, glancing expectantly about, while Pieter follows, locking the front door behind them.

'Where is it?'

'Wait a moment, I'm coming.' He reaches her. 'Here.' He points across the cobbled street at two bikes chained up against the railing. One is black, one fire-engine red.

Clara frowns. 'Where?'

'There.'

'In the river?'

Pieter laughs. 'No, the bike. I bought you a bike. The red one.'

Clara's frown falls. 'You did?'

'Yes. Do you like it?'

Clara grins. 'Do I like it? I-I . . .' Then she hides her face in her hands.

Pieter places a hand on her back. 'What's wrong? Is it too much? It's not – it's just because you said you weren't rushing off home so soon, and I thought, well everyone here cycles, so—'

'No, it's not that,' Clara mumbles into her hands. 'It's a lovely gift, it's very thoughtful.' She looks up, peeking through her fingers. 'I have a confession.'

'What? You hate cycling?'

'No, it's far more embarrassing than that.'

Pieter waits.

Clara drops her voice to a whisper. 'I don't know how to ride a bike.'

'Oh.' He frowns. 'Really? But I thought . . . Isn't Cambridge one of the cities with the most cycles in England?'

Clara sighs. 'Yes, yes. I expect everyone in Cambridge cycles except me.'

'Why ever not?'

She shrugs. 'My parents tried to teach me but I was too scared to learn and, as I grew up, I just preferred to walk places – probably because I was still a bit scared but didn't want to admit it – and then, when I started writing the letters, it was perfect because I needed to walk, or I wrote the letters because I walked, I can't remember which way it happened. But, anyway, there was no need for me to cycle any more.'

'That's perfect,' Pieter says.

'It is?'

'Yes, I can teach you.'

A burst of nervous laughter escapes Clara. 'No, no, no . . . I'm not a kid any more. I'm thirty-three. People don't learn to ride bikes when they're thirty-three.'

Pieter smiles. 'Perhaps it's all a matter of perspective. You're almost a kid compared to me. We could pretend I'm your dad and you're six years old or something, a perfectly acceptable age to learn to ride a bicycle.'

Clara drops her hands from her face. 'No, we won't. That's a little dodgy.'

'What's "dodgy"?'

Clara smiles. 'Highly inappropriate. With connotations of the sexual.'

'Sounds like fun.' Pieter laughs, his low, light laugh. 'But okay then, you can be a fully grown-up lady who's decided it's time to get over her fears, to sit on the saddle and trust me to take care of her.'

He walks over to the bike, unlocks it from the other one and pats the leather seat. 'So, what do you say?'

Clara shifts her weight from foot to foot.

Pieter smiles. 'Are you going to keep your father waiting?'

'Shut up! Okay, okay, I'll do it.'

Clara stomps over to the bike and Pieter just smiles, saying nothing.

'It's okay, you're okay,' Pieter pants as he jogs alongside Clara, who grips the handlebars so tight her knuckles are white. She wobbles along, her eyes fixed on the road. Other bicycles whiz past, dinging their bells.

'Don't let go, don't let go,' Clara murmurs her mantra through gritted teeth.

'I won't, I promise, I won't,' Pieter gasps.

'Are you all right?'

'Fine.'

'We should stop.' Clara veers toward the river and gives a little shriek. 'You'll have a heart attack.'

'I'm not going to have a heart attack,' Pieter wheezes. 'But, but . . . it might be better if I, I . . . wasn't talking.'

'Okay, sorry,' Clara says, still wobbling but not stopping. 'Just don't let go – if you do that thing when you say you're still holding on but you suddenly let go, I'll kill you, okay?'

Pieter nods.

Another bike zips past, dinging its angry bell. Clara veers in the direction of the river again and squeals.

'I want to stop, please,' she pleads. 'How do I stop?!'

'Back-pedal,' Pieter puffs. 'Just pedal backwards.'

'What? I don't . . .' But then she does and, as soon as both Clara's feet are on the ground and the bike is stable, Pieter lets go and leans over, hands on his knees, head between his legs, panting.

'Oh, God,' Clara says. 'Are you okay? Are you having a heart attack?'

He holds up his index finger, signalling her to wait. It takes a few minutes before he can stand straight again.

'I'm fine,' he says finally. 'And this isn't because I'm old. It's because I'm unfit.'

Clara laughs.

'I tell you what,' Pieter says, 'have you ever seen *Butch Cassidy and the Sundance Kid*?'

Clara shakes her head.

'Really? You haven't? I thought all women had.'

Clara frowns. 'Is it a western? It sounds like one.'

'Well, yes, ostensibly, I suppose it is,' Pieter admits. 'But it's extremely funny and very moving, and it stars Paul Newman and Robert Redford. Two of the most, or so I've always thought, handsome men in the world.'

Clara raises an eyebrow. 'I didn't know you were so finely tuned to the female psyche.'

Pieter shrugs. 'There is much for you to learn. I'm deeply layered, like a fine ancient wine.'

Clara smiles, sliding off the bike. 'Then I look forward to tasting you again soon.'

Pieter swallows a grin. 'There is a beautiful scene in the film when Paul Newman takes his girlfriend – or perhaps it's Robert Redford's girlfriend, I don't remember – anyway, he takes her on a bike ride, she sits on the handlebars while "Raindrops Keep Fallin' on my Head" plays on the soundtrack. It's absolutely gorgeous.'

Clara gives him a look. 'You're not suggesting . . . ?'

Pieter nods.

'I think that would definitely give you a heart attack.'

'It wouldn't, I've got my breath back now. And, anyway, cycling is far easier than running.'

'Okay then, it would give *me* a heart attack.'

Pieter laughs. 'Let's just give it a go. I promise, I'll stop the second you say. You've got nothing to fear.'

Clara raises an eyebrow. 'I highly doubt that.'

'Pleaaaase . . .'

'All right,' Clara relents. 'But if you tip me into the river, I'm suing you for everything you own.'

'You can have it all.'

'Deal.'

Clara steps aside and lets Pieter take the bike. He mounts the saddle and waits. She doesn't move.

'Come on.'

'This is a mistake,' Clara says as she hoists herself up onto the handlebars, 'a big, big mistake.'

'Have a little faith,' Pieter says, kissing the back of her head.

Clara smiles. Again the urge to declare love rises up inside her but she holds on to the words, secreting them in her cheek. And then he begins to cycle. At first he goes slow, with long, languorous pushes on the pedals, so they glide alongside the river, the breeze blowing through Clara's hair. She closes her eyes to feel the warmth, the sun splashed on her face as they drift through an avenue of trees. Then she opens her eyes and starts to giggle with the sheer joy of it all.

'All right, hold on,' Pieter says, pushing harder, faster, until they're speeding along and Clara's giggles turn to shrieks of delight. And she can't believe that she's never felt this before. That she's missed out, until now, on the sheer thrill of being alive.

Chapter Twenty-Three

'Isn't Greer here? I wanted to ask her some baby advice.' Alba sits on the kitchen counter, kicking her legs lightly against the cabinets below. 'And where's Till?'

'Tilly's having a sleepover at Megan's, and Greer . . .'

'What?' Alba frowns. 'Am I sensing disquiet in the afterlife?'

Edward snorts. 'Oh, she's fine. She's having the time of her – well, death.'

Alba giggles and even Edward allows himself a small smile.

'It's me who's the total wreck.' He sighs. 'I don't know how to deal with it.'

'With what?'

'With the fact that she's not the same as she was . . . before.'

'Well, you can't expect her to be,' Alba says, crossing her legs. 'She's not.'

Edward sighs again, deep and long. 'Yeah, I know. But I just thought . . . When she came back, I was so, so bloody happy. I thought it'd all be the same again, just like it was before. I thought I'd been given my life back' – he gives a sad little smile – 'my wife

213

back. I thought our family would be fixed again, that we'd been given another chance. But she's changed, she doesn't feel the same way about things any more, about me . . .'

Alba jumps down from the kitchen counter and steps over to her brother, putting her hand softly against his back. 'You can't hold on to her, Ed. Life has changed, it's shifted and transformed and you're trying to relive what's gone, you're trying to grasp something that's already disappeared.'

Edward looks down at Alba. 'When did you get so wise, little sister?'

She smiles. 'I'm preparing for motherhood.'

'Well, by the sound of it, you're going to be good at it,' Edward says. 'Certainly better than I am at fatherhood.'

'Oh, don't be so hard on yourself,' Alba says. 'You've been through a lot, much more than most. You're doing your best and you're doing all right. Tilly seems pretty well settled to me.'

'Yeah, I suppose so,' Edward says. 'Though she's a lot happier now that Greer's back. And she's still a terrific mother, even if she doesn't really want to be a wife any more.'

Alba rubs Edward's back.

'Well, maybe that's why she came back, not for you but for Till. Or, maybe to help you let her go, or teach you something about love,' Alba suggests. 'Or perhaps she just came back for herself, maybe it has nothing to do with you at all.'

Edward frowns and then, suddenly, his face crumples into laughter.

'I'm slightly horrified to admit that hadn't occurred to me at all,' he says, 'that she could be back for a reason that had nothing to do with me. That she might have her own reasons, her own journey, her own . . . Why is love so often monumentally self-centred?'

'Yeah, I think good love is a balance,' Alba says. 'Between two people who take care of themselves and each other, but who don't expect another person to fulfil them, or blame them when they're feeling unfulfilled.'

'How do you know all this stuff?' Edward asks. 'I don't and I've got at least a decade of experience on you.'

Alba smiles. 'Zoë's taught me a lot. Her parents actually have a happy marriage; can you believe it? So it's been a bit of a steep learning curve for me, but then you know what a swot I am.'

Edward grins. 'I'm deeply impressed.'

'You know, we visited her parents for dinner a few weeks back, to tell them about the baby, and her dad said something pretty incredible.'

'What?'

'He said that he'd noticed something, over the thirty years of being married to Zoë's mum – that how "in love" with her he felt on any given day had absolutely nothing to do with his wife and everything to do with him. If he was feeling great then she could do no wrong, his love overflowed. And if he was feeling out of sorts then he felt disconnected and picked on petty things. Either way, his wife hadn't done anything differently. It wasn't her fault – the good or the bad.'

Edward thinks of Greer, probably this minute with his next-door neighbour. 'But, surely, the people we love can do things that make us miserable, right? I mean, saying it's all up to us, doesn't that let the other person entirely off the hook, so they can behave however they damn well please and we just have to swallow it?'

Alba drops her hand from her brother's back and steps back towards the counter again. 'No, not at all. That's not what he meant. He was making the point that, most people in life are

215

dissatisfied and, instead of looking inward, they look outward and blame their feelings on their nearest and dearest. Of course, this works in their favour, for a while, when they first fall in love – then they blame all those glorious feelings on the other person and infatuation sets in. But, once the endorphins have subsided, once the fresh shine has worn off and life settles back to normal again and their default sense of dissatisfaction returns, then eventually they'll make the very person they once made responsible for the good feelings, responsible for the bad ones. Do you see?'

Edward gives his sister a sharp look. 'Have you been writing me letters?'

Alba frowns. 'No, why?'

Edward sighs. 'Nothing, it doesn't matter.'

'Why do men think sex is the answer to everything?'

'What?' Ross stops walking.

They are ambling along King's Parade, eating falafel wraps on Ava's lunch break, having bumped into each other at the falafel van. The coincidence was fortunate since, following the slightly humiliating experience of their last encounter, Ava hadn't planned on seeing him again anytime soon, certainly not outside the dance class. Indeed, she'd even considered looking for another dance class altogether. When she'd seen him in the queue, she'd tried to duck away, but he'd spotted her too quickly and good manners had dictated that she join him, instead of run away, as she'd much rather have done.

'Well, it's true,' Ava says. 'You can't deny it. You think I should have a fling. You think sex is the answer to everything.'

Ross laughs. 'Naw, I don't think sex is the answer to *every*thing, I just think – right now – it's the answer to your thing. Or, the start, anyway.'

Ava scowls. 'The start? What's that supposed to mean? How messed up do you think I am?'

'Naw, not messed up,' Ross says, considering. 'Just in need of a little opening up, a little joie de vivre, that's all.'

'I get that through dancing.'

'Hey, don't get me wrong, dancing is braw. But it's just a part of life, it's not a substitute for it.'

'Yeah, well, so is sex – just part of life, I mean.'

'Aye, true.' Ross smiles, ripping into his falafel. 'But is it a part of your life?'

Ava scowls again. 'Are you this rude to all the people you "assist"?'

'I'm not rude,' Ross says, with his mouth full. 'I'm just straightforward. I'll tell you things other people won't, that's my job.'

'Well, I'm not employing you.'

'Aye, of course not,' Ross says. 'But then most people don't reach out for any sort of assistance until their life has deteriorated into complete disaster. I like to step in before that happens. It's less messy that way.'

Ava rolls her eyes. 'So you're some sort of self-appointed, but very misguided, angel?'

'I wouldn't say misguided,' Ross huffs. 'Aye, I'm very accurate, actually. I have a ninety-nine per cent satisfaction rate among my clients.'

'Oh, yeah?' Ava snaps back, finding she's rather enjoying being slightly feisty. 'So one per cent of them are entirely dissatisfied?'

'I wouldn't say that,' Ross says. 'But you can't please everyone. Anyway, they don't all follow my advice. I canna be blamed for that now, can I?'

Ava can't help but laugh. He's so utterly different from her – brash, cocky, oozing with self-confidence – that being with him brings out traits in Ava she never thought she had. It's as if he has showered sunlight on dark soil and coaxed long-dormant seedlings into sprouting leaves. And, although she's spent her life being a wallflower, scathing of all the swaggering students, Ava has to admit that there's something glorious in it. She'd tasted a snatch of it with Finn – speaking without first filtering her words, being able to blurt without fear – and now Ava realises that she's always hated such self-assured people because really she hated herself for not allowing herself to be like them.

'Oh, I don't know about that,' Ava says with a smile. 'I think I've spent my whole life trying to please everyone.' And, with those words, she realises something else – why Ross doesn't get romantically involved with his protégées. If she was sleeping with him she'd want to please him so hugely, she'd never be able to truly be herself.

'Aye, and did you succeed?'

Ava laughs. 'No, not really. It's pretty difficult, since everyone's so different. Mum wanted me to be prim and proper, get married and have a dozen babies. Dad wanted me to go to Trinity College, like he did, graduate with honours in law, like he did, then eschew all attachments, like he wishes he had, and dedicate myself to becoming a high court judge, or some such thing.'

Ross stops devouring his falafel and looks at her. 'So, what did ye do?'

'I tried to please them both – I became a librarian in the University Law Library and got married very young, failed to make any babies, then got divorced – and, of course, pleased neither. Then I gave up every connection to law entirely and "downgraded"

218

to the public library. So now I'm a great disappointment to them both.'

Ross rests his hand lightly on Ava's arm and she stops walking.

'You may think that,' he says. 'They may even think that. But it ain't true. Deep down, even so deep they're unaware of it, that isn't the way they feel.'

'Thank you,' Ava says softly. 'That's very kind of you to say.'

'Aye,' Ross says, 'but that ain't why I'm saying it. Being kind is not my modus operandi. I'm saying it cos it's true.'

'How would you know? You've never met them.'

'Oh,' Ross says, dragging out the syllable. 'I've got not a wee amount of experience in the area of people's parents, and mountains in the difference between thinking and feeling – most people live their whole lives thinking they feel this and that about this and that. Really, they ain't got a clue. And, if only they'd stop thinking long enough, they'd find that out.'

Ava nods; even though she doesn't entirely understand what he means she trusts somehow that what Ross says is true. She leans towards him and gives him a playful shove. 'I think you're kinder than you think.'

Ross smiles, but says nothing.

Ava takes a bite of her falafel and chews, rather relieved by the silence. It doesn't last.

'Right then, tell me,' Ross says. 'In all this trying to please everyone else, how much did you end up pleasing yerself?'

Ava swallows and smiles. 'I'm guessing that's a rhetorical question, right?'

'Aye, it would be.' Ross laughs. 'Which brings me back to the fling . . .'

* * *

'Play something for me.'

'What do you want?'

'Anything. Something serene.'

Finn nods. This is all they've done for days now. He has played and she has listened. Sometimes they talk. They still haven't touched. Each is perfectly content.

Finn begins with Bach and Schubert. He floats from *The Well-Tempered Clavier* to 'The Trout Quintet' to 'Ave Maria.'

'This one always made me cry,' Greer says, 'when I was alive.'

Finn begins again. 'Would it still, if you could?'

Greer shrugs. 'Now I just feel . . . sublime.'

Finn smiles.

'Again, please,' Greer says. And, when he does, she starts to sing. '*Ave Maria . . . Gratia plena . . . Maria, gratia plena . . . Maria, gratia plena . . .*'

And then Finn is crying, tears sliding down his cheeks as he plays. He laughs.

'I can't remember the last time that happened,' he says softly, still crying, still playing. The notes encircle them, the music drifting on silk ribbons through the air, settling on their shoulders, tugging at their hearts, pulling them towards each other, though neither moves.

Finally, Finn falls silent, his fingers resting on the strings, his hand holding the violin to his chest. He sinks to the floor, legs outstretched, then leans back against the sofa, his head flopping onto the cushions.

'I've never—I've never played this way before, the way I play when you're listening.'

Greer smiles. 'Then I shall always be listening.' She comes to settle close to him. 'Do you play in public, to audiences?'

Finn gives a wry smile. 'Sort of. But all my audiences are under twelve years old. Plus, on occasion, a few teachers.'

'Oh? But, why?' Greer asks. 'I'd have thought you would've been playing in concert halls since you were a kid. I imagined you in London on a stage, at the Royal Albert Hall.'

Finn laughs. 'I guess not.'

'Why not?'

Finn shrugs.

'Oh, please. There must be more to it than that. Your music is . . . divine. I can't be the only person who feels that way, surely? Your teachers, your mother, they must have encouraged you to perform.'

'My mother,' Finn considers, 'was very . . . generous and very proud of me. She listened to me play but she was so, well, set apart, so removed within herself, after my father left, that I don't think she ever really did anything with her whole heart again. Even when she listened it was a bit like playing into a void, into a bottomless darkness that my notes fell into, bouncing, knocking into each other . . . I never felt her deeply moved or touched. I suppose there was always a part of her that my brother and I could never reach. I wanted her to love the music as I did, to meet my passion, but she couldn't. So, playing for her wasn't a very happy experience for me.'

'I'm sorry,' Greer says softly. 'But your teachers? Didn't they meet you?'

'No,' Finn says. 'Well, it wasn't their fault. I don't think I gave anything – I didn't offer anyone my whole heart after that. I'd just give them the minimum and I'd save the rest for myself, in private.'

He sets his violin gently down on the carpet.

'But it gives you joy now, doesn't it, to play for me?'

'Yes.' Finn grins. 'Pretty much more than anything.'

Greer smiles. 'Ditto.'

Finn eyes her. 'What are you thinking?'

'Nothing.'

'Liar. I sense you hatching a plan.'

Greer laughs. 'Okay, all right. I was thinking . . . what a great shame it is, that you don't play in public, when you could bring such great joy to so many people.'

Finn shrugs. 'I don't think so. There are many musicians better than me out there, people go to concerts, they listen to CDs. There's really nothing more I have to offer that's any better than all of that.'

'Bullshit!'

Finn looks at Greer, shocked.

'I'm sorry, but that's total crap,' Greer says. 'It's not up to you to decide what other people want to hear, if you're not offering them the option. If you go out there and play and nobody's interested then, okay, I'll give you that. But you've got to at least give them the chance.'

Finn gazes at Greer, speechless.

'Don't rob them of you,' she continues, 'before they've even had the chance to choose.'

Finn takes a deep breath. 'That must be the most impassioned speech I've ever heard,' he says, still a little breathless. 'Especially involving myself as the subject. I'm enormously touched.'

'Don't be,' Greer says. 'I didn't say it because I love you, I said it because it's true. I said it because it needs to be said. I said it because you need to be heard. I said it—'

'Do you love me?'

Greer frowns. 'Of course. Didn't I tell you that when I came back? In fact, didn't I tell you that yesterday too, and the day before that?'

Finn grins. 'Yes, but I'm not averse to hearing it every day, even more often than that, in fact, if circumstances permit.'

'Okay, well, I'll see what I can do about that,' she says. 'I love you. There you go, that should keep you going for another hour or so.' She smiles.

'Cheeky. If you had some ribs I could tickle,' Finn says, 'this is when I'd be tickling them.'

Greer laughs. 'But you can't, you can't touch me,' she teases, 'you can't—' And then, all of a sudden, she stops. 'Oh, shit.'

'What?'

'Children,' Greer whispers. 'Children.'

Finn leans forward. 'What? Where?'

'How old are you?'

'Thirty-six.'

'And, do you want children?'

Finn shrugs. 'I don't know. I've never really given it much thought.'

Greer sighs. 'Oh, God. When I was your age, I thought of nothing else. Well, not quite, but nearly. And . . .'

'What?'

Greer sighs. 'Well, not only can I not give you any sexual satisfaction, but I can't give you any children either.' She sighs again, deeper. 'Not that I could do the latter even when I was alive, so that's no matter.'

Finn frowns. 'But isn't the little girl next door your daughter?'

'Yes, she is. But I didn't give birth to her, that's all. I was lucky enough to inherit her from Edward's first wife.'

'Inherit?'

'She died, when Tilly was about a year old.'

'Shit,' Finn says. 'And then you . . . Poor bugger.'

Greer sighs again. 'I know. Edward hasn't had the easiest time of it, wife-wise.'

'Bloody hell,' Finn says. 'And now I'm stealing his second – he must hate me. And I can't say I blame him.'

'You're probably not his favourite person in the world right now,' Greer admits. 'But he knows this is all me, that it hasn't . . . that you wouldn't . . . Anyway, in time, I hope the two of you might even become friends.'

Now Finn sighs. 'Sweetheart, I think you're overestimating the human condition right now. I think you've forgotten what it was like to be one of us.'

Greer gives a wry smile. 'I'm trying, but now I—I'm worried.'

'About what?' Finn shuffles over to her. 'What's wrong?'

'I don't want you to regret it. When you're much older and it's too late.'

'Regret what?'

'Not having a real wife, children, a normal life.'

'Oh, hell,' Finn says. 'Forget about that. I'm a self-obsessed musician. I can happily play for ten, fifteen hours a day. I'd make a lousy husband and a worse father.' He reaches out to her. 'Really, you're the absolute perfect, perfect . . . non-wife for me.'

Greer smiles. 'You may think that now, but when you're sixty and alone and—'

Finn frowns. 'I won't be alone, I hope. You'll still be here, won't you?'

'I hope so too,' Greer says. 'But I don't know. How can we know for certain? Really, I have no idea how long I'll be here for.'

'Shush,' Finn holds a finger over her lips. 'Let's not worry about this stuff now. What's the point?'

'The point is to prepare,' Greer says. 'So you can prevent pain in the future and—'

'Look, don't worry about me. I'll be playing this thing' – he nods at the violin at his feet – 'until I drop down dead. I'd drive any normal woman crazy; my kids would be in therapy complaining about their father who never gave them any attention. Believe me, our strange situation is the best of all worlds.'

Greer gazes at him. 'Are you certain?'

Finn nods. 'More certain than I've ever been of anything in my life.'

Greer looks at him, trying to discern a flicker of dissolution or doubt. But Greer can't see any trace of fear or hesitation in Finn's eyes; she can only see her own reflected back at her.

Chapter Twenty-Four

My Otto,

Little Otto is so good, so quiet. I think the force of my fear keeps him silent. It's a shame, truly, that he will not be allowed to run and shout and cause a little mischief. I worry that, if we are here for too long, he will grow into a man unable to express himself or reveal his feelings or, perhaps, even know them in the first place. I pray this will not happen. I am forever shushing him, drilling silence into his bones so now he doesn't even cry out when he's hungry, he simply cries silent tears and, of course, I pick him up (though I am usually holding him anyway – he may also grow up being uncomfortably attached to his mother) and tend to him. But don't worry, he's okay, he's not being deprived because of his silence, I am taking care of him, as best I can, though it just isn't nearly as well as I would like, given . . .

His eyes are still blue, his hair black. He looks so like you that, sometimes, I am scared by it, I think you are a ghost or that you've crept up upon us without warning. Sometimes,

I wake with him in my arms and, despite his tiny body, I – blurry-eyed and only half conscious – think that he is you. I confess at these times I cry, because he is not. Though, not for a second, would I wish him away, that I would take you in his place. I am selfish. I want you both. I will not swap one for the other. One day, we will all lay in bed together, me and my two Ottos, I will have you both in my arms and then all will be exactly as it should be. We wait for that day; we wait for you.

Ever Yours,
Marthe

They are sitting up in bed together, Clara leaning back against the headboard with her eyes closed, Pieter reading letters. He taps her gently on the arm. Clara opens her eyes.

'When will you go?'

'What? Oh . . .' This is something she's been trying not to think about. She's been fending off her mother's phone calls, along with her own doubts and fleeting desires to return to England, along with the very real need to tend to the shop. Clara hates, too, to think of the would-be letter writers and receivers who aren't, because she isn't where she should be.

'It's okay, no pressure,' Pieter looks up from the paper he's holding. 'I don't want to rush you; I'll just need to—'

Clara turns to him. 'Oh, God, you—do you want me to go home right now, you should have said' – she slides her legs out of bed and stands between two piles of papers, searching the floor for clothes – 'I know this is just a fling, I didn't want to outstay my welcome, yes, I really should . . .'

'What?' Pieter puts down his paper. 'Wait. Home?'

Clara picks her T-shirt off a nearby chair. 'Right, you should have said something before.'

'Home?' Pieter says. 'I wasn't talking about home; I was talking about Herzogenbusch.'

'Oh.' Clara pokes her head out of the T-shirt with a sheepish smile. 'Oh, right, that.'

'Yes, exactly. I have something for you.'

'Something else?' Clara continues to smile, flushed with relief. 'You already bought me a bike.'

'True,' Pieter says, reaching into the drawer of his bedside table. 'But that doesn't prohibit me from doing other things, does it?'

Clara shakes her head, stepping back to the bed.

Pieter removes a thin blue file and hands it to Clara who, sliding back under the bed sheets, takes it. She undoes the knot of string tying the file together, then, slowly, carefully, pulls back the blue cover to reveal a small stack of pages swathed in lines and lines of tiny black sentences.

'What is it?'

'Marthe's letters. I translated them for you. I wrote them out, so you can read them yourself to Otto.'

'Oh.' Clara's eyes fill and the desire to declare love rises again in her heart.

'But I'll just need a few days' notice, to make sure I don't have any appointments when you want to go.'

Clara puts her hand to her mouth.

'And,' Pieter adds, softly, 'I don't remember saying that this was just a fling – did you? Am I forgetting, in my old age, this important detail?'

Clara drops her hand. 'I love you.'

Pieter leans towards her, smiling. 'I'm sorry, I didn't hear that.' He taps his left ear. 'My hearing isn't what it used to be.'

Clara grins. 'I said, I love you.'

'Ah, good. That's what I hoped you'd said.'

Pieter shifts forward, until he has Clara in his arms and is kissing the tears, of relief and joy, that slide slowly down her cheeks.

'I love you too,' he whispers. 'I love you too.'

Later that day, they go for a cycle ride. Clara almost crashes several times, whenever she takes her eyes off the road to glance over at Pieter and grin at him.

'I can't believe I'm actually doing this,' she calls out. 'At last! It's glorious, it's truly glorious!'

Pieter laughs. 'Now you can officially say: it's as easy as riding a bike.'

'Yes,' Clara calls, breaking away from him in a rush of speed. 'Yes, yes, yes!'

Still laughing, Pieter stands on his pedals and pushes after her. 'Wait, go easy on me, I'm old and unfit, I might give myself a heart attack trying to catch up!'

He follows Clara, gliding behind in the stream of her scent and laughter, along the canals, through the winding streets until, at last, she stops outside a shop. Pieter looks up at the sign: *De Posthumuswinkel*. He dismounts and crosses the road with his bike to lock it against the railing with Clara's.

'Ah, so you brought me here. You promised lunch, but it was a trick.'

Clara shrugs. 'I'm sorry, I can't help it. I didn't mean to, but I'm like a homing pigeon. And this place reminds me of my own little *Letters*, so I need to visit it every now and then . . .'

Pieter casts her an indulgent smile and then, as he takes her hand to cross the road again, he bites his lip. His grip on her hand loosens. Clara looks over at him.

'Are you okay?'

Pieter nods.

'Really?'

He shrugs. 'I just wonder when you will want to go home. After all it is, as you say, your home and you miss it – your shop, your letters . . .'

Clara stops outside *De Posthumuswinkel*, shifting to let another couple of customers in through the door.

'Well, I've been thinking about it, actually,' she says, treading softly. 'I just didn't want to say anything yet, since I didn't want to scare you off.'

'Scare me off?'

'Yes, I mean, you told me how you don't like to commit, and—'

Pieter frowns. 'I didn't say that. I said I couldn't have children and so I didn't really have relationships either, but that's not the same thing at all. Unless, of course, you do—'

'No, I don't,' Clara says, a little too quickly, fixing her gaze at the pavement. 'Anyway, that wasn't what I wanted to talk about, it was something, something . . . I've been thinking, that it might be possible to close my shop in Cambridge and open one here. I could do the same thing. People could come in and write letters, I could walk the streets—'

'—or cycle,' Pieter suggests.

Clara shakes her head. 'No, cycling is too quick. I wouldn't have a chance to really see people. I need the chance to spot them.' She smiles. 'It's how I spotted you, reading your letters by the light of your lamp.'

'Then I'm glad you hadn't learnt to ride before,' Pieter says. 'Or we might not be here right now.'

Clara nods. 'So, what do you think?' she asks, her heart beating fast, afraid that she's moving too quickly, saying too much, too soon, that he's about to say so, to let her down gently. 'Of my idea?'

'I think it's wonderful,' Pieter says. 'I think I will be your best customer.'

Chapter Twenty-Five

'You are a complete mystery to me,' Ava says.

He's taken to meeting her for lunch every Monday outside the library. They walk through town to sit on the wall outside King's College, so long as it isn't raining, and eat a falafel wrap from the van on Market Street or a thick slice of homemade pizza from Gustare.

Ross grins. 'Grand,' he says. 'I like to be enigmatic.'

She rolls her eyes. 'Yeah, but it's more than just that. I don't see you. I don't see . . .'

'What?'

Ava takes a deep breath. This isn't a spontaneous decision. She's been thinking about it for days, about whether or not to tell him, and she has finally decided that she will. He's the closest thing she has to a friend, after all. And Ava has, at last, had quite enough of being lonely and secretive. Still, even though she's planned out what to say, it doesn't make the saying of it any easier, now that the time has come.

'I – usually – I see things about people. Well, one thing, actually . . .'

'Aye?' Ross fixes her with a gaze of intense interest.

Ava squirms, unused to such undiluted attention, wishing she'd managed to blurt it out all at once. 'I, um, I can see the worst event of people's lives.'

Ross uncurls his crossed legs and sits up straight. He puts down his falafel wrap, which Ava knows is a serious step, since not much gets between Ross and his food. His gaze transforms from intense interest to total fascination.

He grins again. 'I knew there was summit special about you.'

Ava blushes. 'But, anyway, well I can't see yours.'

'And thank feck for that.' Ross laughs. 'I've gotta say, I'm not one of those ones who wants to know when they're gaunnae die.'

'Oh, no, it's not always death,' Ava says. 'There's plenty of suffering worse than death.'

'Jesus,' Ross says. 'I don't wanna know about that either. That's some depressing stuff right there.'

Ava shrugs. 'Imagine what it's like for me. It's impossible to make friends, cos all I can see is the worst of what's going to happen to them and, as you might imagine, it does tend to get in the way of any normal conversation.'

'Shit.'

'Exactly. In fact,' Ava says, thinking this will impress him, 'I was actually attempting to have a fling – of sorts – a few weeks ago, and—'

'Of sorts?' Ross interrupts.

'Well, if he'd proposed marriage, I probably wouldn't have said no,' she admits. 'But, anyway—'

'I think we need to discuss the terms and conditions of a "fling",' Ross says dryly, 'before we let you loose on the male population.'

'Shut up and stop interrupting.'

'Sorry.'

'Right, well, I went to visit my new neighbour. I brought him a plate of blueberry scones—'

'Nice move. I can never resist baked goods. Especially home-made.'

Ava glowers at him. '*Anyway*, he was great. It was the first time I'd ever really, properly talked to someone, let go, stopped monitoring myself . . . There was something about him, so free and liberating. Anyway, then I saw the worst event of his life and, of course, I couldn't just chit-chat after that. I haven't seen him since.'

'What?' Ross exclaims. 'But he could have been prime fling material. He sounds perfect.'

'Not really,' Ava says. 'He's in love with a ghost.'

'Aye?' Ross raises an eyebrow, clearly intrigued, though this piece of information is clearly not as intriguing as the other. 'So, what was the worst event of his life?'

'That.'

'What?'

'The being in love with the ghost. It's going to – for various reasons – give him the greatest joy and cause him the greatest pain of his life.'

'Jesus.'

'Yes. It'll give him the greatest joy when they are together and the greatest pain when she leaves.'

'Leave? Why will she leave?'

Ava shrugs. 'I don't know the why, I can only see the what.'

'So, how long will they have together?'

'I don't know. I usually can see the timing of things, but I couldn't,' Ava says. 'I just saw that, one day, she'll disappear. And it'll break him.'

235

'Shit,' Ross says. 'That sucks. So maybe you should tell him. He might be able to avoid a lot of grief, nip it in the bud now, before it breaks his heart, y'know?'

Ava shakes her head. 'He wouldn't have ended it, even if I had told him. He's in love. Love doesn't end for any rational reason, no matter how much sense it'd make. Love is the opposite of sense.'

'Aye,' Ross says, ruefully. 'You're right there.'

Ava gives him a wry smile. 'Which is probably why I've never been in it.'

'Never? Not even with your husband.'

A shadow of sadness falls across Ava's face. 'No. I thought so then. But no, it wasn't love.'

'Oh, dear, how depressing,' Ross says. 'Then no wonder the thought of a fling doesn't appeal – your heart is probably half desperate to fall in love already.'

Ava looks at her half-eaten falafel, suddenly finding it intensely interesting.

'So, whatever the worst event of my life is – death or worse – you can't see it?'

Ava shakes her head. 'I've been given a reprieve. The chance to make a friend.' She smiles. 'Either that, or you're immortal and will lead an entirely blessed life free from any pain or disaster.'

Ross grins. 'Aye, I like the sound of that.' Then he considers. 'When you were a bairn, how did y' learn to swim?'

Ava frowns. 'Sorry?'

'A bairn. A kid.'

'Yes, I know,' Ava says. 'I was just a little thrown by the sudden and strange shift of subject. Um, I don't really remember, I took lessons, I guess.'

'All right, so,' Ross says, 'in my experience there are two ways to

236

learn to swim. The first: being thrown in the deep end and figuring it out through thrashing and flailing. The second: paddling in the shallow end and building up to it from there.'

'Ah, okay, yes, well, I'm definitely in favour of the second option. I'd probably have been so traumatised by the first that I'd have been scared of water for the rest of my life.'

Ross nods. 'Aye, alright. So y' prefer the more softly, slowly approach? Personally, I was chucked into the deep end of Loch Kilconquhar, and I was the strongest swimmer in all of county Fife. I nearly made it to the regional championships, but I . . . met a girl.'

Ava smiles. 'So you were working your magic on women early on, then.'

'Aye.' Ross grins. 'But, enough of me. Back to you. So, I reckon, when it comes to the fling, we should take the backdoor approach.'

Ava raises her eyebrows. 'Excuse me?'

Ross laughs. 'I'm not suggesting anything dirty. We'll just take a more gentle route, build up y' confidence a bit, before we set off to slay the dragon, so to speak.'

Ava eyes him. 'You have an odd use of metaphors. But yes, okay, gentle sounds good.'

Ross stands. 'Right, then, let's get on with it!'

Ava looks up at him. 'With what?'

'With finding you a new job.'

Edward presses his ear against the wood of the kitchen door. Beyond it he can hear Greer and Tilly giggling. He smiles. Despite his own desires, it gives him the greatest pleasure to hear them both happy. Indeed, the sound of their happiness is probably the greatest sound in the world and, always, instantly, injects him with a flush of great joy. A joy, too, that lasts, that simmers in him like the scent of bubbling caramel in a kitchen long after it's been eaten.

He stands, taking his ear from the door, suddenly struck by something. It's an idea so simple but so radical, that it's a moment before he can make sense of it, filter it down from its lofty heights to plain building blocks that his basic mind can understand. The thought that alighted upon him, that descended from somewhere, settles and stretches and reshapes until, at last, he can see it: clear and bright and true.

The thought is this: is it possible that, what he *thinks* will make him happiest is not actually what will? Could it be that he's been wrong or, at the very least, a little misguided? He's been so certain that having his wife back, just as she was, is what would be best for him. In the same way that he's been certain about every other thing that would make him happy, though he hasn't, in retrospect, always been right. And now he feels, in this moment, regarding this particular subject, that he's been wrong. And, he's missed something vital, the opportunity for an even greater joy than the one he'd been striving for.

Edward has never before doubted his own rightness, not really. He's always been quite certain about things, sometimes in relation to other people and things but mostly when they pertained to himself. Born into the upper classes, Edward was raised in a culture that invested him with a sense of certainty. He attended Eton, followed by Cambridge, excelled at both and stepped into the bright, fresh world already a success, a man always confident of his own convictions.

Thus, Edward was absolutely sure about many things. He liked his eggs fried, with runny yolks. He liked the breast of the chicken but not the leg. He liked cricket but not football. He favoured France, especially Paris, over Italy. He listened to classical music, preferably Mozart, but never jazz or pop. He took showers, not baths. He believed in the power of inspiring architecture to spiritually uplift and thought it was a very bad idea to build functional, uninspired blocks of flats that would depress both their inhabitants and society at large.

And, throughout his life, Edward had never really had cause to doubt his own rightness. He'd made the right choice of study, career, spouse. Of course, the death of his first wife had sent him into somewhat of a spin, the death of his second wife even more so, and her reappearance perhaps most of all. But, even then, Edward was still quite sure of himself, what he did and didn't like, what pleased and what displeased him.

And yet, now, as this new epiphany settles onto the seabed of his knowing, Edward finds himself decidedly askew, the compass of his certainty having been knocked quite off-kilter. It's in this stirred-up space that a long-forgotten memory rises up and resurfaces, breaking through the wet sand: on the Christmas that Edward was ten years old, he received every present he asked for. His stocking was full and overflowing. And he spent a very satisfactory morning, from dawn till noon, playing with, counting up and categorising all his new acquisitions. Then, before the feast of lunch, as was family tradition, he went with his parents and siblings to church. Edward had insisted, much to his mother's chagrin, on taking his very favourite new toy with him: a foot-tall, hand-painted tin toy soldier with full working parts. Edward hardly listened to a word the vicar said, until he accidentally caught the old man's eye and was fixed with a gaze of great disapprobation and displeasure. For a few moments then, little Edward rested his new toy on his lap and heard the vicar tell a story about a saintly orphan who'd given away her only Christmas present to a gypsy girl who was even more deprived than she. The vicar assured his congregation that the gift of the gypsy girl's gratitude and delight was a greater gift for the little orphan than the Christmas present had been. At the end of this story, Edward gave such a loud sniff of disbelief that he earned a look of disapprobation from his mother this time, though that still didn't serve to dissuade him from his surety that the story was silly and wrong. The possession of a new toy, in Edward's decided opinion, was far better than the questionable action of giving away said toy to a total stranger.

And then, in the way that strange twists of fate sometimes have life imitating art, Edward found himself walking out of the church with his mother, behind another mother and son, who seemed to be the same age and height as he, but far more skinny and shabbily dressed. As they all emerged out into the sharp chill of the icy air, Edward's mother leant down to whisper the details of the boy in front. His father had died a month before, in an agricultural accident, and the family were very poor and, no doubt, the boy had received no Christmas presents. Perhaps, Edward's mother suggested, then nodded meaningfully at the precious toy soldier her son gripped firmly to his chest. Edward had responded to her look with his own, one of absolute horror. So, his mother shrugged and they walked on.

Demons and angels fought within Edward as they passed through the gate and turned down the lane. He was mightily relieved when the road forked and the other boy and his mother took the opposite route. Out of sight, out of mind, he thought and resumed gazing lovingly at his toy. And yet, as he walked, he couldn't stop thinking about the other boy and, at the end of the lane, Edward let go of his mother's hand and turned and ran back to the boy. Tapping him on the shoulder, he handed his toy over quickly, so he couldn't change his mind. A look of confused shock passed over the face of the skinny, shabby little boy. And then, when Edward explained his gift, it was passed over by a look of such pure, heartbreaking joy, that Edward actually felt a lump rise in his throat and tears spring into his eyes. He hastily wished the boy a happy Christmas, then turned and ran back to his own mother, who kissed him.

And, though he wouldn't admit it to anyone, Edward had to admit to himself that the vicar had been right. Owning the toy had given him great satisfaction and delight, but its possession hadn't at all swelled his heart in the way the giving away of the same toy had. In that act, Edward had been touched with a depth of feeling he'd never experienced before and it carried him all through Christmas Day on a sort of cloud. It had been a singular lesson in being wrong. One Edward had forgotten until now.

Greer and Tilly's giggles burst out behind the kitchen door again and Edward smiles a second time. He loves his wife and yet he must let her go. He loves his daughter and yet, one day, he must let her go too. When Greer died he raged against it, he thrashed and brawled against the turns of life and, for three years, he refused to let go. This brought him neither peace nor happiness but, as he's now learning, the mind is a belligerent and, clearly, often very misguided master. Now he's been given the miraculous gift of having his wife back, not in the way he wanted, yes, but she's here all the same. And he can either cling on miserably or let go and trust that he might find even greater happiness than he's known before.

241

Edward turns away from the kitchen door and begins walking down the corridor. And, as the giggles fade behind him, he decides that he will take the job offered to him by A&B Associates after all.

'What's wrong with the job I already have?' Ava hisses, as they enter the library.

'Nothing,' Ross says, 'since it's the perfect place to find y' new one.'

'Is that why you came back with me?' Ava regards him with a horrified look. 'You said you wanted to look up a legal precedent on Roe vs Wade.'

Ross laughs. 'And why would I want to do that?'

'*I* don't know,' Ava hisses. 'It's what you said.'

'And you believed me? Silly girl.' Still smiling, Ross strides over to the bulletin board and studies it, rocking back on his heels, absorbing each notice. Then he strides back to the desk behind which Ava is turning on her computer and sliding into her seat.

'Aye, that gave me some interesting ideas,' he says. 'Now I need to see the papers. You have them all on file?'

Ava scowls at him. 'Yes, of course we do.'

'Grand. Shall I wait here while y' bring them up?'

Ava sighs. 'Yes, I suppose so. Though, strictly speaking, you're not a student here, so I shouldn't be bringing you anything.'

'Ah, but you'll make an exception for wee auld me, right?'

Ava raises her eyes to the ceiling but since, strictly speaking, he's stalked her with the intention of helping her out, rather than himself, she can't really object.

'Okay, I'll go and get them.' She stands. 'But please, don't cause any mischief while I'm gone.'

Ross gives her a wicked smile. 'Y' know I cannae promise you that, lassie. So ye better be quick.'

Not needing to be told twice, Ava hurries away and, when she returns, finds Ross sitting on her chair, behind her desk, dispensing life advice to an enthralled young female student who hangs on his every word. At the sight of this, any last hopes Ava had that they might end up together, that Ross might break his rule for her, fades. She would have to be a stronger woman than she is to spend a lifetime with a man whose vocation it is to inspire women to be the brightest most brilliant version of themselves. No, Ava thinks, as she walks towards the desk, Ross is not the one for her. Then, as she gets nearer, Ava finally sees *it*. And the papers she's holding fall, scattering like upturned ships across the floor.

Chapter Twenty-Six

Our Otto,

Our son took his first step today. Can you believe it? Not quite eight months old and already he's making a bid for freedom – but can you blame him? Perhaps this is why he's so quick to walk, because he knows he is trapped and wants to be free. I cannot blame him for that.

I'm sorry to say that, although he's quick to walk, he's hardly speaking. For which I blame myself, since I've imposed silence on him for so long, it's not surprising he barely whispers a single sound, let alone a word. So he still hasn't said 'Mama', though I think he probably should be saying such things by now. Mrs X certainly seems to think so. She is very kind to us, especially since little Otto came. She loves to hold him, to coo and – I think – pretend that he is hers. Of course, I allow this, how could I not? With everything that they are doing for us, I am grateful to be able to offer this small thing in return. When she visits us in the cellar, when she stays while we eat, I try to make myself

*invisible, so she can be just with him, so she can imagine
they are alone together, that he is her son. You'll be happy
to hear that she brings him treats, things from the black
market that she never brought me: a peach, a tiny piece of
cake, a cube of chocolate . . . Of course, little Otto adores
Mrs X in return, for all the attention and the treats. He
reaches for her with chubby, grasping hands when she opens
our door and his face lights up in a grin. It's my greatest
delight to see him happy and we both look forward to these
visits all day. I hope you have some light in the darkness of
your days too, whatever it is, I wish it for you.*

    Ever Yours,
    Marthe

Clara holds his hand across the car. The letters – originals and
Pieter's translations – are on her lap. She presses her other hand
atop them as they bump along.

'Did I thank you, for doing all this?' she asks.

Pieter smiles, not taking his eyes off the road. 'Perhaps a
hundred and fifty times.'

Clara sighs. 'Okay, so I'm starting to get annoying. But I just,
I just . . . It's so kind of you. I'm not sure I'm brave enough to do
it alone.'

Pieter laughs. 'Not brave? You could do anything you wanted
alone. I'm touched that you wanted me to accompany you, but
this is not from weakness, not at all.'

Clara looks out of the window, at the limitless fields, at the
light white sky.

'I don't know what you see in me,' she says, 'but I certainly
don't see it in myself.'

Pieter smiles. 'Yes, well, isn't that always the way? How many of us actually see ourselves clearly?'

Clara considers this. 'I've never really thought about it before.'

Pieter squeezes her hand. 'You're doing a wonderful thing,' he says. 'And I think, somehow, that it will make a difference.'

'What do you mean?' Clara frowns. 'How? To whom?'

'I don't know, I can't explain. I just do.'

They fall into silence, the car speeding along, the fields flashing past, the letters clutched on Clara's lap.

When Herzogenbusch at last comes into view, it is dark grey against the white sky. Clara feels it before she sees it. Her gaze is pulled, suddenly, unexpectedly, from the gentle lull of another wheat field to the horizon of the road. She shivers. And, until Pieter finally pulls into the parking lot outside, the car skidding slightly in the dirt, Clara says nothing. She says nothing as she gets out of the car, clutching her letters. She walks silently, stoically, behind Pieter as he makes his way to the gates. She pretends not to see the offer of his hand, continuing to press the letters to her chest, as if they are her final possession on earth, in danger of being snatched away, and she will protect them at all costs.

Through the gates they enter an office. Pieter signs the guest book for them both and leaves a donation in a large plastic box, a sign above in Dutch and English, inviting visitors to support the maintenance of this memorial to tragedy, to ensure that future generations will be able to visit and won't be able to forget.

'Do you want to take the guided tour?' Pieter asks.

Clara looks up at him, having not heard a single word. 'What?'

'The tour,' he says again, softly, gently. 'We can go around on our own, or we can take the guided tour. Another one is beginning in ten minutes. You could ask questions and—'

Clara shakes her head. 'No, no. I can't.'

'It's okay,' Pieter says, 'we don't have to. We'll go on our own.'

He offers his hand again and, this time, Clara, transferring her grip on the letters, takes it. As they leave the office, Pieter picks up a guide to the camp, dropping a few extra coins into the plastic box. They walk out into a square, dirt ground, flanked by buildings. Neither moves.

'There's a museum and a memorial centre,' Pieter says, softly.

Clara shakes her head.

'There's a preserved section of the old camp.'

Clara nods.

They walk on, Pieter leading the way by a few steps, Clara clinging to him. When they reach the rebuilt barracks, Pieter stops. Clara shuffles up to his side. They stand, pressed together, in silence.

Row upon row of very narrow bunk beds, hard wooden slats covered only with a thin burlap bag stuffed with a few fistfuls of hay, are stacked three rows high.

'Do you . . . ?'

'Tell me.'

Their words overlap. Reluctantly, Pieter lets go of Clara's hand and opens the leaflet he holds. For a few minutes, he reads.

'Approximately 31,000 people, mostly Jews but also Gypsies, resistance activists and Jehovah's Witnesses, were imprisoned here between the beginning of 1943 and the autumn of 1944. Most were transported to the death camps but 750 died here – 421 of inflicted natural causes and 329 were shot.'

'Shot?'

'Yes.'

'Otto,' Clara says. 'I don't know how he . . .'

'Perhaps we can find out,' Pieter says. 'They preserved the place where the prisoners were . . .'

'Shot?'

'Yes, and perhaps they'll have a memorial there, with names. I imagine that would be usual practice.'

'Usual?'

'I only meant, to commemorate the dead,' Pieter says. 'I believe it's the case in all the camps.'

'Oh,' Clara says. 'Then we must go there.'

'Are you sure?'

Clara gives a half-nod. 'I have to go to the place where he died.' She takes a deep breath, then another. 'I'm guessing he won't have a grave.'

'No,' Pieter admits. 'They dug mass graves, unmarked, or they cremated the prisoners, so . . .'

'So, I'll have to read the letters where he was killed. Either where he was shot or, if not, here, where he slept.'

Pieter nods. He folds the leaflet then takes Clara's hand again. Slowly, they step away from the barracks and back out into the dirt square.

'It's this way. Beyond the barbed wire, just outside the prison walls.'

It takes them less than five minutes to reach the place of execution. It is marked by a thick, white stone pillar just a few feet taller than Pieter. Engraved into the stone is a long list of names. Clara lets go of Pieter's hand and traces her finger slowly down the letters, pausing at each one in a minor act of presence, a recognition of their life and death. When she nears the end, Clara crouches down. And then, her finger stops.

'He's here,' she says. 'Otto Josef Garritt van Dijk. He was shot.'

Pieter doesn't say anything, but he crouches down beside her, slipping his arm over her shoulders. Clara doesn't cry or make a sound. She barely breathes.

At last, she stands again. Pieter, his knees cracking in the silence, does the same.

'I'm not going to read them in any order,' Clara says, addressing the memorial stone, rather than Pieter. 'I'm just going to begin with my favourite and then go on from there. I hope you don't mind. And, don't worry, I'll read every single one.'

She waits, as if expecting a response. And then, when none comes, as the wind whistles across the flat fields, Clara unties her bundle of letters. Then she begins.

Our Otto,

Today, October 24th 1944, we had our very first real sign of hope. The first one I allowed myself, anyway. Although I keep it alight in me, although I've never let it go out, hope is, nowadays, a tiny light trapped under a large rock. When I first came here it was big and bright and shone in the centre of my chest. That was when I believed I'd see you again tomorrow or, only a few months after we parted. It's been more than a year. If it wasn't for little Otto, I might have lost hope altogether. But I can't, I have to hope that, one day, I'll be able to bring him to you and we'll be a real family at last, just as we might have been before.

And today, just today, that rock lifted and that hope glimmered free, lighting the whole of our tiny, dark cellar. Today Mr X came to tell me that there was a German surrender at Aachen. Perhaps the war might be over in only a month. Though Mr X doesn't think so. He believes that the

Nazis will fight on to kill us all and they will not stop until they are stamped out with great force. But, this is the problem with hope, once it is let out of its box, or from under its rock, it can be hard to hide again, to push away and pretend it doesn't sneak out to illuminate this little hole.

And so, today, just today, I'm letting myself hope that this war shall be over soon, that the killing will cease, that we will be free and together again before the new year. I hope, I hope, I hope . . .

Ever Yours,
Marthe

Clara doesn't rush on to the next letter, nor does she look to Pieter who stands quietly behind her. Instead, she fixes her gaze on the thick stone memorial.

'It's beautiful, isn't it?' she asks, softly. 'She loved you very, very much.'

The air is still now, the wind having settled, and the sky feels heavier, denser and darker, as if a rainstorm is gathering above them.

'Would you like another?' Clara asks.

She reads the next letter carefully, slowly, enunciating each word, as if her listener is an old man who struggles to hear. She reads the next in the same way, pausing again at the end to converse a little with the memorial, to comment on what she's just read. Then she turns to the next.

And when, at last, Clara's fingertips are white with cold and the last of the light is slipping behind the horizon, she finishes the final letter, Clara stops then steps up to the memorial and places her bare hands flat on the stone.

'Thank you for listening, to Marthe and me,' she whispers. 'And I hope that brings you some peace, to know how very much you were loved.'

All of a sudden a loud crack sounds through the air, like a gunshot. Clara and Pieter both start and she turns to him. And then, the air shifts again, fizzy and cracking, as if an electric storm had just lit up the sky. They look at each other, Clara shocked into silence.

Pieter gives her a startled, astonished smile.

'I think he's thanking you, for reading to him.'

Clara nods, her fingertips tingling, still unable to speak.

Chapter Twenty-Seven

Ava sits at her desk. Students come and go, asking her questions, handing in old books and requesting new ones. Ava nods and responds. She provides them with accurate information and useful literature. But, all the while, she's contained within a smog of sorrow, mourning the loss of her friend, though he isn't even dead yet.

It'll be soon, Ava is quite sure of this. Although why she didn't see it until yesterday, she isn't at all sure. Perhaps her mind blocked it out so that she'd be able to make a friend, so she'd be able to enjoy being free and easy with another human being, for once, for the first time in a very long time.

With the exception of those few hours with Finn, the only friend she'd ever been completely herself with was her sister. This wasn't because Ava hadn't seen Helen's death, she had and she'd blurted it out one afternoon while they were playing in the garden. It was leukaemia, it would strike when she was twelve years old and it'd devour her quickly.

Ava was terrified that Helen would tell their parents, and that she would spend the rest of her years consumed by fear and sorrow.

But she didn't. Helen told Ava that she was glad to know, and she'd have as much fun as possible with all the years of her life she had left: six.

Ava was the lucky partner in most of these activities. They climbed trees, searched for shrews and voles in the undergrowth, went on long bike rides through the meadows . . . They rarely bothered to do their homework but instead had a million imaginary adventures together, staying up late most nights, reading novels with torches under their bed sheets and eating midnight cake. Helen appreciated every lovely little moment of life, so that everyone loved to be around her and even adults commented that she was a particularly joyful child. Helen never complained that she didn't have enough, that she was bored, that she didn't want to eat dinner. Instead she threw herself into life with unreserved passion and brought joy to everyone she met, Ava most of all.

When the cancer finally came, Helen assured Ava that she was okay, that she was glad to have known, to have sucked all the juice out of life before the sweet fruit was snatched away. She was glad it was over quickly too, all the pain of diagnosis and treatments, all the time in hospital. Helen held Ava's hand at the end and smiled up at her through both their tears. Ava clutched her sister's fingers until they went cold.

At first, Ava thought that, given her sister's experience of life and death, perhaps other people might want to know in advance the dates of their own demise. However, following several incidents at school – involving both students and teachers – that culminated in Ava's expulsion at the age of ten and a half, she finally accepted that this wasn't the case.

Ava suspects that Ross might be just like Helen, that he will embrace the knowing and suck all the last juices out of life before he goes. But, since that is the way Ross lives his life anyway – as if every day might be his last day in the chocolate shop – that'd only leave Ava with the miserable duty of darkening the horizon. Which, unfortunately, is something she just can't bear to do.

'Your cooking is definitely improving,' Greer says. 'Judging by the smell of that chicken, anyway.'

Tilly bites into her sandwich and chews. She nods. 'Yeah, Dad, this is actually edible. Well done.'

Edward smiles. 'Gosh, thanks Till, for that highest of accolades, and for showing me the entire contents of your mouth.'

Tilly giggles.

'It doesn't sound like I should trade in being an architect for a career in the catering industry just yet, though.'

Tilly frowns. She shifts on the black-and-white blanket laid across the grass, reaching for her plastic cup of orange juice. 'But you're not an architect any more, Dad, so what difference does it make?'

'Till—' Greer reprimands her.

But Edward smiles. 'Well, actually, the purpose of this little picnic is actually to celebrate the fact that, from next Monday, I will be an architect once more.'

'Really?' Greer says. 'Oh, Ed, that's wonderful, congratulations!'

'No shit, Dad? That's great.'

'Tilly!' Edward and Greer both exclaim in unison.

'Jeez, can the parental unit chill for a sec?' Tilly holds up her hands in defence. The sandwich filling falling out as she does so, slices of chicken and tomato tumbling into her lap. 'Oh, shit,' she says again, picking them up out of her skirt.

Edward opens his mouth to admonish her, then instead starts

255

to laugh. Catching his eye, Greer starts to giggle too, which only lifts Edward's spirits and makes him laugh harder.

Tilly looks from one parent to the other. 'What's going on with you two?'

Edward shakes his head. 'Nothing,' he says. 'I . . . I'm just happy, that's all.'

Tilly narrows her eyes at him. 'Have you got a new girlfriend?'

'What?' Edward frowns. 'What on earth makes you say that?'

Tilly shrugs. 'It'd be a good reason, that's all.'

'But, but what makes you think . . . ?' Edward trails off. 'I mean . . .'

Tilly rolls her eyes. 'You guys think I'm so stupid. I know Mum's got a boyfriend, so, I just thought it made sense.'

Edward looks at Greer. 'I thought we weren't going to tell her, until we'd got it all a bit more figured out.'

'Don't blame me,' Greer says. 'I didn't say anything.'

'She didn't have to, Dad, I'm not a silly kid. I knew something was going on since we saw Mum in the garden with the next-door neighbour.'

'Till,' Greer exclaims, 'you make it sound so sordid! We weren't even touching.'

Tilly nods, knowingly. 'Yeah, well, you didn't have to be. It was obvious. Trust me, I know about these things.'

'*You know about these things?*' Edward repeats, horrified. 'What's that supposed to mean?'

Tilly just shrugs.

'Well, I very much hope you don't mean by personal experience because, however wise you are, you're still only thirteen years old, young lady,' Edward says. 'We don't want to be having the talk with you just yet. I hadn't planned on having to tell you about all that till your sixteenth birthday, at least.'

256

'Oh, Dad, grow up,' Tilly says. 'We learnt about all that in sex-ed class, like a year ago.'

'What?' Edward's eyes widen. 'They're teaching sex to teenagers? That's outrageous!'

'I'm sure they're not teaching them *how* to have sex,' Greer says, 'just how to be safe, when the time comes.'

Tilly nods.

'They shouldn't need to be safe, they shouldn't be doing anything to be safe from in the first place,' Edward exclaims. 'I'm calling the headmaster, first thing in the morning.'

'Oh, please, Dad.' Tilly sighs. 'Just cos you live like a monk, doesn't mean the rest of the world should too.'

'I'm not talking about the rest of the world,' Edward snaps, 'I don't care what they do. I'm just talking about you. And, anyway, I do not live like a monk.'

Tilly meets this protest with another roll of her eyes. Edward looks to Greer for support, but she can only give a little shrug of apologetic agreement with her daughter's statement.

'Huh, well, what do you two know, anyway?' Edward huffs. Then he frowns at Tilly. 'But you don't mind? I mean, that me and your mother aren't . . . That we're not together in the traditional sense?'

Tilly laughs. 'Oh, Dad, we're hardly a traditional family, now, are we? Anyway . . .' She shrugs. 'I don't really care, as long as you're both happy. It was pretty awful living with you before, Dad, you were so freaking miserable all the time. Then Mum came back and you were happy but then she wasn't so much. But now, whatever, whatever, you're both happy. So I don't really care what you're doing, as long as you stay like this.'

Edward and Greer exchange a look.

'Yeah, so, most of my friends, their parents are either divorced or married but constantly sniping at each other,' Tilly says, chewing her sandwich once more. 'But, now, you guys are like best friends. So, the way I see it, I'm pretty lucky.'

Edward sighs. 'How old are you? You sound wiser than anyone I know. Especially me.'

'And me,' Greer says.

Tilly just shrugs and smiles.

Chapter Twenty-Eight

Our Otto,

He is walking — he'd be running if I allowed it, but of course we have to mind the noise, always the noise — doing laps around our little cellar. Sometimes he falls, though he never cries out, silent as ever. I confess, I am worried that he's still so quiet, that he still says no words. But I console myself with the thought that, as soon as we are free again, he'll be able to run down the streets, laughing and shouting like any other little boy. Of course, it'll probably take time for him to get used to such a different way of life, to know that it's safe to be bold and loud, to reach out and touch the edges of life, instead of curling and trying to remain unseen. But I hear that children are resilient creatures — so Mrs X tells me — and it won't be for long that he will be scared and shy, once we are free again.

But are we so resilient? Will we bounce back so easily? I cannot imagine it. These four walls have been my home now for so long, and I have been scared for every minute of every day, so that my skin sweats with fear and my breath smells of it.

Will we ever be the same again? When we finally see each other, will a great deal have changed? Of course. And, perhaps, we will also need some time until we fit together as we did before. But we will. I don't think it will take so long and, if it does, it's of no matter. I was so impatient when I first came. I couldn't bear the thought of just a few days apart from you but, slowly, patience was forced upon me. And now, like fear, it is a part of me. So I can wait now, for any amount of time, for as long as it takes to fit together with you again.

    Ever Yours,
    Marthe

Shit. Shit. Shit.

    It can't be. It simply can't be.

Clara stares at the dates in her diary, flicking the pages back and forth. She's fifteen days late. How can that be? How can she not have noticed? And they've been so safe, so careful, Pieter not wanting to take any risks. Admittedly, the night outside the Herzogenbusch camp, when they'd torn at each other's clothes in the car, in the dark of the parking lot, under the barely visible stars, the electricity of Otto's response still firing through their veins, they hadn't used any protection. But that had only been four days ago. It was far too early and her period had been due two weeks before. So the mathematics didn't add up. And yet, there is no denying that she is late.

Clara was alone in Pieter's house when she woke – all pretence of the B&B having been abandoned weeks before – the bed half empty and cold since he left early for the Institute and an important meeting with his director.

Now she sits in the kitchen, having showered and dressed, with her diary open on the table, staring into her cup of clear, bright herbal tea. For the first time, Clara resents the tea. She wants murky, milky tea. She wants to feel at home, safe, comforted. Instead, she feels alone, abandoned and scared.

Will Pieter think she did it on purpose? That she sabotaged his precautions somehow? Will he resent her for the rest of their lives, for giving him the one gift he never wanted? Will he dismiss her protestations outright, or will he try to believe her but, every now and then, succumb to doubt? Clara can't bear the thought of it, of him hating her or thinking that she's deceptive and untrue.

Finally, unable to stand all the worrying any more, Clara realises that she simply needs to know for certain. So, casting the tea aside and stumbling across the kitchen, nearly slipping on several stacks of paper, she walks along the hallway in a daze and opens the front door. Once on her bike, Clara pedals as fast as she can, her thighs aching as she stands, pushing faster and faster, hardly noticing the wind in her hair, not feeling a single spark of joy at the speed as she soars along the streets, finally screeching to a halt outside the pharmacy.

It's not until she takes the pregnancy test to the counter that Clara realises she has no bag, no purse. It's then that she starts to cry. Mercifully, miraculously, the pharmacist takes pity, nodding as Clara makes desperate promises to return with money later in the day, directing her to his own private toilet and telling her to take all the time she needs.

After a hundred 'thank yous' and an awkward parting, Clara closes the toilet door. Five minutes later she's staring at the unmistakable pair of pink lines on the little white stick she grips between sweaty thumb and forefinger. Clara sits on the closed toilet seat and shakes. *How can this have happened? How the hell can this have happened?* The timing is awful and the circumstances so far from ideal as to be disastrous. She's not ready. She wasn't ready for a baby as part of a loving partnership in which the father would fully and happily participate. She's certainly not ready for single motherhood. This is not something she can do alone. She cannot. She simply cannot.

And yet, even though Clara would give anything not to be in this particular situation right now, nor can she contemplate the alternative. And she knows, even as she stares shakily, shell-shocked, at the twin pink lines, that she will not terminate this pregnancy. Even though the cluster of cells rapidly expanding inside her is now surely smaller than a pea, still she cannot. Instead, in such unthinkable circumstances, she will do the unthinkable and return home and ask her mother for help.

Clara dreads the thought of raising a baby with her mother's assistance. The constant criticisms, the undermining of her every impulse and instinct, the decrees that she's ruined her life. It'll be unbearable. But still, probably slightly less unbearable than trying to do it all alone.

The other thing Clara knows, now that the reality of the facts have set in, is that she cannot tell Pieter. She cannot risk that instead of (or as well as) being angry he'll also be noble and insist on raising the baby with her. And, inevitably, as the screaming days and sleepless nights pass, he'll grow to hate them both with a passion, perhaps the same degree of passion with which he once loved her. And, although Clara imagines she could possibly endure that force of hatred being directed at her, she cannot allow it to be directed at an innocent party, the little soul she is now responsible for protecting, emotionally and physically, for the next eighteen years or so.

Clara sighs. And then, in a flash of mercy, she thinks of her great-grandmother who raised a baby in truly unbearable circumstances. Marthe would have, no doubt, embraced and kissed the ground in gratitude for a snippy mother, had one been offered to her, in exchange for freedom and food and a life without fear.

It is the thought of Marthe that enables Clara to get up and leave the safety of the toilet, to emerge out into the real world to face what needs to be faced. After thanking the bemused pharmacist several more times, Clara steps out onto the street to find that she'd forgotten to lock her bike and it has been stolen.

It's a long, heavy walk back to Pieter's house. Every few metres, Clara wants to sit down on the cobblestones and cry. But she thinks of Marthe and keeps walking. It's not until she opens his front door that the full force of him returns to her: his smell, his eyes, his kindness, the way he looks at her with such unadulterated adoration. And then, Clara finds a space on the floor, squeezing between two stacks of papers and lets herself sob, great big, heaving sobs, fat tears falling into her cupped hands, for all that she's lost, for all that she wants and will now never have.

Clara allows herself half an hour of self-pity and then she stands, wipes her eyes and walks up the stairs to the bedroom. She has to leave before he gets home. She has to write him a note, a letter, a lie that will, ultimately in the long run, prevent more pain than it bestows. She packs her bag quickly. She doesn't have many things. She'd only been intending to stay in Amsterdam for three days and has ended up staying six weeks. She gives herself an hour to write the letter. She doesn't want to rush it. She wants to be as kind and gentle as she can. She leaves the envelope on the kitchen table, since it's the first place he'll come, then picks up her bag, walking slowly along the corridor for the last time. And shuts the door behind her.

Dearest Pieter,

I'm so sorry to do this so suddenly, you'll think it the strangest thing and it is. I have to leave you. I have to go home. We can't be together any more. Not because I don't love you, I do, with all my heart, more deeply and completely than I ever thought it possible to love anyone.

But you don't want children and I realise – rather suddenly and unexpectedly, I know – that I do. And, of course, I can't ask you to change. I wouldn't want to. It's an impossible obstacle, a dreadful one, an immovable one. I should have waited for you and told you tonight in person, I know. But I couldn't, I just couldn't bear it. For this I'm deeply sorry and I do hope you'll forgive me. Though, if you don't, for a good long while at least, I understand. Completely.

I will always think of you with infinite love and affection. And I will think of you every day, for the rest of my life. Of this, I am quite certain.

Ever Yours,
Clara

Chapter Twenty-Nine

Edward stands in his bedroom, before his empty wardrobe and amidst a sea of suits scattered across the floor.

'I've got absolutely nothing to wear,' he moans. 'Nothing at all.'

Greer laughs. 'You've got plenty to wear; you just don't want to. You're worse than a woman.'

'Hey,' Edward protests. 'I'm not nearly as bad as you used to be.'

Greer smiles. 'Well, yes, I've got to give you that, I suppose. Although I'm pretty good nowadays.'

Edward regards his wife's transparent form, in her favourite tight moss-green silk shirt that perfectly matches her eyes and a long light-blue skirt that puffs out to settle just below her knees. She is still the most beautiful woman he's ever seen. He sighs.

'True,' he says, regaining himself. 'But I'll bet, if you were given a choice of attire every day, you'd be just as bad as I am now.'

'No doubt.' She looks down at her clothes. 'I am grateful that you buried me in this. If I have to wear only this for the rest of – whenever – it was a good choice.'

'Well, thank you,' Edward says. 'It wasn't a difficult choice. It was your favourite.'

'Was it? I hadn't remembered.'

'How much do you remember?' Edward asks. 'About us, I mean.'

'Bits and pieces,' Greer says. 'It's all quite hazy, what we did, what we said . . . Even now, since I came back, it's still rather like that. Time is so – vertical, is the best way I can describe it, so different from how humans live, horizontally, with all their memories of the past and thoughts about the future. It's rather amazing, actually: not to feel regret or fear.'

'Yeah, it sounds great,' Edward says, 'I look forward to it. But since I'm still a mere mortal, it doesn't help me out with choosing a suit.' He sighs. 'It used to be that you could make me a bespoke suit and I'd be the envy of all my colleagues. I wish you still could.'

'So do I,' Greer says. 'Not being able to touch anything can be a little frustrating from time to time.'

Edward smiles. 'I thought you didn't have human emotions like that?'

Greer shrugs. 'I guess, every now and then, a blast from the past sneaks through.'

'Well,' Edward says, 'I'm sorry about the frustration but it's quite nice to know that you're not entirely above us all.'

Greer laughs. 'Nearly, but not quite.'

Silence falls between them.

'I'm hoping,' Greer says softly, 'I'm hoping that one day, not yet, I know, but one day you might want to meet Finn . . . That we might all even have dinner together, with Tilly too.'

Edward regards her. 'Seriously?'

Greer nods.

Edward takes a deep breath. He thinks again of hearing her laughter behind the kitchen door. He exhales.

'I don't know, G. Maybe, one day, when I'm . . . I don't know, but not yet.'

'Yeah, of course,' Greer says. 'I know it's a big ask, but I just wanted to put it out there, let you mull on it.'

'Okay, I'll mull,' Edward says. 'I'll mull for a good long while. But I'm still getting used to all this, okay? So don't expect too much of me.'

Greer nods again.

'I'm trying,' he says. 'I'm doing my best.'

'Oh, sweetheart, I know you are,' Greer says, floating towards him. Hovering above the sea of suits, she reaches out and holds her hand against his cheek. Edward closes his eyes, letting the heat and the calm sink in.

Slowly, he opens his eyes again.

'Sometimes I can be all Zen about it,' he says softly. 'I'm just happy that you are, that you have what you want and I'm happy that I have you back. It's a miracle and I'm deeply grateful for it. But, other times, I feel this anger rise up in me and I wish he was gone, that he'd never even arrived, and I had you all for myself again. Just like it was before.'

'I understand, sweetheart. And I think you're amazing.' Greer gives her husband a little smile. 'But I also think it's time.'

Edward frowns. 'For what?'

'To get out there, to give yourself the gift of some aliveness, some happiness again.'

'What do you mean?'

'You know what I mean.'

'I don't.'

Greer gives him a coy look. 'Sex.'

Edward laughs. 'My wife is telling me to start dating, this is funny.'

'Your daughter too.'

Edward sighs. 'True.'

'Hey, most husbands would love this,' Greer says. 'You get your family and you get carte blanche to go out and make sexy time with anyone else you want.'

Edward gives her a look. 'Don't joke, it's not funny. This situation of ours is crazy.'

'It's a little unconventional, true,' Greer admits. 'But I believe we're managing it pretty well, like Tilly said, better than many other "normal" families. Maybe that's what creates so much misery for ordinary human beings – all the rules and expectations – no one can measure up but they keep trying, failing and hating themselves and each other for it.'

'Yeah, maybe,' Edward says. 'But that still doesn't mean I'm inviting your boyfriend over for dinner, okay?'

Greer smiles. 'How about, he can come over when you have your girlfriend over for dinner too?'

'Oh, because that wouldn't be an absolutely insane setup,' Edward says. Then he returns her smile. 'I do love you so.'

Greer laughs. 'I love you too.'

And then, before she realises what's happening, Edward is kissing her. Their lips touch and blend and then, he steps forward to hold her but instead steps right inside her. For a few moments they are merged and then Edward steps out again.

He shakes his head, holding it, pressing his palms against his temples.

'What was that?' Greer asks.

'I'm sorry,' Edward says. 'It was an accident, I didn't mean, I didn't – whatever it was, it wasn't good. I've got the worst headache.'

'I'm fine,' Greer says, 'just a little taken aback.'

'Yeah, well, you're lucky,' Edward says, still holding his head. 'I need pills.'

'You need to get laid.'

Despite himself, Edward smiles.

'With a real, live woman.'

'Yeah, all right, okay, point taken.' He looks up, giving her a mischievous grin. 'Still, it was worth a shot, don't you think? To see if we still had that old magic.'

Greer raises an eyebrow. 'And what's the verdict?'

Edward considers. 'I need to get laid.'

They both laugh.

Chapter Thirty

Our Otto,

The Germans have withdrawn from the Ardennes. What a New Year's gift! It seems, at last, that little progresses are building on each other, that a snowball is slowly starting to speed down the mountain, that the Allies are gathering momentum and weight and that a real victory is in sight. I am no longer hoping, imagining, that this will be very soon. The last great event like this was nearly three months ago now. How many people have been killed since? Too many to count. Too many to mourn. And yet, we fight on.

I have long wished that I could be on a battlefield. I know you'll think I'm crazy for saying so, but I am certain that you wish the same. And why should I be any different from you? I am so passive here, helping no one and only, in fact, doing the opposite, every day putting in danger the lives of the two people who are fighting, in their own silent, secret way, to keep little Otto and me alive.

I think often of the day they took my parents. How I let

them. How I hid in a wardrobe as my mother's screams filled the house. I wish I hadn't. Every night I wish this. I know you said I did the right thing, that I couldn't have stopped it, that I would have died with them, that saving myself would at least give Mama and Papa some peace. But it feels wrong, not to fight, to let death and evil sweep through your land without holding up a hand to try and stop it. I would rip out a Nazi's eyes before I let them take little Otto. I know they would take him anyway, I know it would do no good, really, but I would fight. I would fight with everything I have, with every breath, I would not give up before I was dead.

I'm sorry, I don't think you'll like to read such things. Perhaps motherhood has made me fierce. I have such anger and hate in me now, such force, that I sometimes have to scratch at my own arm until I bleed to keep from screaming out with rage, sometimes I have to dig my nails into my flesh to stop myself from abandoning little Otto and running out onto the streets and attacking as many soldiers as I can before they shoot me.

I think I shan't read this letter to you. It's probably for the best.

Ever Yours,
Marthe

Clara doesn't get out of bed for forty-eight hours. And then, telling herself to pull it together for the sake of her neglected customers, finally gets dressed and goes to the shop. She has to put all her force behind the door to push it open, past the great tide of letters shoring it up. Surprised, Clara eyes the pile. Surely she can't have had that many bills in six weeks? And yet, on closer examination, most of the envelopes seem to be handwritten. She bends down and opens one up. It's short and written on paper – cream with flecks of gold – she recognises, paper she sells in the shop.

Dear Clara,

You probably don't remember me. I came in a few months ago and you helped me to write a letter I was very scared to write – to my husband from whom I was estranged. I sent it. It changed my life, in so many amazing ways. I can't thank you enough. I came to see you, several times, but you weren't here. I hope everything is all right and that you come back soon.

Love,

Lucy Allsden xxx

Clara stares at the letter, perplexed. Then she opens two more letters at random and finds similar sentiments, if very different circumstances, contained within. It's possible, even probable, she considers, that the rest of the letters do too. Clara smiles, quite overwhelmed. She rests her hand just below her belly.

'Maybe this won't be so hard after all,' she says. 'Maybe I won't just have my mother to help.' She addresses her non-existent bump. 'Maybe we've got a few more potential friends here than I thought.' Clara's voice cracks and tears spring into her eyes.

'Bloody hormones,' she says, stepping over to the counter, suddenly eager to reacquaint herself with the pens she's missed so much. She takes the long way round, doing a circuit of the shop, brushing her hand along her drawers of papers, over the letters embossing the walls. On seeing the pens in the little glass cases, the pens her grandfather made, Clara thinks again of Pieter. Not that she's been thinking of much else since she left Amsterdam and, even when other thoughts rear, he never really disappears but just lingers in the background, ever ready to leap back into the spotlight when she's not paying attention.

She will give him one, she decides. He will love it, treasure it. And he deserves a pen – *her* pen – much more than she. Perhaps, too, the gift would help him to think of her more fondly than he probably does right now. Quickly, before she has a chance to second-guess herself, Clara goes to the counter, opens the drawer and finds the pen her grandfather made for her, sitting in its black leather box, untouched. She lifts it out for a moment, a goodbye, an apology that she was never able to let the pen live its purpose, as her grandfather had so wished. Clara twists off the cap, kisses the pure-gold nib then returns the pen to the box. Then she goes to her hundred drawers to find the perfect writing paper to write to Pieter.

The first letter arrives three days later. He must have written it as soon as he received the pen. The next day two more letters come. The day after that, three. On day four it's just one. Clara holds them in their envelopes. She can feel the sorrow, the love and longing wafting from the envelopes as if he has sprayed them with that particular scent. She wants to know what he says, she wants to hear him. The desire to open the letters is so strong that her fingers shake with it. But her fear is greater. She will cry if she reads them. She will sob. She will want to run to London, jump on the next train to Amsterdam and ruin Pieter's life, without thought or care. It took all the power Clara had to be able to leave someone she loved for their own good. Being selfless is not an easy thing, especially under the influence of hormones, and Clara fears that reading them will shatter the last shards of selflessness she still clings to.

So, every day, she picks them off the mat of the shop and places them in the drawer beneath the till. If he keeps up at this prolific pace she'll have to find another place to put the letters, probably a box in the attic, for one day, surely, she'll be able to read them. But, for now, Clara wants them close. Several times a day, she opens the drawer to press her fingers to the paper, imagining she can feel the imprint of his touch as he sealed them and sent them off. So, because she can't read his letters, in a vain attempt to sate her desire for Pieter's words, Clara reads Marthe's letters instead, over and over again. Of course, the love she reads there only makes her cry too, so that Clara has to sit back from the counter and let the salty water soak her T-shirt instead of the inky pages. But at least they don't (nearly, but not quite) make her run out of the shop and all the way back to Amsterdam.

Chapter Thirty-One

It's his first day at A&B Associates. And it's the first time, saving his interview, that Edward has worn a suit in over three years. The shirt collar feels too tight and itchy against his skin. He tugs at it repeatedly, before undoing the top button and hoping that nobody notices. And, for most of the day, while he's orientating himself and organising his new office, nobody does. Until he's standing in the office kitchen, making himself a triple espresso from the very fancy and expensive coffee machine.

'Settling in well already, I see.'

Edward glances up to see what he can only describe as one of the sexiest women he's ever laid eyes on, standing next to the fridge holding something – probably something edible, he doesn't see what and nor does he care – since he can't take his gaze off every other inch of her. She's quite tall and voluptuous, not especially slim, but she holds her weight in a way he's never quite seen on a woman before: with such supreme confidence, as if she knows that she's quite the most desirable female on earth. Her clothes are tight, hugging every curve of flesh, her shirt is unbuttoned just low enough to reveal the dip of her breasts. Her skirt isn't short but, somehow, her legs are all the more enticing for being hidden beneath it, just her smooth ankles revealed, along with feet slid into tall, black, shiny heels.

Looking at her, probably open-mouthed, probably drooling, Edward feels something else he hasn't felt in years. Not since before Greer got sick. He is, suddenly and completely, overcome with pure unadulterated lust. The experience is so surprising, so shocking to him that he's lucky he doesn't spill all three shots of his espresso down his trousers.

'Cat got your tongue?' she asks.

Still, Edward can say nothing. Only stare.

The incredibly beautiful woman laughs, then turns and leaves.

Edward is left staring after her, a ridiculous grin of undiluted joy spread across his face. He will not touch this particular woman, he knows. It would be career suicide, personal suicide too, most probably. But it doesn't matter. She may be a goddess, but making love with her isn't the point. She was a sign. She triggered his reawakening. And, for this, he will only always be grateful.

Ross hasn't seen Ava for three days. She cancelled their Monday lunch. Then didn't turn up to the Wednesday swing dance class. Something is most definitely up, but she isn't answering his calls so he doesn't yet know what. So, there's only one thing to do, other than waiting patiently until she's ready to tell him – something far too passive for Ross to ever contemplate – which is to track her down at the library.

He's on his way there when, for some reason he can't quite explain, he's drawn to take a short detour along a street he never usually walks down. When he discovers that it is, in fact, a dead end, Ross turns to go back. Which is when he spots the little blue door, the window crammed with papers, pens and all kinds of writing paraphernalia. He squints to read the little handwritten note in the corner of the window, inviting him to step inside and *Learn the lost art of letter writing . . .*

Ross has never particularly wanted to write letters. He's quite happy with phone calls, texts and emails. Frankly, he's never given the topic a second thought. And so he can't explain why, despite being headed to find Ava, he does exactly what the little handwritten note has instructed him to do, he turns the handle of the little blue door and steps inside.

Clara looks up from one of Marthe's letters. Fortunately, she's not crying.

'Hello,' he says, looking around, still a little confused.

'Hello.' She tucks the letter away. 'Welcome to *Letters*.'

'Aye, thanks. I dunno why I'm here, though.' He grins. 'I don't think I've ever written a letter before in me life.'

Clara stands, managing a smile. 'Well, then you've come to the right place.'

'O, aye?' He laughs. 'Then I suppose I should buy some paper and a pen.'

'What kind would you like?'

Ross shrugs. 'I have absolutely no idea.'

'We've got plenty to choose from.'

'Why don't you choose summit for me then, lassie?' he says. 'I bet you've got a better eye for these things than I.'

Clara crosses the carpet, stopping in front of the rows of drawers, a few feet from Ross. He watches her as she opens and closes drawers, examining papers.

'You know, lassie, you're a lot stronger than you think.'

Clara stops, mid drawer, and turns to him. 'Sorry?'

'You think you can't cope with things,' Ross says. 'But y' can.'

Clara frowns. 'Do I—have we met?'

'Naw, but I just know things, about people,' Ross says. 'Women usually, it's a gift.'

'Oh?' Clara raises an eyebrow, rather amused despite herself. 'I see.'

'You're pregnant,' he says, matter-of-fact.

Clara's eyebrows drop. She stares at him in amazement.

'But . . . What . . . I don't—I'm not even . . . How the hell do you know that?'

Ross gives a little shrug. 'I told you, it's my gift.'

'Well, bloody hell.' Clara gasps. 'Clearly . . . it certainly bloody is.'

'And I'm telling you, it's only when y' think you can't cope that you can't. Y' can do anything life puts in front of you, if only you believe y' can.' He smiles. 'Even motherhood.'

Clara stares at him.

'Although,' Ross considers. 'Don't let that stop y' asking for help. It takes strength to reach out to others. Don't try to do it all alone, okay?'

Clara nods.

So does Ross. 'Good.'

'Thank you.'

'You're welcome. Now, back to me letter . . .'

Clara returns to the moment and matter at hand. 'Oh, yes, of course.' Refocusing on the drawer, she picks out a piece of paper and hands it to him. 'Here you go.'

Ross examines it: blue as a bird's egg with a white lace trim.

'Oh aye,' he says with a grin. 'She'll love that.' He still has no idea what he'll write, though he expects it'll come to him.

'I'll get you a pen,' Clara says, and she does.

She shows him to the little writing desk and he sits. And, when he finally puts pen to paper, he finds that, yes, the words come to him easily, so easily in fact that he hardly knows what he writes.

Thirty minutes later, still smiling, still bemused and still wondering quite what happened, Ross closes the door of the little shop behind him. Realising he's now late for Ava's lunch hour, he hurries along the little cobbled cul-de-sac, and back towards the main road. At the intersection, he pauses, turns his face up to the sunshine and steps out onto the street. The driver sees him too late and is speeding too fast to be able to stop. Ross is still looking skyward when he's hit.

'You've got to play for people, in public.'

Finn shakes his head. 'No, I don't.'

'But why not?'

It's a conversation they've been having in circles for days now. Neither will budge. Until, finally, Greer lowers herself to using her one bargaining chip.

'If you do it, I'll do it.'

Finn frowns. 'You'll go busking? How would you even hold the violin? And you don't even know how to play, I don't—'

'No.' Greer gives him a meaningful look. 'I'll do *it* – the thing you suggested before, when . . .'

'Oh. *Oh.*' Finn brightens visibly. 'You sneaky little minx.'

Greer grins. 'I know. I'm very, very naughty. Especially since I want to do it too.'

'You do?'

She nods. 'Yes, but, being unburdened by earthly desires, I can hold out a lot longer than you can. *Infinitely* longer, in fact.'

Finn scowls.

Greer waits.

'All right, then,' he huffs. 'I'll do it.'

Greer claps, though, of course, her hands make no sound.

'Excellent,' she says. 'Then so will I.'

Finn laughs. 'I'm going to have to watch out for you, aren't I?'

Greer nods. 'Yep, I'll resort to anything when I want my own way. Just ask Edward.'

Finn smiles. 'I think it's a little early for that, don't you?'

'Perhaps,' Greer says. 'We'll see.'

Edward is walking home, hurrying along the street in order to get there as soon as he possibly can. He found the train journey from London a little stressful. He'd forgotten what rush hour on the Underground was like, all those sweaty bodies pressed together, too many armpits exposed. Of course, he hadn't been able to get a seat on the King's Cross to Cambridge train so had stood all the way. But he doesn't care, so long as he gets home to see his daughter before bedtime and, hopefully, Greer too.

And then, much to Edward's surprise, he sees her right there. He's standing on the pavement, waiting at the crossroads to turn onto Mill Road, and he looks up to see her hovering on the roof of a three-storey Victorian house, looking down across the street. He follows her gaze and it rests on a busker standing outside a little shop, holding a violin under his chin, tweaking his bow. Strangely, he has no open case, no empty hat, no place for passers-by to drop coins. And then, all at once, Edward recognises his next-door neighbour. He's suddenly hit with a rush of jealous hatred, stunned into immobility, just as he had been by lust only a few hours before. He clenches his fists and grits his teeth.

And then, the musician begins to play. The music is so beautiful, so sorrowful and sweet that it brings tears to Edward's eyes. He watches the musician, this other man his ghost wife loves, play. And, try as he might, as the music soaks into him, Edward can no longer conjure up any hatred, any loathing for this person, someone who can create something so entirely sublime. Instead, he listens and watches. Memories rise up, pain pulls at his heart, opening it wider and wider until joy begins to seep in. Tears slide down his cheeks as he stands at the crossroads. And, for the second time that day, Edward is suddenly overcome with gratitude.

Chapter Thirty-Two

Our dearest, darling Otto,

I cannot quite believe I am writing this. I can't believe I am writing at all. I should, surely, be out in the streets, dancing, shouting joy and victory from the rooftops. And yet, I have become so used to writing now, it is part of my speech, my expression, and so I feel I have to write this momentous moment down, to commemorate it, to be sure that it has really happened.

Mr X was the one who told me. I've only seen him half a dozen times since coming here but, occasionally, he visits the cellar to tell me when something significant happens, something to give us hope that the end might be in sight. In the last few months, since the start of the year, he's visited the most often of all. On January 27th, when Soviet troops liberated Auschwitz. On April 12th, when the Allies liberated the Buchenwald and Belsen camps. On April 30th, when the Führer committed suicide. And today, May 8th, to say that yesterday was the unconditional surrender of all German forces.

Tomorrow I will leave this place. Tomorrow I will see daylight for the first time in nearly two years and Otto will see it for the first time in his life. Tomorrow I won't have to whisper, I won't have to shush and keep Otto silent any more. Tomorrow I will come to find you.

Ever Yours,
Marthe

Ava receives the letter and the phone call on the same morning. The phone call to tell her that Ross has died and the letter he has written. The phone call comes first, so when the letter arrives it is laced with an extra layer of poignancy. The letter is a surprise, though the phone call is not, since Ava knew it was coming. She didn't know exactly when, but she knew it would be soon.

She had spent the past week debating with herself, every minute of every hour of every day, whether or not to tell him. Although, even then, even as she tore herself apart, Ava knew that the answer would always be 'no'. She wouldn't tell him. He'd said, once, that he wouldn't want to know particulars of his death, nor the fact that it was imminent, and she would respect that. She understood. She wouldn't want to know either, and so she understood.

Now she sits in her hallway, leaning back against the front door, eyes closed, for the entire afternoon until, at last, she opens the letter. She decides it's either now or at three o'clock in the morning and, Ava well knows, that even minor upsets feel significantly worse at three o'clock in the morning. She certainly doesn't want to face a major one. For this letter, she'll need the slight uplift of sunlight. She'll need all the help she can get. And so, as the last of the evening light falls through the windows, Ava opens the letter.

Dear Ava,

Why am I writing to you? Probably because you won't answer my calls. Joke. I jest. Don't take offence. Have I said something typically rude, brash or annoying and now you're punishing me for it? If so, please stop. I miss you. Anyway, I'm just on my way to track you down, nay, stalk you, so I'll find out what's up soon enough, I'll wheedle it out of you. I have my ways of making people speak, my means, but I promise not to use any of my very worst instruments of torture on you. At least, not at first . . .

But, before we get to the good stuff, I have to tell you this. I've been thinking a lot about what job you could do and I've hit on it! A counsellor or, more precisely, a grief counsellor. Aye, now, I know that sounds like the most bloody depressing job in the entire world. But think about it for a wee sec. You'd never — at least, not often — have to censor yourself, you'd be working with people who'd probably already experienced the worst event of their lives and you'd get to chat with them about that. Well, not 'chat' maybe, but you get my point. Anyway, the idea came to me in a lightning strike of inspiration, as all my best ideas do, so you should really pay heed to it. Promise?

All right, now it's time for me to scuttle off and stalk you,
Tallyho & all that,
Ross

Of course, Ava should have realised that she wouldn't have been able to sleep after reading the letter, anyway. She wouldn't be able to think of anything else. She almost — but not quite — laughs at the irony of his suggestion, given her current situation.

It's the second great grief she's suffered now, after her sister, so she'd certainly be experientially qualified for the vocation, if not yet practically. Though that'd only be a matter of learning and Ava has always loved learning. She only wishes that Ross had been able to tell her himself. And so she sits in her hallway, until long past three, until, at last, she falls asleep, still clutching the letter in her lap.

Clara sits behind the counter in her little shop. Still she's receiving a letter from Pieter every day and the pen drawer is nearly bursting with them. Still she hasn't opened a single one. She is exhausted. Not just because she can hardly stop crying, though of course that doesn't help, but the impact of pregnancy on her body is something she simply hadn't imagined. The baby is still so tiny, but Clara is so tired all the time that she has to close the shop for a few hours at lunchtime and sleep on the floor or at her chair. It doesn't matter where, she's out like a light in less than a minute. Mercifully, she hasn't actually thrown up yet, though nausea sweeps over her constantly, not simply in the morning.

Unfortunately, the tiredness means that she hasn't been taking her evening walks. Which is a shame, since she misses sitting at her writing desk and she misses writing the letters. It's also a shame since she's still curious to see the man who lives on Riverside Drive, the one with the daughter. Clara wants to double-check that her letters have taken effect, that he's happier now. She also imagines that she might ask him for a little parenting advice, as she still hasn't told or asked anyone anything about the baby, not even her mother.

Her customers keep her fairly distracted and she's now read every one of the seventy-eight letters she received while in Amsterdam.

It was so touching to take delivery of all that love and appreciation that Clara hasn't been able to look any of her customers in the eye for several days, for fear she might spontaneously hug them or, more likely, cry.

She's been waiting for food cravings, but hasn't been struck by anything strange just yet. No desperate desires for pickles and ice cream or bacon dipped in peanut butter. But she does get seized by sudden unexpected urges every now and then. Last Wednesday she stayed up until three in the morning reorganising her bookshelves into alphabetical order. Yesterday she spent nearly an entire day trying to remember how to knit so she could begin a baby blanket. Today, as she sits behind the counter, Clara is grabbed by an instant impulse to force open the locked drawer of the little writing desk. She'd quite forgotten about it since returning home and, before she'd left, she hadn't felt desperate desires or insatiable curiosities regarding anything much, not the greater things in life, certainly not inconsequential things like locked drawers. And yet, now, all of a sudden, she *has* to know. No matter what it takes, Clara will open that drawer.

Three hours later, having tried everything she can think of, including attempts to pick the lock as well as prise it open with a pair of scissors, Clara is truly exhausted and thoroughly fed up. If the desk wasn't the most precious object she owns in the world, Clara would right now take an axe to it, or a crowbar. But, of course, she won't. Not only could she not bear the idea of hurting the ornate little writing desk, but she also imagines that even a scratch on its intricately carved surface might spoil its special powers altogether. And so Clara sits on the floor beside the desk, legs outstretched, contemplating her next move: tears or sleep.

Just as she's starting to nod off, the door to the little shop opens and a customer steps inside. Clumsily, drowsily, Clara stumbles to her feet.

'Oh, sorry,' the customer says, 'I didn't mean to disturb you.'

'No, no, you're not.' Clara blinks, rubbing her eyes. 'I was just . . . Oh, hello.' She recognises this woman, though for a moment, Clara can't quite place her. And then she remembers. 'You came in a few months ago; you wrote a letter to your sister.'

'Yes.' Ava nods, surprised to be remembered. 'I did. Thank you. It . . . It helped me a great deal and, soon after that, well, my life changed a great deal too.'

'Oh,' Clara says. 'For the better, I hope.'

Ava smiles. 'Oh, yes.'

'Have you come to write another letter?'

Ava nods again. 'Yes. To a dear friend who died a few weeks ago.'

'I'm sorry.'

Ava takes a deep breath. 'It's okay. I mean, not for him. But I don't really feel like he's gone, silly as that sounds. So much of what he wanted for me has happened, so I rather feel like he's still with me, same as he ever was. I still talk to him in my head, all the time, though I know that's silly too.'

'No,' Clara says, 'not silly at all.'

'Actually, he wrote me a letter, before he died. And I think, by the paper, that he wrote it here.'

'Oh? When was that?'

'Sometime between two and three weeks ago. He's Scottish. Cheeky. Handsome.'

'Oh, yes,' Clara exclaims. 'I remember him. He was lovely. In fact, he . . .'

'He told you something?' Ava asks. 'He gave you some great

290

life advice? It's okay, don't worry, I won't ask.' She smiles. 'It was his thing.'

'He was very good at it.'

'Yes, yes, he still is too, judging by the answers I hear in my head,' Ava says. 'I'm writing to thank him for that, for everything.'

'That's lovely, I'm glad,' Clara says. 'I might write to thank him myself.'

Ava smiles again. She looks at the writing desk, then her gaze drops to the floor, to the instruments and implements strewn about.

'Um, what are you doing?' The old Ava, the pre-Ross Ava, wouldn't have been so bold, so intrusive and impertinent. But the new Ava just says what she thinks, within reason – she isn't quite as outrageous as Ross was, not yet.

Clara follows Ava's gaze to the floor. Her first impulse is to lie. To protect her family secrets from this virtual stranger. But there's something about Ava she likes and trusts, even more so than the first time she saw her, so many months ago. She would, Clara thinks, probably make a rather perfect friend.

'I was trying to force open a locked drawer in my desk.'

'Did you lose the key?'

'No,' Clara admits. 'I never had it. It was locked when I got it.'

Ava's eyes brighten with interest. 'Have you tried to open it before?'

'Not really. I—'

'No? Gosh, you're so patient – I'd have been at it with a hammer the first day I bought it.'

'Well, yeah, I used to be accepting, apathetic. Boring.' Clara gives a wicked little grin. 'But now I want in.'

Ava claps her hands. 'Excellent!'

'The only thing is, I can't take a hammer to it, since I can't damage the desk in any way. So my options are a little limited.'

'Ah.' Ava regards the desk. 'Okay, so perhaps here's where my skills come in use at last.'

'Oh?' Clara asks, feeling a spark of hope rise in her chest.

'Well, I used to be a devourer of cryptic crossword puzzles and a gobbler of the written word,' Ava says. 'I work in a library, so that helps.'

Clara grins. 'You're a reader.'

'Yes. And I've read about how these old writing desks were often built with hidden drawers, and that their visible drawers were sometimes designed with a secret catch that would unlock it from behind—'

'Really?' Clara asks, open-mouthed.

Ava nods. 'Yes, I suppose it was in case the owner lost the key and didn't have a copy. It was a quick, easy safeguard.'

'Do you think this desk has one?'

Now Ava returns Clara's wicked grin. 'Well, there's only one way to find out now, isn't there?'

Both women dart towards the writing desk. Very gently, they lift it and place it carefully in the centre of the carpeted floor. Clara stands, watching, as Ava gets down on hands and knees to examine the back of the desk. Clara holds her breath, then quickly exhales once she starts to sway a little with dizziness.

A sharp, quick click sounds in the silent shop and Ava rises, a triumphant look on her face. 'That's it, I think. Try the drawer.'

Slowly, postponing the moment in case it's all about to evaporate into nothing, Clara bends down and gives a little pull on the handle. It slides open.

The drawer is deeper than it looked from the outside, though it's empty, save for a single envelope. A letter. And on it, in her great-grandmother's handwriting is written: *Otto Josef Garritt van Dijk*. Clara picks it up, turns it over, and sees that it is still sealed. It has never been opened, never been read.

Chapter Thirty-Three

'Are you sure?'

Greer nods.

'You're not scared?'

She shakes her head, then smiles. 'Well, maybe just a little. But what's the worst that can happen? I'm already dead.'

'Hey,' Finn says, 'you joke, but there's a lot worse pain than death. Hell, death is a mercy in some cases.'

Greer regards him. 'Are you trying to talk me out of it?'

'Oh no,' Finn exclaims, realising his mistake. 'I was speaking abstractly. Not about us. This will be fine. This, I'm imagining, will be wonderful.'

Greer remembers what happened with Edward and only hopes that Finn's right, that he won't be about to suffer in the same way. 'So, how's it going to work?'

Finn only pretends to consider this question. Truthfully, he's been thinking about it every night since the day he first suggested it. 'Well, I figure, I'll play and then, when you're ready, you just step inside me. Like you did with the tree in my garden.'

'I like the way you say that, so cavalier, so casual,' Greer says with a smile. Then, all of a sudden, she worries that, for some reason, Finn might have an even more extreme reaction than Edward. After all, what if he has a weak heart, or something of that nature? 'But, what if something awful happens?'

Finn frowns. 'Like what?'

'Like you die of a heart attack or something like that.'

Finn shrugs. 'So, then I'll have a heart attack and we'll both be dead. We've got nothing to lose.'

'*Nothing to lose?* You'd be dead.'

Finn shrugs again. 'We'd still be together, though. That's all that matters.'

'I'm not sure it works that way,' Greer says. 'I don't think all dead people come back as ghosts. I don't know that we'd be able to find each other. I don't know how it works, I'm no expert on the afterlife.'

'No expert? You're living the afterlife. Or, not exactly "living" it, but you know . . .'

Greer laughs. 'Yeah, but that doesn't make me an expert. I don't know how it works in the grand scheme of things, I don't know—'

Finn holds up a hand. 'Okay, enough! Enough procrastinating with ridiculous reasons—'

'—hardly ridiculous,' Greer objects.

'I don't care. Let's just do it and see. You promised you would.'

Greer sighs, reasoning that he probably won't die. 'All right, then. But, since this is such a risky endeavour, this means you have to play in a park tomorrow too, and—'

'Hey! No renegotiating of the terms,' Finn protests. 'That's not fair.'

Greer smiles. 'I know, but still, worth a try.'

'You really are a cheeky minx.'

'That reminds me,' Greer says. 'Did I mention, Edward invited you round for lunch on Sunday?'

'Did you mention?' Finn sits up straight. 'No, you certainly did not.'

'I know,' Greer says. 'But, apparently, he heard you play – see, I told you it was a brilliant idea, didn't I? – and then—'

'Are you sure he doesn't just want to beat me up?'

'No, quite the opposite, in fact. Bizarrely, he seems to be really looking forward to meeting you properly.'

'That *is* bizarre. But great, I mean . . .' Finn frowns. 'Hold on a sec, is this another sneaky distraction technique designed to throw me off my game and make me forget about what we were about to do?'

'No! Of course not. I wasn't lying. What do you take me for?'

Finn raises an eyebrow. 'You've already warned me that you stop at nothing.'

'Yes,' Greer admits, 'true. But I draw the line at lying. Even I have my moral standards.'

Finn eyes her. 'Do you? But still, why are we talking about your husband when we're about to try making love for the first time?'

Greer holds up her hands. 'Okay, you're right, bad timing. Chalk it up to a fear of intimacy – and death.'

'But you're already dead, I thought we'd established that.'

'Not my death, silly, yours.'

'All right, okay, well, as I've said, that doesn't matter.' Finn stands. 'Now, I'm going to go and get my violin, before you can come up with any other cunning diversion tactics.'

'Wait!'

Finn turns back. 'What now?'

'One more thing. I wasn't totally telling the truth, at least, not the whole truth. The reason I brought it all up, the death thing, well . . . I sort of kissed my husband.'

Finn frowns. 'What?'

'Well, he kissed me. And then, sort of accidentally, sort of on purpose, he stepped inside me.'

Finn's frown deepens. 'He did?'

Greer gives a little nod.

'Did you try to stop him?'

'It was over really quickly,' Greer says. 'But no, I didn't.'

Finn narrows his eyes. 'How did it feel?'

'How did it feel?'

Finn nods.

'Well, he got a huge headache and I didn't feel anything.'

'Nothing?'

'No, not really. It was rather similar to walking through the tree.'

'Oh,' Finn says, then he smiles.

'You're not angry?'

'No. Hell, he's your husband. I don't blame the man for wanting to try. But, at least this way, he won't try again. And, anyway, it's a good sign. A sign that you're not meant to be.'

'You don't worry that it might be the same for us too?'

Finn shakes his head. 'No, I don't. Not in a million years.'

He chooses Mozart. *The Marriage of Figaro*. He builds slowly, drawing Greer in, winding long silky ribbons of music around her as she listens, pulling her towards him. When she stands and steps forward, Finn plunges into the greatest aria ever written. The notes soar high and strong above their heads, the strength of the music tugging at their hearts and pulling them towards each other. When she steps into him, for a split second Finn stops. It's as if he has plunged into a waterfall on a blistering day, cool rivulets running down his scorching skin, as if he's breathing in the softest, sweetest scent he's ever smelt and it's seeping into every cell of his body, as if he's free-falling through the air with all the beauty of the world beneath him . . . And then, Finn doesn't know what he plays. It's a wonder, in fact, that he manages to keep playing at all, since the sensation of having Greer within him is so intense, so extraordinary, that he might forget to breathe. It's quite unlike any physical pleasure he's ever felt before while, at the same time, being an infinite magnification of every orgasm he's ever experienced – as if he's standing in the centre of a firework display, as if he *is* every firework, exploding with joy, over and over again.

Finn finally drops his violin, just as Greer steps out of his body. She shakes herself off and floats above the floor, bathed in a beatific smile.

'So,' Greer says, 'was it wonderful for you? Because it was pretty bloody wonderful for me.'

Finn collapses on the sofa and gives a slight shake of his head.

'No headache?'

'No,' he says, his voice barely a whisper. 'And, I mean, it wasn't wonderful for me. It was the most magnificent, most glorious, most sublime experience of my life.'

Greer smiles.

'In that case,' she says. 'Shall we do it again?'

Finn manages a slight nod.

'And, perhaps,' she suggests, 'like physical sex, it gets even better with practice.'

Finn closes his eyes and sighs.

The day after she received Ross's letter, Ava signs up to take an introductory course in grief counselling. Five days after that, she attends his funeral. Perhaps unsurprisingly, it had been a rather uplifting affair, considering. Ross's friends, all the people who knew him – of whom there were, also unsurprisingly, a very large number – were keen to celebrate his life with great gusto and cheer. Eulogies were filled with jokes and loving anecdotes. Swing music was played. Pop songs were sung.

And yet, underneath all the cheer ran an undeniable river of grief. Ava inhaled the breath of over five hundred hearts heavy with sorrow and, by the time she's shuffling home, she feels so heavy with mourning that she can barely put one foot in front of the other. On her doorstep, she fumbles with the key and drops it into the rose bush next to her door.

'Oh, hello.'

Ava turns to see a man she vaguely recognises, wearing a very smart suit and carrying a briefcase. It comes to her, through the fog of her sorrow, that he lives on her street.

'Hello,' she says, beginning to scrabble about among the leaves, trying not to get pricked by the thorns, hoping the man won't linger.

'Can I help?' he asks.

'No, thanks, I'm fine.'

Not seeming to hear, Edward walks over, puts his briefcase down on her doorstep and starts to help Ava search.

'Ouch!' Edward sucks his thumb. Then he laughs.

Ava looks up at him. Her sight is still hazy through the fog of sorrow, but even she can't deny that her neighbour is really rather handsome. Something stirs inside Ava and, all of a sudden, she desires nothing more, nothing else, but sex. With this stranger. A fling. She wants to be flung. Preferably, with great gusto and passion onto her own bed. The desire is so sudden and so surprising that

Ava is rather caught off guard. She's read somewhere that people often want to have sex after (and even during) funerals. Something to do with death and the reaffirmation of life. But, whatever the reasoning, she wonders if, by any chance, he might want the same thing. The way he looks back at her, she thinks she might just be in luck.

'I don't suppose . . .'

'What?'

'You might, you fancy coming in for a drink?'

Edward gazes at her. 'I, um, I know we only live a few doors away but I'm afraid I don't even know your name.'

She reaches out her hand. 'Ava.'

'Edward.'

'Nice to meet you. Now, how about that drink?'

'Well, um, I was . . . Yes, of course, I'd love to.'

'Great.' Ava looks down into the rose bush once more and there is the key, caught by the fading summer sunlight, glinting up at her. She picks it up and unlocks the door. And then, she laughs. A pure, sweet, lovely sound that catches the breeze and lifts them both up.

'What?' Edward asks.

'Oh, nothing,' Ava says. 'I just realised something. I can say: *This is what Ross would have wanted*.' She giggles again.

'Who's Ross? He's not your husband, is he?'

'Oh, no,' Ava says. 'Just a very dear friend.'

Edward smiles. 'I'm delighted to hear it.'

Chapter Thirty-Four

My dearest Otto,

I have a story to tell. I'm afraid it will probably shock you, perhaps upset you, but hopefully it will touch you too. So, I once wrote these words: 'my dearest Otto', to your father but, of course, you won't remember that you were once called Otto too. You have long been Lucas, after your adopted father. I hope you will not hate me for this, for this choice I made. I hope you will understand why and that you will forgive me for not telling you the truth, for not telling you your story, until now.

You were born during the war. On the 8th March 1944. You are, in fact, a full year older than you believe, I apologise for that too. I didn't register your birth, I was hiding in a house on Herengracht, 389 and so, of course, it was impossible. Mr & Mrs Borst risked their lives to keep me, and then you. We lived in their cellar for nearly two years. We didn't see the sunshine or the stars. For the first nine months you lived inside me, thankfully, and for the first four of those months I didn't realise you were there. Mrs Borst was terrified, when at last I told her. She hadn't planned on taking an even greater risk, for the chances that you might accidentally betray us, that someone might hear you were great indeed. Mercifully, you seemed to realise this – perhaps you absorbed my own fear through my milk – and hardly ever made a sound.

We were fed as best as they could provide, we were kept alive, though sadly my milk dried up after only three months. Mrs Borst grew to adore you. She had no children of her own but had always longed for them. She spent many hours with us, holding you and singing softly. Perhaps this was why they kept us. I think, if she'd been younger, she would have taken you and raised you as her own. Perhaps that would have been for the best. But, as it was, they halved their rations with us and it was just enough.

On May 9th 1945 – two days after the German forces in the Netherlands surrendered – we finally emerged from our hole. We were both quite sick from malnourishment and lack of real light. I had nothing to give Mr & Mrs Borst, for all they had given me. And they gave me everything, my life and yours. It is not possible to say how grateful – what an inadequate word – I was, I am, I always will be to them. Even if I'd had everything in the world to give, it could not have been enough. And I had nothing. Only myself, and you.

And that was how I met your father – the man you have always known to be your father, though he was not. Lucas Bastiaan Janssen was Mr Borst's nephew. He was fifteen years older than me, not particularly attractive, but I was deeply grateful – that inadequate word again, do we have no others? – to say that I also owed him my life, our lives and I could never repay him – that he had helped and also risked his life *for us, coming very close to losing it on two occasions.*

But I rush on too fast. Of course, after the war ended, I went looking for Otto, for your true father. I will not tell our story here. I have neither the strength nor the ability to tell it any more. So, separately, I am leaving you my other letters, letters that I wrote to him while we were apart, letters that he never received, never read. You will find them in our attic. They will tell you so much, not enough, but a great deal about your real father. I wish I could have given you more, I hope you will understand why I could not. I wish I could have given you him.

I lived in hope for a few months. When I went to the house where he'd been kept, I found that he'd been discovered, that he'd been taken to Herzogenbusch in July 1943. I went to the camp, I waited for weeks as lists of the dead were uncovered and families were informed. Three months after we'd been freed, I learnt that my love, your father, our Otto, had been shot by the Nazis in Herzogenbusch on 23rd of December 1943. I later learnt that he'd stolen three slices of bread to feed a little girl whose mother had died of starvation a few days before. I am happy to tell you that the girl, Miep Gies, survived and we knew her while we still lived in Amsterdam. She told me about the last weeks of your father's life. He was a very brave – yet another entirely inadequate word – man.

It was over a year before I finally agreed to marry Lucas. We still lived with Mr & Mrs Borst, though could now do so openly. We ate our meals with them, we slept in the attic. Every morning I held you up to the sunlight and we breathed the fresh breeze from the open window. Every night I opened the window again and showed you the stars. I found work in a shop. When I worked Mrs Borst cared for you. When I returned from a day away, I saw how happy she was, blurting out the details of all that you'd done – a new step, a new sound, a new smile – and I felt her slight sorrow when you saw me again and stumbled joyfully from her arms into mine.

When she first suggested Lucas, I confess I pretended not to hear, I pretended to be lost in wiping peas from the floor that you had spilt. But I knew, once we knew that we couldn't hope for our Otto any more, that I couldn't pretend for ever. Now there was something they wanted, these people who'd saved our lives, and now there was something I could finally give them in return and I gave it gladly.

I married Lucas Janssen on 1st April 1946. You were two years old. You'd never met your father and so, of course, you believed that this man, who you'd known all your life, was he. Lucas formally adopted you and we registered you, at last, with his names. I wanted to keep Otto's name with you, at least as a second name, but it would have hurt Lucas's feelings and I didn't want to do that. He was a good man, and a good father. You know that. He loved me and he loved you too, very much. He always thought of you as his own. I'm afraid that I was never able to love him, not really, not as a wife should. But my gratitude for the second chance, for the life we'd been given when we otherwise would have had none, kept me through those years.

I confess, even after I knew he was dead, I still looked for Otto every day. I still hoped that a mistake had been made. I dreamt that he had escaped somehow, that he had defied death in order to come back to me, to us, just as he'd always promised he would. I looked for him even after we finally left

Amsterdam – when Mr and then, two years later, Mrs Borst died. I looked for him in the faces of strangers when I walked through the streets. Once I pulled at a man's arm and scared his wife with my voice, my tears. Now that I know I won't be in this world much longer, I am happy in the belief that I will, at last, see my Otto again. And now, at last, I feel it's time to tell you. I'll leave the letter locked in my little writing desk and you will find it, after I've gone. I'm sorry that I cannot tell you myself, face-to-face, but I'm so used to writing everything of importance in my life now that I cannot speak these words, only write them to you.

I'm sorry you never knew your real father. I'm sorry I couldn't give you the gift of that. I hope that what I, we, gave you was enough. I hope that this story, this letter, and the ones I have left in the attic, will give you a part of your father and a part of yourself. You were born of great love and you survived against great odds. You were cheated but you were also blessed. I hope that I made the right choices. I made them for you.

Your loving mother,
Marthe

Later, Clara doesn't know how long she sits with the letter in her lap. Slowly, everything is falling into place. Her grandfather had found the letters in the attic, but he'd never found the final letter locked in the desk. So he never knew about Otto, he never knew that Lucas wasn't his biological father. Indeed, he must have assumed that the baby Otto was his half-brother who'd died. Clara feels sad at this, wishing he'd known the truth. But what can she do? Except, perhaps there is something. And, in that moment, Clara decides she will do it. Even if it won't make a blind bit of difference. She will go to her grandfather's grave and read him his mother's final letter.

Just as Clara is mapping out the particulars of this venture, there's a knock on the door. She glances up with a frown. Customers don't usually knock; they simply push open the door and walk in. Still heavy with sorrow and the fog of first-trimester exhaustion, she refuses to get up, so just waits on her seat for whomever it is to come in. Then they knock again.

'Oh, bloody hell.' Clara pulls herself up from her seat, placing the letter carefully on the counter, smoothing the pages, before shuffling across the shop floor.

As Clara puts her hand on the doorknob she feels, for the very first time, a twinge in her womb. She's never felt anything like it before. It can't be the baby, of course, it's too early for that. And yet . . . She presses her other hand lightly to her abdomen, waiting, hoping. So, when, distractedly, she pulls open the door, she's not actually looking up at the person standing on the other side of it. And so, he sees her first.

'Hello.'

Clara drops her hand and, before she even looks up, her eyes fill.

'You didn't answer any of my letters,' Pieter says, before she can speak, before he's even stepped inside. 'So I'm afraid I've been forced to take more drastic action. It's quite unlike me. I do hope you won't mind my turning up uninvited like this.'

Clara simply stares at him, shaking her head.

'Does that mean: "No, you don't mind" or "No, you don't want me here"?' Pieter asks. 'I did ask for an invitation in many of my letters. And did warn you, in the last one, that if you didn't reply I'd take that as a "yes".' He gives her a hopeful smile. 'So, really, you've only got yourself to blame.'

Clara gives a little nod, tears slipping down her cheeks.

'I must admit,' Pieter says. 'I played out this scenario in my mind many times. I thought, worst case, you'd slap me and send me packing. I thought, best case, you'd embrace me and smother me with kisses. I can't say I envisaged making you sobbing and speechless. I am sorry.'

He reaches a tentative hand towards her and, suddenly, Clara steps forward onto the pavement and hugs him, hard and tight.

'That's better,' he whispers into her hair, 'that's more like it.'

Then she steps back, wiping her eyes.

'But, why are you here? You don't want a . . .' she trails off, finding herself unable to say the word, lest she upset the one she's carrying within her. 'And I, I . . . haven't changed my mind. Nothing's changed.'

Pieter frowns. 'Haven't you been reading my letters?'

Clara is silent, unwilling to admit that she has not.

'Really? *Really?*' Pieter's frown deepens. 'I thought it'd be impossible for you not to read a letter, given' – he nods towards the shop – 'your profession.'

'You're the reader of letters,' Clara says softly. 'I write them.'

'But, after what Marthe wrote, after you read her letters to Otto, I thought . . .' Pieter says. 'So you let me go unheard. I spoke and you didn't listen.'

Clara glances at the pavement. 'I'm sorry, I wasn't trying to be cruel. I didn't mean to punish, to make you suffer. It was just . . . too painful.'

'But,' Pieter protests, 'if you'd read them, it might not have been. I told you I'd changed my mind, that I wanted you to come back, that I wanted to give you – us – everything, including . . .'

Clara gives him a sharp look. 'What?'

Pieter nods. 'After you left, I thought that I'd cope, I thought I'd survive, I've been doing it for long enough. But I found I couldn't, I can't . . . I don't want to be without you. I need you near me. I need to read to you, I need to have you listen. It's not the same without you, nothing is. It's really all quite . . . unbearable.'

Clara's eyes fill again, but she shakes her head. 'You can't agree to have a baby as a bargain, because you want to be with me. I'm deeply touched, of course, but that's not a reason, it's not enough.'

Pieter holds up his hand to stop her but she ignores him.

'You should know that, you grew up with a father who wasn't there and so did I, and' – tears drop down her cheeks again – 'I can't let my child go through the same thing. It wouldn't be fair. No matter how much I want to be with you, it just wouldn't be fair.'

She turns back to the shop, blinking away her tears, fumbling to open the door. Pieter reaches and takes her arm, but Clara pulls away and pushes her way into the shop. Pieter follows.

'Wait,' he says, 'wait.'

Shaking her head, Clara stumbles towards the counter and leans against it, catching her breath.

'You're not giving me a chance to explain,' Pieter says. 'I had a whole, very long speech, prepared. I've barely got through the first few lines. I still had much more. I still had to tell you that I don't simply want a baby because you do. You . . . You've ignited something in me, something I'd never felt before. I want a baby because *I* want one. With you, yes, but not as a bargaining chip. I want a baby because it feels like the greatest expression of my love for you. I want to create life with you. I want, I hope to be blessed enough to be able to love, not just you, but any children we might create together. To have the chance to do that . . .'

Clara pulls a sleeve across her wet nose and gives him a sheepish smile. 'I'm sorry . . .' she takes a deep breath.

Pieter reaches into his pocket and pulls out a handkerchief. It's wrapped around something and he unwraps it, holding the object in his other hand while he steps towards her and, very gently dabs her cheeks. Then he gives her the small square of embroidered cotton.

Clara sniffs. 'I'm a mess.'

'Not at all.' Pieter smiles. 'In fact, I must confess, I'm rather flattered. I never imagined I could have such an effect on a woman.'

Clara sniffs again, wiping her nose on the handkerchief. 'I'm afraid you can't take all the credit. My emotions are all over the place at the moment.'

Pieter nods. 'Ah, you've got your . . .' he trails off, looking slightly disappointed. Then he opens the palm of his other hand and holds it out to Clara. 'It's yours. I can't keep it.'

Clara takes the pen. 'But, I wanted you to have it. I've never written with it anyway. It's such a waste. I thought—'

'That I could learn to write letters with it?' Pieter finishes. 'And I did. All of them to you. And, if I do say so myself, they were rather beautiful. But clearly wasted on you.'

Clara smiles. 'I said I was sorry. I'll read them all today, okay? I'm sure they are very beautiful.'

Pieter grins. 'Good, I'm glad to hear it. And now you have the pen back you can write something of your own.'

'I don't have anything to write.'

'Not yet, perhaps, but you're still young. You've got a thousand stories still waiting for you, a thousand wonderful, incredible, unexpected moments of joy, sorrow, delight, disappointment, laughter—'

311

'Hopefully more of the good than the bad,' Clara says, rubbing the pen between her thumb and forefinger.

'Yes, of course,' Pieter says. 'I'll try to give you at least a hundred delightful days for every disappointing one. And, as soon as you've finished your menstruation, I can get to work on giving you some particularly delightful moments, and perhaps we might even get—'

Clara laughs.

'What?'

'Menstruation? You're so formal.'

Pieter frowns. 'Not at all, I'm simply old-fashioned.'

'Well, anyway,' Clara says, 'I'm not on my menstruation.'

'No? But you said . . .'

'Yes, I know. But, in fact, I haven't had it for nearly eight weeks now.'

It's a few moments before Pieter's frown transforms into a look of shocked joy.

'Really?' he asks, his own eyes now filling with tears. 'Truly?'

Clara nods.

'Oh, my good God,' Pieter says. 'Oh, my—'

And then, all of a sudden, he bursts into sobs. Clara holds the handkerchief out to him.

'It's okay,' she says. 'No need to have a nervous breakdown. I know you're old, but you can still learn a few new tricks. Changing nappies isn't all that hard, I hear, we can practise . . .'

Pieter lifts his head and looks at Clara with such total adoration that it leaves her quite speechless. Tears still falling silently down his face, he places his hands gently on her cheeks.

'I have no idea what's going to happen next,' Pieter says, taking a deep breath. 'Nor in the millions of moments to come. But, of all those I've had so far, I've never been as utterly, utterly happy as I am now.' He kisses the tip of her nose. 'Thank you, my sweet, sweet girl, for finding me and bringing me home.'

'Ditto,' Clara says, softly. 'Ditto.'

Acknowledgements

Many thanks to my agents, Andrea and Christina. Infinite thanks to all at Allison & Busby for championing all the books. Especially to Susie Dunlop, Publishing Director, for her indefatigable support. Also, Lesley Crooks, for her editorial eye and social media assistance. Great thanks to Ash, for reading every chapter as I wrote it and writing me glorious letters in return. Massive thanks to Al, as ever, for never missing a single mistake of mine. Huge thanks to all my readers – your loyalty and passion continue to inspire me. Enormous thanks, as ever, to Artur, for always making everything possible.

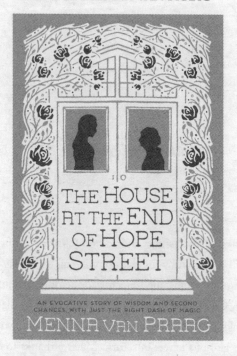

When tragedy strikes Alba Ashby, she finds herself at the door of a house she's never noticed before. Number Eleven, Hope Street in Cambridge is no ordinary house. Its walls are steeped in the wisdom of past residents: Virginia Woolf, Dorothy Parker and Agatha Christie to name a few. Alba accepts an invitation to stay, offered to her under the condition she has ninety-nine nights, and no more, to turn her life around.

Guided by the energy of the house, where portraits come alive, bookcases refill themselves and hot chocolate has healing properties, the enchanting experience Alba and her new friends share will change their lives for ever.

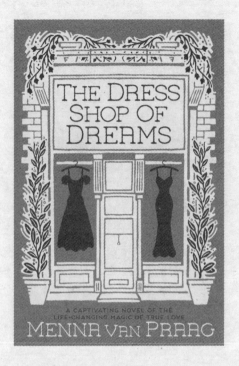

THE DRESS
SHOP OF
DREAMS

A CAPTIVATING NOVEL OF THE
LIFE-CHANGING MAGIC OF TRUE LOVE

MENNA VAN PRAAG

Scientist Cora Sparks spends her days in the safety of her university lab or at her grandmother Etta's dress shop. Tucked away on a winding Cambridge street, Etta's store appears quite ordinary to passers-by, but the colourfully vibrant racks of beaded silks and jewel-toned velvets hold bewitching secrets: with just a few stitches from Etta's needle, these gorgeous gowns have the power to free a woman's deepest desires.

Cora's studious, unromantic eye has overlooked Walt, the shy bookseller who has been in love with her forever. Determined not to allow Cora to miss her chance at happiness, Etta sews a tiny stitch into Walt's collar, hoping to give him the courage to confess his feelings to Cora. But magic spells – like true love – can go awry . . .

THE
WITCHES OF
CAMBRIDGE

BE CAREFUL WHAT YOU WISH FOR
IF YOU'RE A WITCH, YOU MIGHT JUST GET IT
MENNA VAN PRAAG

Amandine Bisset has always had the power to feel the emotions of those around her. It's a secret she can share only with her friends – all professors, all witches – when they gather for meetings on the college rooftops. Although lately she senses the ties among her colleagues beginning to unravel. If only she had her student Noa's power to hear the innermost thoughts of others, she might know how to patch things up.

Mathematics professor Kat is struggling with unrequited love, but refuses to cast spells to win anyone's heart. Kat's sister, Cosima, is not above using magic to get what she wants, sprinkling pastries in her bakery with equal parts sugar and enchantment. But when Cosima sets her sights on Kat's crush, she sets off a chain of events that turns each of the witches' worlds upside down . . .

To discover more great books and to
place an order visit our website at
allisonandbusby.com

Don't forget to sign up to our free newsletter at
allisonandbusby.com/newsletter
for latest releases, events and exclusive offers

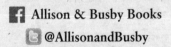 **Allison & Busby Books**
@AllisonandBusby

You can also call us on
020 7580 1080
for orders, queries
and reading recommendations